THE AMERICAN

*Frederick Faust
(Max Brand)*

THE AMERICAN

MAX BRAND

INTRODUCTION BY

WILLIAM F. NOLAN

ILLUSTRATED BY

V.E. PYLES

STEEGER BOOKS • 2019

TABLE OF CONTENTS

INTRODUCTION BY

WILLIAM F. NOLAN

FAUST HAS NEVER been given his due as a historical novelist despite the fact that much of his best work was done in this genre. Indeed, his robust narrative of Richard the Lionheart, The Golden Knight (written by "George Challis" in 1937) stands out as his finest achievement. The Ivor Kildare pirate novels (The Naked Blade and The Dew of Heaven) also rank near the top as does The Sword Lover, "The Hammer," and The Splendid Rascal—not to forget his superb Tizzo series. An impressive body of work!

Which brings us to *The American*, Faust's fictional treatment of the French Revolution 'a massive uprising that erupted in 1789).

Sensing the rich potential for strong drama, Faust began making extensive notes on the event as early as 1921. By 1925 he had compiled two million words of research, and began what he hoped would be a major novel (again writing as "Challis"). The end result depressed and frustrated him.

"I set out to conjure up a lion," he declared, "and ended up with a mouse."

He was being unfair to himself. While admittedly not the literary masterwork that he had envisioned, *The American* is not without solid merit, and deserves serious consideration.

The story begins when John Hampton of Virginia, a 30-year-old soldier of fortune seeking adventure in France, becomes involved in a deadly tavern brawl, during which a rich land-owner dies. This death puts Hampton on the road to a new life.

Rather than centering the novel's action in Paris, the heart of the Revolution, Faust stages the action in a small French village, allowing him to dramatize the larger event in a tighter, more concentrated form. Spurred by the revolution in the French capital, there is an equally violent local uprising among the village peasants against the royals, led by John Hampton. He soon regrets his participation in the resulting mayhem; the bloodshed sickens him.

Faust's battle scenes are particularly effective in delineating mob violence, and the final pages of the novel are beautifully rendered as Hampton is forced to choose between two women who love him equally. His choice is surprising. In sum, *The American* offers a vigorous, rousing narrative.

It is well worth reading.

Prolific award-winning author WILLIAM F. NOLAN (best known for **Logan's Run***) is the leading global authority on the life and career of the legendary Frederick Faust ("Max Brand"). Celebrated as "The King of the Pulps," creator of Dr. Kildare and (among 250 Western novels) Destry Rides Again, Faust was killed in action in 1944 while serving as a war correspondent during the Italian Offensive in World War II. (Kildare was named after county Kildare in Ireland—and Faust had used the name earlier for his pirate hero Ivor Kildare.) Nolan's collection of works by and about "Max Brand" includes 1,100 books and nearly 600 full-issue pulps, and remains the world's largest.*

CHAPTER I

A TAVERN BRAWL

A SMALL CHICKEN stuffed with little Alsatian sausages and a bottle of red Burgundy raised to exactly the temperature of the tavern room had brought upon the soul of John Hampton, of Hampton Hill, Virginia, a moment of warm meditation and calm during which his fingers itched neither for the sword nor for the dice box, his feet did not yearn for the exquisite precision of a French dance and in his ear there was no passion to hear the music of the latest opera.

He was content to sit back with his long-stemmed clay pipe and look through the delicate mist of smoke at the stir of life in the big room of the hostelry. There were not many guests, but from one table, where a man from Hampton's own country was playing the host, so many expensive orders issued that from the kitchen the voice of the cook could be heard shouting orders and curses at his assistants, and Monsieur René himself, the host of "The Flying Stag," kept hovering about the big table to give the savor of his own special courtesy to every mouthful of food and to every swallow of wine.

Since 1783 had brought the dreadful monotony of peace to the new United States, John Hampton of Hampton Hill had found diversion for half a dozen years in roaming the Old World, tasting wars of many vintages with the delicate appreciation of a connoisseur; and he had learned enough to be half-amused and half-concerned on account of the outspoken frankness of the big American at the other table.

In the course of the conversation which Hampton over-heard he discovered that the name of his compatriot was Hugh Massey, from Philadelphia; he was of about Hampton's thirty years; he was fully as tall as Hampton, also, and had shoulders equally broad, though the rest of his body was more solid and massive and lacked the greyhound suggestion of suppleness and tireless speed.

At his right sat a dark, handsome young Frenchman who seemed to be Massey's special friend in the party; he was a viscount, and his name was Jean-Pierre, Viscount de Charlevain. He attempted from time to time to control the tongue of his American friend because it was apparent that the talk of Massey gave offense to the four other men at the table and particularly to one Albert Coutenay, a very sour fellow whose mouth was

*The wine struck
Massey's face. Swords
sung from their sheaths*

continually pulled to a one-sided smile by a scar which seamed his right cheek.

But Massey kept pouring more wine, and with every glass of it his tongue waxed more eloquent as he discussed the probable future of the States General, which were meeting at that time in Paris, and the future of all of which might be involved.

"Read Tom Paine," said Massey. "Then you'll see that there's no room in the world for kings and nobles. Titles must go down! They must go down—even titles of empty courtesy—"

"Perhaps," said the scar-faced man, "you come from a country where courtesy is not important, *monsieur.*"

JOHN HAMPTON, as he heard the insult, took a longer pull at his pipe and smiled a little. He drew closer to him the chair on which his sheathed sword was lying. Hugh Massey had straightened in his chair and was scowling at Albert Coutenay.

"Courtesy?" he asked. "What did you say about courtesy and my country, *monsieur?*"

"Hugh, be quiet," said Jean-Pierre. "We are with new friends in a tavern, and therefore you should remember the old proverb."

"Why," said Hugh Massey, "it's a friendly act for me to give you all warning of the time to come. See the picture for your-self. A starving France covered with titles like a beggar covered with medals and now, at last, the people meeting to talk over their troubles with the example of the United States of Amer-ica shining in their eyes to prove that the Third Estate is the Nation, and not the lazy nobles, not the fat clergy—now at last the unprivileged people will see their power—they will waken—they will revolt—"

Some smack of this same prophecy in his own blood had brought John Hampton of Hampton Hill all the way from the service of Turkey to the Western World, scenting the old game of war like a hawk in the air. He had made the journey so swiftly by sea and by post that the slippered, whispering, turbaned Orient was still like a bright ghost in the back of his mind and he had to look around him again to reassure himself that he was actually sitting in "The Flying Stag" at Le Havre, with its time-darkened walls, its small, leaded windows, its atmosphere of kitchen steam, tobacco smoke and wine savors.

"—and the world," Massey was saying, "will see another people liberated from the mediaeval dream of emperors, kings, and nobles who fatten—"

The scar-faced man lifted one hand, and pointed it like a pistol at Massey.

"Pardon me, *monsieur,*" he said. "You make one dreadful mistake."

"Of what sort?" asked Massey, frowning.

"Of a sort that will sicken all French men," said the other.

"Monsieur?" demanded Massey sharply.

"You speak of fat nobles," said Coutenay.

"Well?" said Massey.

"Observe the noble viscount."

"And what of him?" asked Massey.

"Is he fat?"

"I speak of types, *monsieur*, and never of my dear friends," said Massey.

"The pure blood of the most ancient nobility in Gascony flowed in the veins of my grandmother. But am I fat?" asked Albert Coutenay.

"Monsieur, I do not follow you," said Massey.

"It may be difficult for an American to understand," explained Coutenay, "but in France no noble is fat."

Massey was about to speak but Jean-Pierre lifted a finger and silenced him.

Monsieur Coutenay continued: "I have heard ignorant fools hint that even his sacred majesty, Louis the Sixteenth, sometimes called Louis the Wise, or Louis the Watchmaker, is slightly, ever so slightly inclined to plumpness. But do you understand why that is impossible, *Monsieur* the American?"

Massey shrugged his shoulders.

"I have seen the king and he is simply—fat," he said.

"You speak," said Coutenay, "like an American. But every Frenchman knows it is impossible that his divine majesty should be fat, not because he is the king but because he is the first noble of France. And a French nobleman never is fat except in the eyes of fools or—Americans!"

AS HE made the final point, his three companions broke into a loud laughter. John Hampton, half-closing his eyes, drew long and delicately upon his pipe and seemed to find a special savor in it.

Massey said: "Gentlemen, it seems that I have been insulted, but a host should be slow to resent the remarks of his guests."

"Monsieur," said the man with the scar. "I remove that unpleasant limitation. When this glass of wine is finished, our meal and your hospitality have both ended."

He lifted the glass and drained off half of it. Then he poised it between thumb and fingers adding: "But since I never drink alone, let me present you, my dear friend, with the dregs."

Saying this, he flung the remainder of the wine in the face of Massey.

The big American sprang to his feet with an oath and kicked away the chair which he had overturned. The Viscount de Charlevain was already on his feet as the four other Frenchmen leaped up. Their swords came singing out of their scabbards as Monsieur René cried out in a lamentable voice: "The chairs—the furniture—the glasses and crockery—ah, my God! Gentlemen, I entreat you to use the yard for your exercise—"

Hugh Massey had snatched up his sword by the hilt and flung off the scabbard so that it went crash through a window. He barely had time to throw up his blade to parry the long lunge of Albert Coutenay.

There was no question of honorable tactics in this tavern brawl. One of Coutenay's companions came in toward the side of Massey and made the American give ground with a leap that sent the table crashing to the floor. One of the wine glasses spun all the way across the floor to the feet of John Hampton. He leaned and picked it up.

In that moment the fight had developed along set lines. Coutenay and an active little jumping-jack were crowding Massey into a corner. The other pair attacked the Viscount, but with much less venom. It was plainly their idea to keep him out of the battle while Coutenay paid Massey home, with the help of his swift-footed little companion.

The servants came running into the room, some of them to stand and grin at the good show, and others to throw up their hands and yowl. Monsieur René, in a corner, had turned his face to the wall and covered his ears with his hands so that he might not hear the sound of more breakages.

In the meantime the beat of lunging feet on the floor kept up a stammering thunder and raised what was more offensive to

John Hampton of Hampton Hill—a fine dust which made him sneeze. He therefore knocked the dottle out of his pipe, rose, and pulled his sword from its sheath. It was a backsword with a very meager blade, a mere sliver of light, but the steel was the finest that Damascus armorers could forge and it shone with a singular grey-blue light. With it the skill of Hampton knew how to touch away the side-sweeps and downright cleaving strokes of the heaviest scimitars. Still he looked at it with a touch of regret before he entered with it into a common tavern brawl.

UP TO this moment Charlevain had been upholding his end of the battle very well, though he could not break through his two opponents to come to the aid of the American friend. Hugh Massey fought with a good, manly passion, a long reach, and a surprising amount of agility for such a heavy man, but probably he could not have matched either of his opponents, for France was the school of fine swordsmen at that time.

Coutenay in particular seemed a master. Twice his lunges made Massey grimace as death shone in his eyes; and it was on the latter Frenchman that Hampton called as he crossed the room, saying: "Monsieur Coutenay, will you honor me with your attention?... Monsieur Coutenay, I wait here at your service!"

Coutenay sprang back to clear himself from the danger of Massey. Then he turned his scarred face on Hampton and shouted above the thunder of the trampling: "What is this to you? Are you going to be a fool? Will you keep your hands for your own troubles? *Monsieur*, he is only an American who needs a lesson in manners."

"Then I can share the lesson with him at the same price," said John Hampton.

Albert Coutenay, in place of arguing further, thrust suddenly full at the breast of Hampton. The American turned the stroke by perking up the hilt of his sword; then he stepped in to the attack. He moved with a thoughtful air; Coutenay found his best attacks touched aside as their elders often put by the remarks of children; and every time the counterstroke of Hampton made him leap for his life. Within half a dozen passes he was already sweating with agony and with effort. He was being driven relentlessly towards a corner, at the same time, and he commenced to cry out: "Jules!—Louis! Pierre!—Help! This devil has a sword made of quicksilver!"

"Ah!" said Hampton, at the same moment, as the solution to his problem appeared to his mind's eye, and instantly his blade was inside the Frenchman's guard.

A violent backward leap saved his life, but it penned him at the same time right inside the angle of the corner of the room. Here there was a crash on the floor in the opposite side of the place and then a French voice yelping: "Coutenay—away for your life! We have killed the Viscount!"

Footfalls fled noisily from the room and Hampton deliberately stepped back to let Coutenay bolt after his friends, for it was not dead Frenchmen, no matter how noble, that he was fighting to save, but the same big American who had spoken so loudly and frankly in a foreign land.

He watched Coutenay run for his life and then turned to find big Hugh Massey standing near the wall to which he had been driven, holding his left arm close to his side.

CHAPTER II

NO BODIES

ALL THE APARTMENT had grown silent. Footfalls clattered on the wet cobblestones outside and then both inside and outside there was stillness except for the wheels of a heavy peasant's cart in the distance and the pounding hoofs of some great Norman horse. Even the servants, even Monsieur René, had disappeared. All was so quiet that Hampton could hear the rain dripping from the eaves into the courtyard.

He said: "Well, Massey, you see there isn't much sale for American ideas in some parts of France."

Massey bowed, or seemed to bow, in a formal assent; but his body continued to incline until he pitched forward. Hampton got to him with a leap and caught the falling weight. He laid big Hugh Massey on the floor and saw the wet red spot that was springing out on his left side; far more significant, he saw the little rosy bubble form and burst into spray from the lips of Massey when the American tried to speak. No words would come. There was only a wheezing and a gurgling noise, a dim effort toward articulation, and then a sudden flow of blood from the mouth.

Hugh Massey jerked out a folded letter and began to point toward it, then at his own breast. He sat up with his eyes thrust out of his head by strangulation and his mouth straining wide in the effort to speak, but only succeeded in uttering that horrible red babbling. John Hampton of Hampton Hill dropped to one knee and signed for Massey to write his message on the floor—there was blood enough at hand to serve for ink.

Understanding appeared in the face of Massey and he turned to obey that suggestion even while the last desperate need for breath was turning his body rigid, but the last flurry seized him at that moment. He began to wag his head rapidly from side to side and pat the floor with his hands. His legs drew up beneath his body and kicked out violently, once; then he fell on his face and was still.

John Hampton looked grimly down at the dead man; then he turned his head and stared into the shadows on every side. Nothing lived in the rainy gloom of the tavern room except two lamps and the low weltering of the fire on the hearth. The rank tobacco smoke was still so thick in the air that it seemed as though the breaths which had blown it forth were still speaking audible words, also. The foolish quarrel rang in the brain of Hampton; he could hear the deadly voice of Coutenay begin the quiet insult; he could see again the red flash of the wine that had been thrown in Massey's face; and once more, in his mind's eye, the big American was stamping and lunging with the sword which was so unfamiliar to his hand. It spelled, clearly, murder. They had murdered Hugh Massey almost at the moment when his feet were first placed on the soil of France.

Hampton strode from the room into the wet court. The cobblestones were wet and slippery with small lichens and the wings of the old building stretched out on either side like arms to restrain him. Lights burned in two or three windows, only; the rest looked out at him like darkened, blinded eyes.

HE LEFT the court quickly. The rain, falling very fine, now, laid cold hand against his face. It covered the grey streets of Le Havre with a false, green twilight and dirtied even the rays of light that shone from houses. He was close enough to the waterfront to see the tall masts of ships lifting above the roofs, but even in this busiest part of the town, not a soul was out walking the streets. He had to pass square after square with his naked sword in his hand before he encountered two gendarmes descending the steps of a wine-shop. He stopped them with a cry.

"Murder!" said Hampton. "In the Flying Stag—"

They came back with him, hurrying their steps as though in great haste, but walking with such short strides that they length-ened the way. They were full of questions.

Hampton merely said: "I'll show you the picture that was painted in The Flying Stag. You'll find two dead men on the floor. Afterward I'll tell you about the way they were killed."

Presently they saw the old signboard of the tavern with its ridiculous stag spreading out wings that hardly would have carried a heron through the air. They passed through the court and straight into the big room.

It was dimmer than ever. Only a single lamp burned in a corner and an old woman was scrubbing the floor, wringing her mop into a bucket, and then scrubbing again on her hands and knees. As she worked, she panted out faint fragments of an old song from time to time; neither the words nor the tune meant anything to Hampton.

"Well?" asked the gendarmes, standing close together and peering about them. "Well, *monsieur?*… And the dead men?"

"There!" said Hampton. "Where the old woman is scrub-bing. One of them lay there. And another yonder near the window…. Ah, I see what's happened! Our host has had the bodies removed…. *Monsieur* René! *Monsieur* René!"

The host came quickly into the room, his round black skull cap nodding as he bowed and clasped his hands together.

"Yes, *monsieur?* You called me, gentlemen? Will you have wine?… Marcelle, you fool, leave off scrubbing the floor when gentlemen come into the room!"

The hag stood up and peered at the three with a sagging grin.

"René, where are the dead men?" asked Hampton.

"They are with the saints, all the dead, if my prayers can help them to heaven," said the host. "To what dead men do you refer, sir?"

"The American who lay here, and the other by the window…" said Hampton.

"The American? Who lay here?" echoed René, apparently bewildered. "But what American, my dear friend? You are the only one who has been here today?"

The two gendarmes began to talk rapidly and softly together.

Hampton crossed the room to the window under which he knew that Jean-Pierre, Viscount of Charlevain, had been fighting when he fell. There was no sign of him on the floor. He took the lamp and held it close. There was not even a drop of blood to show the spot where Charlevain had gone down, though the scrub-woman had not yet cleaned this part of the floor.

Behind him, he could hear one of the gendarmes murmuring: "Have you seen him before?"

"Ah, my friends," said René, "you know what Americans are when they drink. And this one has been here all afternoon drinking rum punch…."

"Rum punch? Ah, ha!" chuckled the gendarmes.

Hampton lifted his head and snapped his fingers.

"Very well," he said. "I understand, Monsieur René. Every good tavern-keeper wants to keep his reputation and the floor of his inn perfectly clean…. Bring me my score."

He turned to the gendarmes.

"Put it this way," he said. "I was simply drunk. I did not watch a fight here. I did not use my own sword in it. It was all a drunken dream. And the harbor waters have closed over the results of that dream quite a while ago. The fish in Le Havre harbor should have quite an American taste for some day to come…. And so, adieu!"

"You shall have a drink, first," said Monsieur René. "When a man has been listening to a nightmare, he needs something strong to warm his belly and his blood."

He led the two away to the taproom, and Hampton sat down by the fire to examine the letter which had concerned the dying Hugh Massey so much.

THERE WERE, in fact, two letters in the single envelope. The first, addressed to one Marceau, landlord of The Red Horse, in the village of Charlevain. It ran:

"My dear Marceau,

"This letter is carried to you by a friend dear to me. His name is Hugh Massey. If he does not stay at the château, he will patronize your inn. Treat him kindly, give him the best wine in your cellar, do not rob him except on Sundays and holidays, and oblige me.

Charlevain."

The second letter was addressed to the Marquis d'Alenton at the Château de Charlevain. It read:

"My dear and patient father,

"I have returned to the edge of France but dare not come any closer without your special permission. God knows that my heart yearns to see you and that my knees desire to drop to the ground while I beg your forgiveness. The truth is that the money I took to the new United States walked out of my pockets in the most amazing manner. I cannot explain. Perhaps my kindest of friends, Mr. Hugh Massey, of Virginia, will be able to give you reasons and put me in a slightly better light. I beg you to use him well. I have had his house, his money, his friendship. I have written about him before, but when you see him you will understand at once that I have not been able to do him justice. If he finds it in his heart to say a few kind words about me, I entreat you to listen to them.

"But this brings me to a thing which I have written to Marguerite and which she of course has told you. Now I attempt to explain it a little. I know that every inch of our family estate is to you as dear as your own flesh, and every hill is like a finger of your hand, every forest is like the hair of your head; in spite of this, I have sold my rights to the village of Charlevain to Hugh Massey, and transferred to him all the rights over the place which are pentailed to me for the space of twenty-five years.

"My dear father, control your anger for a moment. Let me

explain. I found myself in America with the money which you had furnished me disappearing overnight and nothing but bankruptcy before me. And it seemed to me that I was in the land of opportunity, where money is made quickly. Therefore I determined to become a merchant, as the Americans often are. The fortunes which they accumulate are not to be believed.

"From Hugh Massey I borrowed, therefore, on no better security than my word as a gentleman of France, enough money to fit out a tall ship and load it with the products of Virginia until it rode deep at the wharf. Then it was despatched for the West Indies; but at the very crossing of the bar of the river's mouth, it stuck in the sand, a gale came screeching out of the northwest, and in a few hours the crew were ashore, but my beautiful ship was smashed to pieces by the waves and the cargo lost forever. What could I do, therefore, except place some security in the hands of Mr. Massey? And what security did I have except the village of Charlevain?

"So I transferred all rights to it into his hands, legally. I trust that you will understand and forgive what I have done, but even as I write, the fear of your anger is coldly about my heart. I leave Mr. Massey to talk with you and learn your mind about the matter before I dare present myself at the château.

"In the meantime, I salute you, sir. I kiss the hand of that delightful Marguerite, and remain

"Your obedient and loving son,

"Jean-Pierre."

A shadow crossed the mind of Hampton. He looked up and saw a servant tendering him his bill. He paid it with silver and remained a moment in thought.

It seemed to him that the gestures and the attempted words of Hugh Massey as he lay struggling on the floor, dying, could be interpreted very clearly. He was pointing out to Hampton the letters which would identify him; he was trying to beg Hampton to carry those letters to Charlevain and there ask for all the power of the marquis in revenging this horrible murder in the dimness of an obscure tavern in Le Havre.

Hampton slowly refolded the letters and replaced them in his pocket. A darkness of conscience was coming over his heart. He had grown too accustomed to brawls and violence. Tavern scenes were all twice-told tales to him; and therefore he had delayed too long in intervening in that murderous fight. He should have been on his feet at once. Or, when he at last entered the battle, he should have pressed home a swift attack.

He had failed... two men, perhaps, had died on account of his carelessness....

He should have entered the brawl sooner, should have let Coutenay's belly feel his sword.

The conscience of that gentleman adventurer, John Hampton, was the least active part of his soul. This attack of penitence, therefore, wrung his heart in an unexpected way and made him start up from his chair. The death of two men burdened his spirit and he knew that he could not rest in peace until he had done something about it. As for attempting to find justice in Le Havre, he knew well that without patronage to help him he would find the French courts the slowest and blindest machines in the world. Charlevain, suddenly, became his goal.

CHAPTER III

HAMPTON'S DOMAIN

THE BIG BLACK Norman horses drew the diligence rapidly over a road which ruled a white line through France, through May, through the forest where the spring of the year shone in level sprays of yellow green.

John Hampton of Hampton Hill, once a brilliant young colonel in the army which fought for the Continental Congress and George Washington, once commander of a privateer in the Dutch service, once major in a Russian cavalry regiment, and lately a full-fledged general in the army of the Divine Porte, began to throw back his heavy shoulders. He smiled, and his face, which in repose was as grim and rugged as that of some Indian in his native Virginia, lighted with a sudden warmth. He tasted to his soul the spring of the year.

Toward the end of the journey there were no other passengers, so Hampton rode on the high seat beside the driver, because he believed in company. The driver was a man of thirty, built on a scale so vast that beside him even big John Hampton felt as slim and bodiless as a child. The fellow was a monster with a pock-marked face. He had the heavy mouth of an ape, the flattened snout of a boar, the eyes of a tired lion. A big scar pulled his mouth awry into a brutal sneer when he talked. For the most part he was in a deep reverie from which he half-started with wordless mutterings from time to time, or a whip-stroke for one of the horses.

He addressed Hampton in the manner of one speaking in the midst of a steady conversation.

"But as an American you see this French madness with a special eye—our States General, our Third Estate toying to swallow the other two, and our king. Tell me with a stranger's clear eye, what is wrong with our France?"

"It seems to me a happy place to travel in," said Hampton.

"And you don't look deeper than the skin for the sickness of others, eh?" asked the driver. "Well, perhaps you're right.... One of our troubles I know. We talk too much. We all read books. We all chatter about them, afterwards. Every man in France thinks that *he* could be king and do a better job.... Now, my father before me was a good, hard-working, silent man, but he gave me too much education to make me contented as a diligence driver and not enough education to keep my hands clean, like a gentleman. So I take it out in talk, and wonder what I would do if *I* were king. And by the way, what do you think of our king?"

"I hear that he is the best watchmaker in France," said Hampton, smiling.

"No, don't smile," said the huge man. "You are not in Paris, and therefore you need not smile. You are not at Versailles, either, and therefore you may use the word 'no.'"

"Thank you," said Hampton.

"You find that our king only sweats with his own fat."

"I did not say so," said Hampton.

The voice of his companion burst out into an overwhelming roar that thundered: "You find us on the verge of a Revolution *à la* America, unless the Third Estate opens its maw and swallows the higher orders. You fear it will do so. Your heart burns for *la belle France*. You feel nausea. Your brain whirls. *La belle France*, like a beautiful girl, swallowed by a sea monster."

"*Monsieur*, I do not share your emotion," said Hampton. "In America we have nothing but the Third Estate."

"Bah! There are no beggars in your land. What do you know of the Third Estate? You have your Washington like a great mountain. You have your hard-faced Mr. Adams from Boston. You have your Mr. Jefferson who *does* read too much. They are all gentlemen—and they do not have to talk to beggars. My God, how fat your people will become with nothing to do but eat! *Monsieur* the American, what will you say of our Third Estate?"

"In my country, we are less than two million common people," said Hampton. "We have nothing *but* a Third Estate."

THE DILIGENCE was topping a small hill at this moment with a rumble of wheels and rattling of chains.

"We have all of this beauty," cried the driver, waving his hand, "but we have other things, also! Hai, there! Come out of the woods, you rascal!"

A one-legged cripple stood up from the brush in which he had been crouching and, leaning on his crutches, dragged off his rag of a hat. His clothes were so tattered that they dripped away from a half-naked body; his hair spilled down across his eyes.

He waved his hand at the diligence.

The diligence, which had slowed almost to a complete pause at the crest of the hill, now lurched forward on the downward slope with a noise that dimmed the shouting of the cripple, while the rolling dustclouds fogged the picture of him.

"Two million common people," bellowed the driver, "but how many as common as *that* one? We have twenty millions like him. Twenty millions."

"Not of cripples," said Hampton.

"Crippled souls, *monsieur!* Crippled souls! Punch a man's belly hard enough and you will bruise his soul! That fellow on crutches has not sat down to one of the king's meals. It would last him half a year. I have seen one of the royal menus—rice soup and onion and chicken soup—pate de foie gras, a bit of stewed rabbit, salmi of red partridges, spring chickens *a l'allemande,* veal kidneys glaces, blanquette of chicken with truffles, turkey *a' la Pe'riguen,* a duck from Rouen, a chicken from Caux...."

"Well, God bless the good king if he can eat all of that!" said Hampton, laughing.

"True," said the driver, peering at him. "You are far from Paris and therefore you may laugh…. But if he could not eat all of everything, he can eat a good part of every dish."

"What a stomach!"

"Say not a word! There is room under his ribs for all of France. He has digested a good part of it already."

"Monsieur," said Hampton, "you are a liberal. I esteem and admire your liberality. But it would change France, I'm afraid. And at this moment France seems to me perfect. And if the king devours the rest of the kingdom tomorrow, I hope he will leave the green on those trees and the blue in that sky."

"You are young, *monsieur,"* said the driver, chuckling, an effect which was like distant thunder. "And you are right."

"I am exactly thirty," said Hampton. "And I don't think you're a whit older."

"Not in years; but years have nothing to do with it."

"In what way am I sure to be right?"

"Because when he is young a man cannot be wrong."

The direct, clear eye of Hampton, which looked each moment squarely in the face and paid no heed to the distances in life, regarded the driver for a moment. Then they laughed together.

Then the driver said: "Watch, now. We'll see the Château de Charlevain around the side of that hill."

The white face of the castle flashed at them a moment later. The Château de Charlevain was strangely built. It is not one of those Gothic fortresses with arrow slots for windows and high towers heaped around a dungeon keep, for it was erected after Louis XI at last gave peace and unity to France. One portion stood on the island in the middle of the lake of Charlevain, the other climbed the mainland hill, and the two parts were joined by a series of galleries which ran out over the water, supported by round arches over massive piers.

When John Hampton saw it the stone was marble white, the roof a deep blue; and the cones of the turret tops were relieved gently against the roof itself, springing as they did just above the cornice. He was enriched by the beauty of wide, carved windows, chimney clusters, noble walls, and the balustraded terraces and shining fountains of the island garden. It was most beautiful of all in the image that sank trembling into the lake. A banner floated over the château to give token that the Marquis d'Alenton was in residence.

"We have such things as that château, such things as that cripple," said Hampton's companion. "That is France… as she may not be forever, *monsieur*." He pointed.

"There is the village… there… there!" said the driver. "You should not come thundering up to it in a diligence, like this. Unless you steal upon her, you never will see Charlevain smiling."

THE VILLAGE lay by the side of the lake, formed like a cross of two intersecting streets and so over-bowered with trees that there were only glimpses of roofs, here and there, and the rugged tower of a church. Where the streets joined in an open plaza, Massey saw the skeleton form of a gibbet and a stocks beside it. All of this he saw through a veil for though the sun still lived on the château the village was drowned in western shadows. Then they dipped under the trees into the main street. The last of his view had been the narrow strips of cultivated land to the landward side of the town, an irregular patchwork of many colors.

Children, tumbling in the deep dust, scattered before the horses and stood aside with open eyes and mouths ringed with black grime as though they had been feeding in the ground; geese, chickens, pigs ran out of his path and a few scrawny curs came out to bark at him timidly, their tails between their legs.

The team of the diligence went on at a walk as the villagers appeared in every doorway. Hampton had passed through other towns of misery on his way from the sea-coast but he had seen nothing so clearly. Charlevain was a lovely name towards which he traveled; now the unhappy reality walked straight into his heart.

A crowd of the villagers had gathered in front of one of the houses down the street. They looked like beasts out of caves, scratching their bodies through their rags, and turning hopeless eyes, without curiosity, as the diligence rumbled toward them.

They were so indifferent that they did not stir when the lead horses of the diligence threatened to trample them. The driver thrust down his brake and stopped the wheels.

"It's a dispossess case," said the driver. "These people will stand here for hours enjoying the sight of somebody more miserable than they are.... See how busy the bailiff is, eh?"

This small and active man was nailing boards crisscross over the lower windows of the house. The door of it still stood open and in the street was heaped the furniture. Some rags of bedding, a few iron pots, a stool or two—there was hardly enough to furnish a one-roomed hut. The dispossessed could be picked out easily from the rest of the crowd, above all the man of the house. He was a big man with sooty marks on his half-bare arms and he stood beside his wife and two children, all with their heads bowed. A woman lay on a bit of bedding at their feet, her hair white, her face starved with age.

The bailiff, as he finished nailing up the windows, slammed the front door and locked it. He turned with the big key in his hand and waved it like a truncheon to illustrate his words.

"Now you will see, all of you," he said loudly, "what happens to people who will not pay their just rent. They must be gone into the world without a roof to cover them. It is the law of France and the will of our young seigneur, the Viscount of Charlevain.... I want you to take this lesson home to your hearts...."

"Take it home to your hands, sharpen your knives with it, you fools!" growled the driver of the diligence.

"Observe this Jacques Cartier," said the bailiff. "A strong man and a clever blacksmith. But he *would* buy a new young horse last year. For what? To plough his land? No, only because he wanted to be carried about by the beast. His two legs were not good enough for him. And now, today, he has lost horse and home and all! Remember it! It is a good lesson! And what, also, will become of Mother Anne, here? She must suffer because her son was a fool! But the will of the seigneur must be served...."

Jacques Cartier lifted his head, and there was something in his face that made the bailiff shrink back a step or two.

"My friend, the bailiff!" called John Hampton.

"Yes, *monsieur?* Yes, yes?" answered the bailiff, seeing Hampton on top of the diligence.

"It is *not* the will of the seigneur," said Hampton.

"Monsieur, I have the special injunction of my lord the marquis in person to dispossess Jacques Cartier today," answered the bailiff.

Hampton jumped down from the high seat. He walked through the crowd and looked down into the grey face of the old woman and saw the clear, young blue of her eyes.

"The marquis is not seigneur in the village, I believe?" said Hampton.

"He is not," said the bailiff. "His son is the actual owner of this place.... You will kindly permit the father to act for the son in the absence of the latter?"

He bowed and grinned with satisfaction as he delivered this stroke. The villagers gaped at Hampton as at a man from another world. And he felt himself suddenly drawn vitally into this quarrel. If his interference was only good enough for a day or two, it would nevertheless give the old woman time in which she could die peacefully, perhaps.

"You know the handwriting of the viscount?" asked Hampton, taking the letters from his pocket.

"I know it as well as I know my own," said the bailiff.

"The viscount has transferred his claim on Charlevain to an American, Hugh Massey," said Hampton. "And neither the marquis nor Jean-Pierre himself have the slightest right to rule the village or dispossess a single householder in it. Read here...."

He held out the paper, folded so that the bailiff could see the significant part and the signature.

THE BAILIFF read and re-read, long enough to memorize the words. And the villagers, silently, packed themselves closer and closer about the scene, staring with a singular hunger on the face of Hampton. As for the blacksmith, Jacques Cartier, he had crouched to the ground beside his prostrate mother and was cherishing her with his big hands, now and then glancing up at Hampton with a sort of desperate hope.

"True," said the bailiff, at last, stepping back from Hampton so as to view him from head to foot more clearly. "It is true that the viscount had alienated this part of the estate for twenty-five years… and you, I presume, are *Monsieur* Massey?"

Hampton overlooked the last words, merely saying: "Get the boards off those windows and unlock the door. Cartier, the house is yours again, and the back rent is forgiven you. But don't be buying more horses, you poor devil!"

Jacques Cartier, jerking up his head, stared at Hampton in a frozen amazement; his wife, with a sort of howling cry that was between sobbing and laughter, dropped on her knees in front of the American; and all at once the entire crowd was shouting.

Cartier suddenly was at the side of Hampton.

"Do you know, *monsieur*," he said, "that by doing this you are pulling down the wrath of the marquis like a high wall on your head?"

"And what of it?" asked Hampton. "It is not the wrath of God, after all."

Jacques Cartier was struck to a staring awe.

"I think I understand," he said at last, very slowly. "God has sent a father to us at last!"

Hampton turned suddenly and waded through the mob toward the tavern with its sign of The Red Horse, grotesque as a Chinese dragon, hanging above the door. The diligence, pulled up before it, already was unloading his luggage. He stepped lightly, with a sense of guilty joy. But even if this act of his remained in force for only a week, he knew it would be seven days of joy to the blacksmith.

A man was crying out inside the tavern, trouble making his voice wail like a woman's: "My God, there is a new seigneur, and he is here! Diane! Diane! Pierre! Where are you? Run to stand by the door—give him a welcome! How can the diligence be so early? Clear the tables! Stand up, louts! It is the new master!"

HAMPTON STEPPED into the doorway towards which a flurry of people were streaming from the taproom on the right and the waiting room on the left He had a sense of clean floors and of windows curtained in bright patterns. The wailing voice ended abruptly as a little man with a starved, weary, intellectual face turned towards him. Within the tavern silence spread in a swift wave to join the deadly stillness of the village street.

Hampton said: "Tell me your name, friend?"

"I am Camille Marceau," said the little man, "and God forgive me!"

"I'm happy to see you," said Hampton, and held out his hand. Camille Marceau, bowing until one knee was almost on the floor, received that hand in both of his and kissed it.

"If I had dreamed that you would honor us today…" began Marceau.

Hampton put the heel of his left hand against the forehead of the tavern-keeper and pushed him erect. Then he patted little Marceau on the shoulder and said: "We don't do that in my country, except to ladies, Marceau. If you think you're not ready for me, I'll tell you that I'm ready for *you,* if you have some cheese and a loaf of bread and a glass of wine; and if your rooms are filled, I can sleep on a table."

"Filled? God forbid!… Will *monsieur* go to his room first, or will he honor a table here while I offer him the best that heaven permits in my kitchen?"

"Food! Food!" said Hampton. "And there's dust in my throat, Marceau, but by one look at you, by the light in your eye, I know you have the very wine that will wash it away."

Marceau began to laugh a little but still he was afraid. That fear never left him as he waited on Hampton at a corner table in the dining-room, anticipating the wishes of the new master with nervous hands. It was a big, cheerful room and Hampton could not help asking how such a fine inn happened, to stand in so small a village. It was, he learned, because Charlevain was such a convenient stage from Paris and wealthy travelers were sure to pause here when they saw the broad face of the inn. Particularly they enjoyed stretching their legs in the garden at the rear.

Hampton, as he ate and listened, grew sleepily content. An atmosphere of awe was attending him. Stealthy whisperings stirred in the doorways, cautious eyes peered in upon him. He finished his supper slowly. He hardly could recall a situation which had pleased him more. He had been endowed quite against his will with a new name, and a small domain that went with it as a personal possession. On the morrow or the next day, of course, he would let the truth appear to the marquis; but in the meantime he tasted the relish of a new sort of power; and it made him want to laugh. While he was playing this rôle in Charlevain, he would allow each moment to bring what it pleased to him, and have no thought for the shadows which his actions might cast before him. If he were breaking the law, it was not far to a frontier, and he knew how to ride by night and hide by day.

Marceau said: "*Monsieur,* if you will permit me, you shall have a fire in your room, tonight."

"Is a fire a very special thing?" asked Hampton.

"Such a fire as I can offer you, *monsieur,*" said the host, "I hope you will find very special. I go now to prepare everything!"

HAMPTON, SIPPING the wine, yawned and drowsed till Marceau came again to show him to his room. It was just at the head of the stairs. The innkeeper paused and held up the lamp so that he could see the face of the master. Thereby he illumined his own grin.

"I hope you will be pleased," said Marceau.

"I'm already pleased," answered Hampton. "Everything was

perfect. The chef is a jewel and you are the best host in the world."

When he took the lamp and went into the room he saw the flowers, first, which were ranged in bowls and vases in front of the window, carrying the sweet air of spring into the room; afterwards the light fell on the sun-stained face of the girl who was in the bed.

"Mademoiselle, I beg your pardon!" he said, hurrying back towards the door.

"No, no! *monsieur!"* called the girl. "The night is so cold—"

He stopped with his back to her, remembering the smile of Marceau; then he put the lamp down on a table and went to the bed. She was sitting up, the covers held to cover her.

"This was a kind thought of Marceau's," he said. "Who are you, my dear?"

"Julie, *monsieur."*

He sat down on the bed. She moved her feet to give him more room.

"You're a lovely thing, Julie," he said.

She made a gesture with her hand and slender brown arm.

"I am as God made me for *monsieur,"* she answered.

"Well, how long has He been in the making? How old are you, Julie?"

"I am twenty, *monsieur."*

"Are you, Julie?... How old are you, my dear?"

"But," said the girl, her forehead puckering a little with curiosity, "well... I am eighteen, if you are pleased to have me so."

"Of course I'm pleased, but I am sorry to see that Julie has been crying."

"I? No, no! Only, when the flowers begin, dear *monsieur,* and the bees start humming, in the spring of the year I always have a little cold in the nose...."

"Julie!"

"Monsieur? Are you angry?"

"You are a servant in the inn?"

"I am the niece of Camille Marceau."

Hampton started up from the bed and strode to the window. Disgust darkened his eyes for a moment, then by degrees he was aware of the view across the lake, the great château and the long, splintered images of the lights upon the water.

"It is true!" cried the girl, "I do not lie. He *is* my uncle! I am not just a poor thing from the streets, *monsieur.* I swear to the kind God who sees me that I am a good girl!"

Hampton came back to the bed and made himself smile at her.

"Marceau said to you: 'Quick, Julie! *Monsieur* must be content! Quickly up to his room and into his bed!' So you came here and slipped into the bed. But afterward your thoughts began to catch up with you... all the Sunday thoughts... about kind saints and good girls. Eh?"

A pair of big tears got away from her eyes and rolled down her face, yet she said: "It is only because you are so wise and kind that I am crying. Now that I have seen you—when I heard your good, deep, gentle voice I was happy—it was only that as I lay in the darkness...."

"Hush, Julie!"

"Yes, *monsieur.* But see how the tears are gone! Now I can smile easily. I could laugh, too, if it pleased you. My heart is happy, except that I see you are in pain for me."

He thought of other faces, out of the years of his life. From that a depth of remembering he said, slowly: "You must get up and go back to your room."

"Ah, no!... How should I dare to face Uncle Camille? He can be terrible. *Monsieur,* be kind!"

She turned on her face and began to sob into the pillow, beating her head with her brown hands. Hampton closed a Louis d'Or into one of those hands.

"If he thinks I am displeased, show him that," said Hampton, and watched with a queer, grinning pain in his heart as she sat up, suddenly, holding the coin before her as though it needed to be felt and breathed of to be believed.

"Is it gold, *monsieur?*" she whispered.

"It is, Julie."

"And for me?"

"Yes, Julie."

"Ah!" said the girl. Her head fell back a little; her eyes closed. "When he sees it! When Uncle Camille sees it!… Is it true that I must go!"

"Yes, Julie."

She hesitated, growing very hot of face.

"Kind *monsieur,* will you forgive me?"

"For what, Julie?"

"If I beg you for one instant to turn your back?"

He went to the window and heard the swift rustling behind him.

"Adieu, *monsieur,*" said the girl. When he turned again, she was at the door holding a thin, blue mantle about her.

"Julie," he said. "You are lovely."

She smiled at her shoulder. "No, *monsieur,*" she said. "I am only a poor, sun-burned thing."

"Would you change a golden color for silly white and red?"

"Not if you are pleased, *monsieur.*"

He saw the flattery enter her and shine again at her eyes.

"Have you entertained the guests of your uncle like this very often, Julie?"

"*Monsieur!* Never!… Camille Marceau's own niece—oh—"

"Of course I understand, Julie. Now go!"

She moved back into the hall very slowly, then jerked the door shut as though in a sudden panic. He heard her slippers whispering down the hall. She was gone.

Afterward he lay for a moment awake in the warm place in the bed and heard the last voices in the street dying down, moving away into infinite quiet, at last. It was then that he could distinguish for the first time the thin voice of strings from the château, where they still were dancing. He was listening to this music, no louder than thought, when sleep came over him.

CHAPTER IV

JEAN-PIERRE'S LETTER

LADY MARGUERITE DE FRERON, now that she was the chatelaine of the castle, so to speak, and official hostess for her great cousin, the Marquis d'Alenton, refused to have in her own apartments the heavy forms and pompous furnishings which had filled the rest of the Château of Charlevain, since the dull, magnificent days of Louis XIV. She preferred the soft, gay fashion which Marie Antoinette brought into France, a little girlish, a little insipid, but marvellously new. No determined colors glared in this room. Red appeared as an exquisite cherry, white turned to delicate cream, and the blue became that of the sky in spring, breathed upon by a pale mist. Instead of brocade hangings or satin as rigid as carved wood, tender silk draped the windows. Above the fireplace, a gilded statuette by Clodion kissed its fingers to the upper world and on the wall opposite the bed Monsieur Watteau had painted white sheep and brown shepherds, bowing gentlemen, curtsying ladies, and a quiet little river which took their images and laughed beneath them.

Lady Marguerite turned from her side to her back, pushed away the gold of her hair, and with her eyes still closed murmured: "The chocolate, Victoire."

The maid went to the door and pushed it open to take the steaming tray from the hands of the servant who waited there. Since eleven o'clock he had been waiting, returning every ten minutes with newly frothed chocolate so that the drink might be fresh and hot the moment milady asked for it.

As Victoire returned and put the tray down on the little painted table beside the bed—Monsieur Girardon had painted it with his own hands not for money but for love—her mistress said: "Now, before I look at the day, tell me, Victoire: Are there shadows around my eyes?"

"The good sleep has rubbed them away," said Victoire.

"Look closely. I know there are a thousand little wrinkles in the corners, and between the eyes."

"Mademoiselle, have I not massaged them away every day? And at eighteen how can wrinkles come and stay?"

"Oh, when they begin to come, they will stay, no fear.... Is the sky clear, Victoire?"

"It is clear enough for April, and it is April-blue, too."

She had piled up the pillows and now helped Marguerite de Fréron to sit up against them. She brought a wet towel and with it tenderly and then more vigorously washed the face and hands of her mistress; after that she roughed the hair into shape and drew over the shoulders of Marguerite a dressing-gown of figured Chinese silk.

When the lady had the first cup of chocolate in her hand together with the first bite of buttered, crusty bread, she said: "How soon before the American arrives?"

"Within an hour, *mademoiselle,*" said Victoire.

"Heavens!" cried the girl. "How shall I be bathed and dressed and my hair done in that time? We must fly!"

"Yes, *mademoiselle.* We must fly!"

"However, I'll read first the letter that Jean-Pierre wrote about this Massey. In the second drawer from the top left in the desk in the boudoir," said the girl. "Bring the entire package."

When Victoire returned with the bundle. Marguerite turned over the letters one by one, in the most leisurely manner.

"Now that we know we have truth in the purse, why shouldn't we spend some of it?" she asked. "Tell me frankly, what you think of the young Count, that Lasnieres?"

"He has only a certain amount of money."

"He has a charming presence."

"Manners are cheap in our France, *mademoiselle*."

"True," said Marguerite, and turned the letter face down. "This Berryer, then?"

"It is said that the queen cannot endure him; which cuts oft all advancement, *mademoiselle*."

"True again," said Marguerite, discarding that letter in the same fashion. "But Gossec?"

"He is a good, hard man who will go far in the world, but he will leave his wife with his money, both under lock and key, and the key in the hand of some fierce Norman shrew."

"I agree with you entirely," said Marguerite. "Ah, Victoire, how useful it is to speak openly—and how hard it is to find a proper husband!"

"*Mademoiselle*, all things are hard when we turn our backs on the will of God."

"You mean that I should take the rich count?"

"The Count of Duperret is so rich that his wealth is a glory. Out of his own pocket, last year, he gave to France the frigate...."

"I know! I know! But he is so old!"

"He is not more than forty. And he is a Gascon."

"He has such an ugly face."

"He is rich, he is of a great title, and he loves you."

"For that reason he will be jealous."

"When the right man comes to you after your marriage, *mademoiselle*, trust that love will always find out a way. If not, there is always Victoire!"

"Do you think, Victoire, that a girl should choose her lover before or after her marriage?"

"Ah, my God! To choose him before, how immoral that would be."

"I mean only to choose him in the mind, Victoire."

"Never, never! What a sin that would be!"

"Well, I dare say you're right... Here's the letter about the American.... What a strange thing, Victoire, that the cold-blooded marquis with the ice in his smile and the poison on his tongue, should have such a wild runaway horse of a son as my cousin Jean-Pierre!"

"Ah, but his mother was a woman. What an eye she had!" said Victoire. She sighed heavily.

"**READ ME** the letter aloud," said Marguerite de Fréron. "I can see the picture better when I hear a thing read aloud."

Victoire began:

"My dearest Marguerite,

"Last night I thought of you. If our relationship were two degrees removed, I would come home and marry you, or be damned."

"I forgot that it began in that way," meditated Marguerite.

Victoire continued her reading:

"I have not been seriously in love more than two or three times in the last month or so. The fact is that these American girls are too frank and open. In clothes—can you believe it?—they are much above the English *and* the French. I have seen the daughter of a shop-keeper put such money on her back that it was a thing to stare at. And all in good taste, also. A thing to wonder over. They are clean, too. There are not many people in this new world but I dare say that they use more soap in a day than *la belle France* consumes in a month. I commend you to your bath-tub and a scrubbing brush instead of the damned powder and perfumes with which most of our beauties cover up yesterday."

"That is a trifle vulgar, Victoire," said the lady.

"No, *mademoiselle*. For a viscount, no."

"Perhaps you're right. Yes, I think it is all right for a viscount. Go on."

Victoire continued:

"I have had a duel...."

"This is the part!" said Marguerite, settling herself, and nodding.

"I have had a duel and by the grace of God and a kind antagonist I have escaped with my life and a small hole in my right arm. In a land of coonskin caps and long rifles, how the devil should I expect to find a fencer who is a true hero out of Rabelais? But I forget that you cannot read that great book."

"I can, though, and I have," said Marguerite.

"For shame, *mademoiselle*," said Victoire, blushing.

"I can tell by your face that you have read it yourself," said Marguerite.

"But it is my duty and my birthright to have a thick skin," said Victoire.

"Every girl has the duty and birthright of learning what she is not supposed to know. Go on, Victoire."

"We fought at dawn, a week or so ago. That is why my writing staggers. My arm is doing very well, but I have been drunk *every* day since with my American.

"His name is Massey. Hugh Massey. He has the shoulders of an ox, the legs of a horse, and a heart of gold. The insult was mortal. If I had had him at advantage, I would have run him through the heart; but after I was wounded he stood back and smiled at me. Yet I truly was helpless. I stood before him as naked as one day I shall stand before my God. But he only said: 'We are both so hot, Charlevain, that I think we could use a bottle of Madeira between us. Perhaps that would wash the hard feeling away?' I could say nothing. I could only open my arms and embrace him—and by doing so I dripped blood over his good clothes. But what was that to such a hero? He merely laughed. I have sworn to love him forever, and he has said that he will endure me as well as he can, for a damned Frenchman. (At this I was ready to fight again, but discovered it to be a bit of American humor.) In short, we are brothers.

"He has taken me home to his plantation and introduced me to the artist who taught him to use a sword. It is a lean, hard old Frenchman, Claude Epivent, who also gave him the French language as pure as the speech of Lyons. When I sank the third time in the sea of my debts, he caught me up by the hair of the head and presented me to his uncle, a fat, soggy, white-grub of a semi-paralytic who spends his life in a chair and yet has spread the net of his business all over the world and constantly catches in his web the riches of China, India, and Africa.

"From this Oliver Massey I have borrowed enough to clear me of debt and leave in my hands enough to make a big merchant adventure. In return for it—God forgive me for it, my father the marquis never will—I have pledged the village of Charlevain out of the family for fifty years. The point of my news and my letter is that Massey goes abroad now to receive the village and to be its landlord for a time. Be kind to him. Keep the marquis from killing him with hired cutthroats or poison. And farewell, my very beautiful and dear cousin.

"Your obedient and faithful servant,

Jean-Pierre."

CHAPTER V

A VISIT WITH THE MARQUIS

VICTOIRE HAD MISNAMED the time for which the American was invited by almost an hour; the result was that Marguerite in spite of herself was at hand in the salon before Hampton arrived. The Marquis d'Alenton greeted her with his usual cold, effortless irony.

"If you arrive a little late, my dear," he said afterward, "you have the advantage of appearing in motion."

"Is that an advantage?" she asked. "To come all in haste and out of breath?"

"To seem all in haste but never to be out of breath is the better way of putting it," said the marquis. "When I was a child the clothes of a woman were so complicated that she hardly dared to move but the new democracy of ideas has lightened her burden and you in particular, Marguerite, should be in motion as much as possible; for then we seem to guess at the rest of your beauty."

"Should I blush?" asked the girl.

"No, you should thank God for the grace He gave you. It is the one talent of the queen."

"I didn't know that you allowed any virtue to Madame Deficit," said Marguerite.

"A talent is not a virtue," said the marquis. "By the way, how do you intend to receive the American?"

"He had at the point of his sword the life of Jean-Pierre—"

"I forbid the name," said the marquis, calmly. "I do not wish to hear it."

Marguerite was silent for a moment, but an emotion was growing in her.

She broke out: "I *cannot* keep from speaking of my dear Jean-Pierre!"

"Marguerite!" cried the Count de Fréron. He was a man of fifty but he carried himself with such a straight back and walked with such a light step that at a distance he seemed no more than a youth. By this outbreak on the part of his daughter he saw his entire existence and all her future threatened, for his estate was so small that nothing but the charity of the marquis provided for his life as a gentleman or assured the girl a marriage portion.

The marquis, however, showed no anger behind his smile, cut with precision in stone.

"I cannot ask you to leave the room, and you will not force me to go myself," he said. "But I take it that you intend to receive *Monsieur* Massey with a good deal of warmth?"

"I do, indeed," said the girl.

"Good!" said the marquis. "You may smile on him, Marguerite, because it may be necessary to soften him a little."

"But tell me—is he a gentleman? Are there gentlemen in America?" she asked.

"What do you think yourself?" asked the marquis.

"They have Indians and things," said she, frowning. "But at least a few of them know how to fence very well indeed. Yes, I suppose that General Washington is a gentleman. Or would you say so?"

"The country is infected with liberty," said the marquis, while the count laughed a little, discreetly. "Liberty is only a fever of the mind, but it is catching and therefore dangerous. In the new United States, every clodhopper holds up his head like a peer, I am told."

The Count de Fréron explained even more simply: "Where there is no sense of caste, there cannot be a gentry."

Young Georges Francois de Poncey, who had spent most of his life in the household of the marquis as a sort of gentleman retainer, said: "They come from America, I understand—most of the idiot ideas that the Third Estate babbles about."

"New ideas are dangerous except to cultivated minds," said the marquis. "Words! Words! Words! They are shot that fly around the world timelessly until they strike a target. That Voltaire; that Rousseau with his vulgar twaddle; their ghosts still speak in the world. Democratic gibberish is afloat like dead stuff in a river. But here in Charlevain we will maintain the old regime, Armand, as one good example in a tainted world."

"And Charlevain village?" asked the count.

"I must buy it back," said the marquis. "The possession of it may have gone to the head of the American. And they are a nation of shrewd traders. But of course I must buy it back. I shall go again to the money lenders and leave some of my blood behind me!"

AND AS he spoke he looked fixedly towards the place on the wall where the portrait of the young viscount, painted only a year before, had been hanging. The space now was vacant. It had been empty since the marquis heard of the alienation of a portion of his estate, which he valued like a part of his body.

At this point Hampton was announced and entered the room. He was dressed as for the street in the new English fashion, that is to say, his clothes were a dark blue stuff and his white stockings were striped with pale blue. When he saw the gentlemen of the château for one instant he paused in embarrassment. The marquis in particular was dressed in the older style. In fact he had not changed his fashion to follow the times but distinguished himself by remaining in the rear of public taste, as many of the foremost gentlemen in France also were doing. He wore today a coat of grey silk and small-clothes of the same material, with a particularly brilliant waistcoat of white satin all embroidered in silk with roses and green leaves, and buttoned like the coat with silver. Point d'Alenton furnished his ruffles and he rested his hand on a long cane with a carved, golden head.

The count and de Poncey were much less shining examples

of nobility in full dress but Hampton felt like a shop clerk as he came in among them. However, he was a determined man who knew how to face a difficulty when he found one.

He was being welcomed by the marquis. He was being presented to the others. Their names rang in the hollow of his ear and hardly reached his mind, for the girl grew on him like a great music. He could not have described her, afterwards, except the kerchief of white gauze that made a mist about her throat, but a door opened in his heart and some great chamber was filled with her and closed and sealed forever.

They went in to dinner almost at once, which was a mercy for him, and he found the calm, steady voice of the marquis proceeding in gentle modulations. There were people in the world who declared that the voice of d'Alenton had never been raised in all his life.

"There were some differences of opinion in your country during the war of your revolution, *Monsieur* Massey. Was your family for the king or against?"

"We were against," said Hampton.

"Interesting!" said the marquis. "And the new liberty; and General Washington as your president, how do you and your family take to the regime?"

"My father died at the head of his brigade for the new liberty," said Hampton. "And General Washington sat in the mud and held him in his arms."

The girl bent her head a little and half closed her eyes. Vaguely Hampton saw her through the vision of that day when he had seen from an upper window Captain Thornton galloping toward the house and, afterwards, he had heard the man's voice speaking to his mother. And he remembered how he had known then that something was subtracted from his world. He wondered what the truth might be concerning Massey. Very possibly it was a Tory family.

Recovering from the rigid moment, he found the courteous eyes of the Frenchmen avoiding his face. The marquis lifted a wine glass toward him with infinite grace and touched it to his lips. So the instant passed and young de Poncey broke in with something that started the conversation again.

Hampton said to the girl: "I'm sorry that I showed that emotion. That was back in 1776 and usually I can talk about him at ease."

She considered him and his remark with that sudden detachment which makes the French, at times, seem the only civilized people.

She said: "I think I understand. You talk about him in a strange house, in a strange country, to strange people: and it makes a small boy of you, suddenly. You could feel that day again as a boy."

This insight startled him.

"That's true, though already I was a soldier at seventeen," he said. "I could see the messenger riding up the road again. I could see the way his horse labored in the mud and knocked out splashes of water. There's an avenue of tall trees in front of the house and I could see the wind bending them, and letting go, and bending them again. The whole room, just now, was around me the way it was then, with woodsmoke stuffing up my nose and the fishing rod still wet in the corner. It touched me when I thought I was perfectly guarded."

To this description she listened carefully, lifting her eyes to him once or twice in appreciation as he made his picture clear. He felt sure that like those Virginia girls she could bubble and chatter through an entire evening, but in the blue of her eyes a mind could work, also.

"You'll want to know about Jean-Pierre," said Hampton to the marquis.

D'ALENTON LOOKED toward him, but not at him. The Count de Fréron bit his lip and stared down at the table. Hampton observed these signs but it was impossible that a man's son and heir should be an unwelcome topic for the table. "And I can tell you a good deal about him," went on Hampton, "although one has to have a quick eye to follow him. He's been from Georgia to Maine and back again but when he whizzed through Virginia I had a few glimpses of him."

The men at the table took these remarks in silence but the girl asked: "Can you tell us all about him in five words?"

"Yes," answered Hampton after an instant of thought. "I can tell you this: He is a good friend!"

The girl smiled at him for saying that but the next moment Fréron was shifting the topic of conversation; de Poncey joined in with a cheerful anecdote, and in the mind of Hampton remained a distinct impression that this was not the day to talk about Jean-Pierre, Viscount of Charlevain. Yet he felt, also, that the name was a key which had opened something in the mind and the heart of the girl. But above all he found himself a little mystified by the extreme kindliness with which the entire group received him. His supposed friendship for Jean-Pierre was not the basis of this kindly attitude. It seemed merely that the French aristocracy overflowed with the most cordial hospitality for strangers; or was it the kindly interest of people who were to be his neighbors?

Sometimes he felt in his throat the desire to tell them how Jean-Pierre had fallen in that tavern in Le Havre; sometimes he felt that he must say that the fish of Le Havre bay probably had devoured the son of the marquis long before this, but there remained in his mind a strange feeling that it was a game in which he must play a part, no matter how unfairly.

If he were cheating, it was through the cheat that he kept touch with the girl, and every moment he sat in her presence he was more and more determined to keep upon her whatever hold he might possess. He began to feel, also, that something more than chance was thrusting him forward, as though he had stepped into the shoes of another man and was being carried on without his own volition. Disaster, he was certain, lay ahead of him, but he could not resist the fascination of the unseen road.

CHAPTER VI

AMERICAN NONSENSE

IT WAS THE most beautiful garden John Hampton had ever known. He felt a warm delight when he saw it, a delight which was also born of the beauty of Marguerite de Fréron. Plainly, her uncle, the marquis, had other things on his mind. And as they strolled through the exquisitely-nurtured lanes, the marquis dismissed the entire display with a brief smile and the words:

"You explain everything, Marguerite." That permanent smile of his which might have implied pleasure or the most exquisite irony.

"Of course," said Marguerite, "the new idea is that a garden ought to be something more than greenery. We ought to be able to walk through a greater space and a greater time…. Come down here at the water's edge and you can see the grotto. It looks really wild, don't you think?"

She crouched to peer into it. Sponge stone dripped from the roof and the water glinted for some distance into the interior. John Hampton watched her.

"There lives nature's wild man," said the marquis. "You are to imagine, Mr. Massey, a burly fellow dressed in lion skins and fighting the wilderness with his club. How primitive is he, Marguerite? Does he have the use of fire?" He meant the miniature shepherd on a miniature hillside in the grotto.

"No, he simply lives on roots and herbs," she said, "and never does any harm to a living creature. He is in the state of innocence, *Monsieur* Massey! He is alone with nature."

"Then what earthly use are these sheep to him?" asked the marquis.

He pointed out a flock of three muttons, their porcelain wool freshly washed so that it glistened like white fire in the sun. A broad ribbon of red satin set off the cleanliness of the ram; blue decorated the ewes.

"Yes, Marguerite," said the marquis, with a smirking smile. "Why does he keep sheep if he isn't going to cook and eat them?"

De Poncey put in: "Perhaps he likes his meat raw. It saves his time."

The girl laughed at the joke against her.

"But you know," she explained to Hampton, "the primitive man has not gone on to the ugly thought of *using* his fellow creatures. He simply has made them his friends. They have no fear of him. The birds fly down and sit on his shoulders. When he calls, the deer come bounding out of the woods."

"The three little trees yonder are the wild woods," pointed out de Poncey.

"I'll know how to torment you when your turn comes, Georges," said the girl, calmly. "Maybe it's just silly make believe," she went on to Hampton, "but it's the very newest idea in gardens."

"I like it," said Hampton, looking fixedly at her.

"These are the ruins of a Doric temple," she said, pointing out three small, broken marble columns near the grotto, with some of the architrave still remaining. "So that rushes the mind from wild mankind to the classic age. Then to take one far away into the Orient on the other side of the world, there's the little Chinese pagoda. I think it's rather sweet, don't you?"

"I do—yes," said Hampton, watching her eyes.

"That pointed arch," she went on, "is the last of a great Gothic cathedral, and it pours such a great deal on the mind. Don't you think?"

"Crusades, and knights in armor, and all that," said Hampton, gravely.

"Yes, exactly. How charming that you really feel it!" said the girl. "That heap of rocks and soil is the mountain, all bare at the summit; this runlet is the river; and of course the lake makes the great ocean for my garden. And so one may walk out here through the whole world and its history, if one wishes to use the imagination a little."

"Be careful!" called the marquis. "You're about to trip on the Great Pyramid."

"Well, Egypt had to be done rather in the small," admitted Marguerite.

"I like it, though," said Hampton.

THEY WERE walking back into the château when the marquis said: "I'm thinking of buying back the village, *Monsieur* Massey. I suppose you will put a price on it?"

"I don't know what it's worth," said Hampton. "I've only got a glance at it but I don't see how it can offer much of an income, really."

"It can't, unless one knows how to work it," said the marquis. "But there's a traditional lore in my family that teaches us how to turn peasants into gold."

All except Hampton laughed. The girl added: "You know the tradition, *monsieur*? One toad in a million has a diamond in his head? Well, we say that every French peasant has a golden purse, if you know just where to look for it!"

"I'll come down to see you tomorrow," said the marquis, "after you've had a chance to look over the entire property. But as for terms, why shouldn't we say the money your uncle advanced for the village, plus a good round sum of advantage money? Wouldn't that be equitable?"

"Entirely," said Hampton, but his face was overclouded by the last remark of the girl.

After he had said his adieus, the marquis took her a little to task about it.

*Hampton smiled behind his mask and
brushed aside the Gascon's thrust*

"You have made a conquest, Marguerite," he told her. "Did you notice, de Poncey?"

"The poor American was lost in amazement," nodded de Poncey. "The only garden he saw was your face, Marguerite."

She laughed as she answered: "I thought he was very charming and attentive. But silent, except in spots. And such a brown, ugly face. Put feathers in his hair and he could serve as a red Indian, don't you think?"

"I think he'd wear feathers and turn into a wild man for you," said the marquis, "but it seems that he is sensitive about the poorer orders. He turned as dark as a rainy day when you spoke about the purse of gold and the peasant."

"But isn't it a saying?" she asked.

"They have another one in their country. One Tom Jefferson put it down on paper, that all men are born free and equal."

"All men? I never heard such ridiculous nonsense!" she cried. "Or is it good Rousseau?"

"American nonsense," said de Poncey. "It means that you're equal to the peasant's daughter, Marguerite!"

And they all laughed together, merrily and in relief; for they had made an unusual effort to entertain Hampton.

CHAPTER VII

JUSTICE FOR RABBLE

THE MARQUIS, AS he had promised, rode down the next day to buy back the village of Charlevain. He took with him the count and Marguerite. For he said to her: "I may need your pretty face to help lower the price."

"I owe you so much," said Marguerite, "that at least I can keep smiling when you wish…. Does Count Duperret come tomorrow?"

"He does, child," said the marquis. "If I could tell you how much you please me by taking him as your fiance—"

"A girl must be married to some one before she is free in the world; of course I know that," said Marguerite. "But I wish that I knew a little more about him."

"I can tell you everything in a nutshell," answered the marquis. "His wealth is of the first degree, his family of the second, and his manners of the third. Is there anything else you need to know?"

"No," sighed Marguerite, "I suppose that I can do with that, but sometimes I wish that the silly fairy-land of Rousseau could come true and that weddings could be something better than mere politeness and law!"

"Child," said the marquis, "do you wish to mend your own clothes, scrub your own floors, nurse your own child, bend your back with labor, and turn your face old before you're thirty?"

"Heavens, no!" said Marguerite.

"That is all Rousseau amounts to, however," said the marquis.

"So let's have no more talk about the way of nature. The way of France is what concerns you, and I assure you that Duperret is a proper match. That should suffice you."

"It must," said Marguerite, and yet she sighed a little as she spoke.

As they entered the village two of the retainers who accompanied them rode ahead to clear the way of children and pigs. The peasants ran out of their houses to bow to their masters and Marguerite, like a good Christian, made herself smile on them. The marquis and de Fréron, of course, gave them not a glance.

A great shouting exploded around the bend of the street. People began to run toward the uproar and the marquis rode into view of a billowing dust cloud through which a big bay horse flashed like gold as it pitched and bucked, fighting with the savage anger of a cat. John Hampton sat in the saddle. He had thrown off coat and cravat, so that his shirt billowed around his shoulders and made him look a giant.

"Watch the peasants," said the calm voice of Marguerite de Fréron to the marquis. "They like the fight but they're afraid for their master. Did you ever before see a peasant who cared a whit about his lord's neck? There's a woman on her knees for him! How extremely odd! But I wish they'd stop the screaming. The American seems to like the fight."

FOR HAMPTON, while the pigtail of his wig danced and leaped like a snake behind his head, shouted and laughed till the bay reared suddenly and flung itself on its back. A long cry burst from the villagers, the shrill of women screeching and the groaning of men. However, the horse had hurt itself, not the rider. As the bay struggled to its feet, Hampton sprang back into the saddle but the fight was over.

The gelding stood with hanging head while the dust settled rapidly and turned to trickles of mud on the sweating flanks; the forelegs were braced wide apart and trembling at the knees. The villagers began to shout with whole hearts for *"Monsieur Massey."* They ran in joyously around him as he dismounted and gave the reins of the gelding to its owner, the blacksmith saying: "He'll be a kinder horse from now on, Jacques. Be good to him. The negro who taught me how to ride used to say that a horse must respect himself or he can't respect his rider."

"*Monsieur*, you have doubled his price for me," said Cartier. "How shall I thank you? But my heart died in me when I saw how this wicked, beautiful devil was throwing you up at the sky!"

The wind now had blown the dust away and Hampton saw the people from the château for the first time and was aware, as the villagers scattered back before such nobility, of the sweat and dust which begrimed him.

Marceau already was there, bowing like an automaton, begging them all to enter the inn as the villagers scattered to a respectful distance.

The marquis said: "Why should we miss this beautiful day, Marceau? There are seats here under the big tree.... You know, *Monsieur* Massey, that Saint Louis is said to have sat under this same oak to give judgment to the people? Shall we sit here for a moment?"

"As you wish," said Hampton. He was a little embarrassed at that moment because Cartier, the blacksmith, was helping him into his coat and big Rolland, the cooper, was dusting off his clothes while Julie adjusted and tied his cravat with wonderful, swift fingers and then gave him a towel moistened at one end so that he could clean his hands.

"If you will pass your fingers through your hair once or twice, *monsieur*," she whispered. And then: "Yes, is she not lovely?"

Perhaps the last words were an adroit hint to him not to stare like a gaping jackass but he still was uneasy when he took one of the rustic seats beneath the oak and told Marceau to bring them some of that white Bordeaux that was cooling in the spring.

"What I hope now is to relieve you of the burden of this wretched village," said the marquis.

Here the girl smiled on him, and Hampton felt his entire life become a thing of peace.

Said the marquis, drawing his riding whip through his hands: "You will understand that Charlevain has been in the hands of my family for certain hundreds of years and that no one who looked from the windows of the château could see land that was not a portion of the estate. To realize that the village itself is in other hands, no matter how distinguished, no matter how friendly, is a misfortune."

"I understand perfectly," said Hampton.

"This excursion of your money into a foreign land," said the marquis, "is in the nature of an experiment, an adventure, I dare say."

"Monsieur le marquis," answered Hampton, "I only begin to be a man of business."

"What I wish to offer," said the Marquis d'Alenton, "is the amount of your investment together with good interest on the sum. Like you, *monsieur,* I am not a man of business... and when you are freed from this burden, we want you to come and stay with us at the château for as long as you may. Business and friendship we shall mix, like wine and water."

The girl, who seemed to enjoy the last remark, smiled upon Hampton again with the frankest eyes in the world.

"It seems to me that my uncle could ask no more than you offer," said Hampton.

"In that case, *monsieur,* we may write out the terms and sign them together; the money will go forward to you at once; and you will be freed from Charlevain.... May I drink to you, to your country, to your freedom, and to the great General Washington!"

"—to you all, sir, and to your beautiful France!"

Marceau had served the white Bordeaux, a sweet, fragrant wine, and Hampton drank with it the courtesy of the marquis, the white beauty of the old château, and the smile of the girl.

Count de Fréron, taking pen and paper from Marceau, was beginning to write sweeping capitals and flowing script.

Hampton began to sweat. For he found himself hurried forward into a transaction which he had no power to conclude, of course. Yet to resist the marquis seemed impossible; and not to resist him was totally absurd. He had caught himself neatly in a net.

"You know the terms, cousin?" asked the marquis. "And aside from the original sum, perhaps a profit of ten per cent, *Monsieur* Massey?"

AN OUTCRY down the street interrupted the marquis. Instead of speaking against it, he folded his arms and endured with his customary smile. A moment later Louis the cripple came into view swinging slowly along on his crutches and looking more bedraggled and dusty than ever. Beside him stepped three men with tufts of red and blue feathers in their caps to signify that they were in the service of the marquis. One of the three stepped out before the others and called: "Who saw this Louis last in the village? There's a reward in good hard cash for testimony. Who wants the money?"

A crowd of the villagers poured around this important procession. One lad ran backwards before the gamekeeper, who carried a fowling piece on his shoulder. The boy shrilled: "I saw you go away in the gray of this morning, Louis. I saw you go!"

Louis stopped short and shook a crutch at the lad, yelling:

"You lie! And you're the son of a liar and the grandson of a—"

The gamekeeper struck him a backhand blow across the mouth. Louis stopped talking and began to lick the blood from his lips.

"I saw him go stealing away! I saw him!" cried the boy in a triumph.

"Then the next time he sees the gray of the morning will be through the bars of a prison window," said the gamekeeper.

Hampton with a few big strides reached the group. The anger in him was as though he had seen a servant in his house struck by a stranger. The cripple, seeing him come, held out a hand and cried out something in a plaintive voice.

"Keep your hands from him!" exclaimed Hampton. "He belongs in *my* village."

The gamekeeper drew back half a step only before this big, angry man. His voice was perfectly cool as he answered: *"Monsieur,* I am the gamekeeper of the Marquis d'Alenton!"

He spoke it with the finality of a man pronouncing an important judgment.

The street had been thickening with people during the last few moments. The riding of the horse had turned most of the village out of doors and they remained with a whispering rumor passing through them.

"They came running on me in the highway, which belongs to no man except the king!" cried Louis. "They seized me, noble and kind *monsieur,* and they—"

"We will find out the truth," said Hampton. "Come with me."

He walked back towards the group of the marquis under the huge tree and heard Mademoiselle Marguerite say quietly: "It is the loathsome cripple again!" Her head was raised with a look of disgust slightly covered by a smile. The brother of that smile was on the lips of the marquis.

The gamekeeper was saying: "There is someone here with more authority than *Monsieur l'Americain!"* and took off his cap with a very low bow to his master.

"This fellow who struck the cripple—is he your man?" demanded Hampton.

"A very good, faithful man, too," said the marquis, "who must have a reason for the blow. But let us come quietly to the truth."

"By all means, to the truth," said Hampton.

"What is it, Jean?" asked the marquis.

"This lame rat," said the gamekeeper, "was caught with the bones of a newly-killed pheasant. He'd been singeing the meat over a fire by the road and it was plain that he'd gone into your domain to kill the bird. You see we tied the bones—and some of the flesh still on them—around his neck. If there is such a thing as right and wrong in the world, he is a poacher!"

"Certainly," said the marquis. "Bundle him up to the château and give him a cell in the lower tier. There is too much of this wretched poaching, *Monsieur* Massey. If we don't keep it in hand our poor dogs will not be able to put up a bird for our guns in a whole morning's walk. Take the worthless fellow away!"

LOUIS DROPPED to the dust, crying out: *"Monsieur, monsieur!* You are a father to Jacques Cartier. Be my father, also. Don't let them take me to turn green with mold in the château!"

Here a booming voice spoke over the heads of the crowd, saying: "It is true. He is your man. He should be judged by you, *Monsieur* Massey."

That was the huge fellow, Cartier, who spoke.

"Is it true?" asked Hampton of the marquis. "Should I be his judge?"

"My dear friend," said the marquis, "in another moment Count de Fréron will have finished drawing up the legal deed of purchase and with your signature the village passes back to me. It is true that for this passing moment the right of justice in Charlevain is yours."

He waved that thought gracefully away.

"Monsieur—have pity!" screamed Louis.

"Are you a man?" roared the angry thunder of Cartier. "Stand up, dog!"

Louis, frightened out of his wits, rose to his feet. The bloody bones of the pheasant swayed back and forth beneath his chin.

"This man of the loud voice," said the marquis, "is he a friend of yours, *Monsieur* Massey? He is the blacksmith, is he not?"

Hampton stared helplessly at the sooty face of Cartier. Then he said: "It is true. I have an esteem for Jacques Cartier."

Hampton turned to Julie. There was no need to wait for her eyes, since they were always upon him.

"Julie," he said, "wipe the blood from the face of Louis, if you please. Louis, you shall have exactly what justice I'm able to find you." He added to the marquis: "Permit me to hear what he has to say and to give the judgment."

"My dear friend!—but of course!" said the marquis.

The smile of Lady Marguerite returned, but it was coldly intermingled with contempt. Those eyes of hers were almost too straight and deep-seeing, he thought. Pride was so much a part of her that she would look at king or beggar or angel or devil in one way only.

Julie had finished wiping the bleeding face of Louis.

"Now stand forth, Louis, and be a man," said Hampton.

"Yes, *monsieur*," said the cripple. "But God prevents me from being a *complete* man, as you may see."

He moved the stump of his right leg a little and ventured the faintest of smiles. From the semi-circle of villagers his sally brought a good, hearty laughter. But the laughter stopped suddenly. They were too anxious to follow every step of these proceedings.

Hampton, scanning their faces, noted those who laughed not at all, four white-bearded elders. In a village of similar size in Virginia there would have been five times as many old men and most of them straight and vigorous, still, not bending over sticks and creeping into the sun of midday like animals out of caves.

He said: "You four, my friends—you, Antoine, and Simon, Philippe, and Theobald. There are chairs for you under the tree. Sit down here, if you please." The names came to him freely. He seemed to know them from of old. "You will know the customs and the unwritten law and you shall help me to reach the truth!"

CHAPTER VIII

NOT FOR SALE

THE FOUR OLD men drew out from the crowd and looked at one another. An outburst of hand-clapping from the villagers encouraged them forward. They bowed repeatedly to the people from the château but at last they sat down.

Hampton heard a woman exclaim; "Poor *Père* Philippe! He does look grave enough to be a judge, if only I could wash some of the yellow out of his beard!"

The excited murmur of the crowd was saying: "This is strange—like an old legend—like the golden age—to be judges of ourselves—God give long life to our American!"

"If I am right," said Hampton, "the thing we wish to find out is whether or not Louis killed the pheasant on the open road or in the woods of *monsieur le marquis*. You four are judges to help me. Here are the witnesses for the prosecution. Afterward, we will hear Louis. And that boy also must be heard who saw Louis, he says, leave the village at dawn. The gamekeeper, there, can begin…. Louis, you must not keep standing on your one leg. A chair, Julie."

She already was bringing a high stool on which the cripple sat down and looked about him, frightened by his importance but proud of it. At this moment Hampton heard Lady Marguerite say quietly, "It *is* a little wearisome, Father, after you have spent more on the wooden leg of the poor wretch than his whole life is worth."

"Have you a wooden leg, Louis?" asked Hampton.

"Thank God and the purse of the noble Count de Fréron," said Louis, "I have a very fine wooden leg that came all the way from Holland. But who am I to use up such a wonderful leg on ordinary days? I keep it for Christmas and the other feasts!"

The villagers did not laugh at this. They had taken their positions where they could view both the accused and his judges and has assumed attitudes of ease, particularly the blacksmith, for having brought with him into the street the sledge which had been in his hand, Jacques Cartier now rested the haft of it on the ground and sat on the iron head. At this simple speech of Louis' they nodded their heads in thrifty agreement.

"You are the first to speak," said Hampton to Jean the gamekeeper.

The man took a step forward and bowed to the marquis.

"Tell your story, Jean," said the marquis, yawning a little.

"It is perfectly simple," said Jean, when he had this permission. "The road is clear of brush. How could Louis have come close enough to the pheasant to strike it dead if he had found it on the road? But the fields on each side have plenty of just the sort of brush that a pheasant loves. We found him on the road but the poaching dog certainly had killed it in the brush."

He bowed again to the marquis, put on his cap again, and stepped back.

"What do you say, my lad?" Hampton asked the boy who had accused Louis.

He was frightened by this formal audience but managed to shrill out that he had looked out the door of his house early that morning and seen the cripple slinking off from the village, far too soon in the day for honest men to be astir.

Cartier's booming voice exclaimed: "What is early and what is late for a man too hungry to sleep? Look at him."

As he spoke he pulled aside some of the rags of Louis' and showed the naked ribs of the cripple which clasped his body like attenuated fingers. Louis dimmed the effect somewhat by scratching the exposed surface.

"Now speak, Louis," said Hampton, "and Cartier, be still."

HE WAS aware of the stone-cold smile of the marquis and of Marguerite de Fréron smiling also though her eyes reserved a judgment and seemed to imply a comparison between the big American and poor Louis. The whole affair, plainly, was disgusting and contemptible to her, and he felt as though a wind were drifting him farther and farther from her esteem. He knew her value to him by the ache that began in his heart and throbbed there steadily, but he forced his mind to a better concentration on the problem of Louis, for it was not Louis alone whom he considered but the long, densely packed semi-circle of villagers who listened to the proceedings with a desperate eagerness.

"Monsieur knows," said the cripple, "that the road is clear of brush, as Jean the gamekeeper says; but it is not clear of grass. It is true that I left the village early this morning; and it is also true that I was very hungry. Now when I saw the head of a pheasant just behind a tuft of grass on the road, I hardly stopped to thank God. I raised the crutch, here, with my right hand. *Monsieur* knows also that we grow skillful with the tools which are constantly near us. This crutch is to me like a longer arm. So at the first cast I struck over the pheasant. Before it could get to its feet again, I had it by the throat, and in that very place I made a small fire out of the stalks of last year's weeds and cooked the bird bit by bit and ate it. The roast for a hungry man is soon ready, noble and kind *monsieur.*"

"Also, a lean rogue has a keener wit than a fat one," said the marquis. The count and Marguerite laughed a bit at this remark, the girl in a clear, sweetly continuing voice that sent cold through the blood of Hampton.

"You have heard them on both sides," said Hampton to the four old men. "What have you to say?"

Old Antoine Honat stretched out his arm.

"The right crutch!" he called. "Let me have it."

Julie, whose bright eyes understood before words were spoken, carried the crutch at once to the old man.

"Perhaps the wood will tell us the truth," said Antoine Honat. He pointed to a thick patch of dust near the tip of the crutch. "This wood was wet," he went on, "before the dust settled on it. That which wet it was not water. Water and dust make a mud which dries quickly and the mud flakes away. This is dry but more sticky. It holds more dust. I rub it away with the tip of my finger—and you see, *monsieur,* that the tip of my finger is stained a little with red. There was blood on this crutch, *monsieur.*"

"He already has told us," said Hampton, "that he knocked over the bird with the crutch."

"True, *monsieur,*" said ancient Philippe Lenoir. "But blood does not spring quickly through thick feathers. If one flings a stick at a chicken and hits it, is blood ever drawn?"

He looked proudly at Hampton, who listened with a frown.

Antoine made matters clearer: "But if he had waited in the brush near one of the little trails that the birds follow through the thickets and then if he had brought down the crutch with a great blow the blood might very well have sprung out."

"It is a lie!" screeched Louis. "After I wrung the neck of the bird, some of the blood fell on the crutch—"

"Be silent!" said old Philippe, sternly. "You left the village at the hour when hunters leave; you did not hunt on the bare road; you poached on the land of my lord the marquis. *Monsieur,* he is guilty."

"He is guilty!" said Simon Dejean, Theobald Sirpe, and Antoine, in one voice.

"Very well done, my friends," said the marquis. "As you see, *Monsieur* Massey, the French mind is not easily beclouded. And now that the judgment is given—"

Here Gartier bawled out: "Louis, tell *Monsieur* Massey in what manner you lost your leg."

"What has that to do with the matter?" asked the marquis.

Hampton said: "But do you in the first place admit that you poached, Louis?"

"The eye of God must have seen me," said Louis, sadly, "and He told the four old men what I had done. Yes, I have poached."

"A leg for a pheasant—tell *monsieur* how you lost your leg!" insisted Cartier.

"Be quiet, Jacques," said Hampton. "But tell me about losing your leg, Louis."

"*That* was a day," said Louis. "It was a clear morning. I remember how the frost lay on the hills like snow until the prime. It was at about that time that I was holding the horse for *Mademoiselle* Marguerite to mount—I was then a stable boy for Count de Fréron, *monsieur.*"

"And a lazy, shiftless one," said the count.

"In other words, a boy," commented Hampton. "Continue, Louis."

"But when *mademoiselle* was mounting, the English mare stepped to the side and *mademoiselle* fell on the gravel and hurt her hands. When *monsieur le comte* heard her cry out and saw what had happened, he was very angry, of course, and naturally kicked me. I, *monsieur,* was young and stupid and let loose of the reins to catch at the place where *monsieur le comte* had kicked—"

He illustrated with a gesture at which the villagers laughed, briefly.

"And the mare galloped off," went on Louis, "which of course enraged the Count de Fréron because it was a valuable animal. And he struck me across the face with his whip—"

"Ah!" murmured Hampton, and glanced aside at the count and his daughter. With immobile faces, they eyed the cripple.

"The lash was heavy," said Louis, "so that it cut through the flesh of my face. You still can see the scar just missing my eye, when my face is very clean."

"I thought this case concerned a stolen pheasant," said the marquis.

"*Monsieur* the judge!" exclaimed Cartier. "Doesn't the leg pay for the pheasant? Go on, Louis!"

Hampton, staring earnestly, saw not the face of Louis but a whole dark world of evil, centuries old.

VAGUELY HE was aware that the villagers were glancing at one another and then at him with a keen glint of hope, or suspicion, in their eyes.

Louis continued: "The weight of the blow staggered me, the pain of it blinded me, and as I jumped back I mistook my footing and fell from the high ground in front of the stable to the low ground beside it. In that way, I broke my leg. But the Count de Fréron did not see because he was busy catching the mare. *Mademoiselle* was helping him. I was stunned, so that I lay there for several hours, because my head was cracked as well as my leg broken. Finally the pain wakened me, because you must understand that the bone had broken through the flesh. At last my groaning was heard by the grooms, who took me to a doctor; but from lying on the ground the wound had caught cold and the leg was cut off. It is a very beautiful piece of work as everyone admits. The stump is as flat as the palm of your hand, *monsieur*. . . . But God knows how all of this talking will help me now from the prison!"

"As you see," said the marquis, "the fellow always was a worthless, shiftless rascal and today you have already heard him lying. There are cells in the château that will quiet his spirit, however."

Hampton looked straight at Marguerite. Her glance was turned to the sky in smiling boredom.

Cartier cried out again: "He was made a cripple for life, and hungry for life by the same token."

"What has that to do with the law?" asked the Count de Fréron.

"There is a law of God, *monsieur le comte*," said Hampton.

"The laws of France will suffice for us," said the marquis.

Hampton swallowed a glass of wine and then dragged a handkerchief across the wet of his forehead. Somewhere—was it in the château or in the next village beyond it?—bells were ringing, and the sound made him think of the cheerful singing of the slaves in far away Virginia. For even slaves were not as these feudal serfs, he thought.

He said to the gamekeeper: "What is the penalty?"

"For the pheasant, a franc," answered the man. "For the poaching—why, as many years in prison as you care to name."

"Or else?" asked Hampton.

"Or else five hundred francs payable to my lord the marquis," said the gamekeeper, with a gesture that terminated the case.

"I shall give you the five hundred francs," said Hampton, turning at last to the marquis; the whole village behind him gasped.

He had all three of their faces before him now, but it was the girl that he chose to watch as the amazement opened her eyes. The marquis started up. His anger was the merest shadow which flicked across his eyes and was gone again; only the cold sun of his smile was shining as he said to Hampton: "My dear friend, your wish is my law. If you pity the poor wretch, he is as free from fine or prison as the angels. No more of that, if you please! But here is the deed of sale, if you are ready—"

"I cannot sell Charlevain," said Hampton.

"What?" cried the count. "Impossible, my dear *Monsieur* Massey."

THEY STOOD up, all the three from the château, and in their rising Hampton felt himself repulsed from their lives by a great wave of incredulous scorn. He could tell clearly enough that their courtesy of the day before had been calculated carefully to make him amenable to the wishes of the marquis, but his hands were tied. They must have in their hands, by this time, a copy of the deed which alienated Charlevain village, signed both by Jean-Pierre and by the real Hugh Massey. That was one reason he dared not put his signature on the paper which Fréron had drawn up. He felt, also, that he owed to the dead American in some mysterious way a continuation of his interests and the only way Hugh Massey continued as an influence in this world was through his ghostly possession of the village of Charlevain.

Yet again, and perhaps stronger than everything else in the mind of Hampton, there was a singular sense of paternity which had been growing up in him toward the villagers.

For so many years he had fought his way through so many countries that he had come to feel no more obligation to other people than he could hold on the end of his sword, but the mute, animal-like affection with which the people of Charlev-ain regarded him had worked on his heart.

Beyond a doubt, his deception would be revealed before long, but every day he kept them from the vindictive hands of the marquis was, he thought, a separate blessing bestowed on the villagers. In his mind, beyond all this, there was a rising anger as he marked down the hypocrisy, the incredible pride of the three from the château. Only the girl seemed to regard him with more curiosity than contempt and disgust, but even to her he was a creature from another world.

He took some gold from his wallet and laid it on the small rustic table.

"That is the price of Louis, I believe," he said. "There are five hundred francs, *monsieur.*"

The marquis had been drawing and redrawing his riding whip through his fingers all this while; now the lash of it sang as he struck the coins into the dust.

"You cannot pay me for a gift I already have made, *monsieur*," said the marquis. "And for this fine stroke, I hope to find the reposte."

"I have no doubt that you are a master of your weapons," said Hampton.

"I have the advantage of a long reach, at least," answered d'Alenton, calmly. *"Adieu, monsieur!"*

The entire village had drawn back before this sudden anger of their masters. Not a voice stirred as the three went to their horses. Marguerite de Fréron came suddenly to Hampton, still watching him with that troubled curiosity.

"What is it that you wish to do?" she asked. "Do you want to be father to the whole village? To all these creatures? Won't they keep your hands unclean, *monsieur?*"

Julie had come close to look into the face of the lady.

"If I can't be a father, *mademoiselle,*" said Hampton, "I'll try to be one of the poor relations."

"That is a very odd and rather pleasant thing to say," answered Marguerite. "And if—"

She paused as her eye fell on Julie, who curtsied instantly at the side of Hampton. For a moment they regarded one another.

"Marguerite!" called her father, sharply.

"And so, *adieu, monsieur,*" she said coldly, and turned away with a sort of insolent leisure that left Hampton a thousand leagues behind. When she mounted, the horse began to dance but she called out to it cheerfully and humored it with a light, skillfull hand. The white mist, of the kerchief blew out behind her and the long feather wavered on her hat.

"Ah, yes, she is beautiful, *monsieur,*" said Julie.

He had an excuse for turning his back on her as Cartier approached like an enormous shadow. For once his voice was softened to a deep, humming murmur: "We cannot speak; we only can love you. But you are a fool, and our kind father, *monsieur.*"

The three from the château were already out of sight around the bend of the street, as Hampton grew aware of Louis, the cripple, who had crouched by the table and was placing upon it one by one the fallen coins, cherishing each in his hands for an instant like a sacred symbol.

IN THE little garden behind the tavern there was a pool; and beside the pool there was a stone bench where Hampton sat down. The walls of the garden gave him privacy and he needed to be alone. In the still water lay the images of the brush, and a tall poplar tree pointed far down in the hollow of a blue heaven where clouds moved no larger than sheep on a mountainside. Hampton tossed in a pebble which overwhelmed the sky with mighty waves so that all the images leaned and wavered to rubbery distortions. Gradually the picture composed itself again so that he could make out all details down to the steep image of himself at his feet and, near it, the gleam of a girl's face that appeared at the shoulder of a rounded bush.

"Julie!" he said.

The face by the shrubbery disappeared.

"Julie!" he commanded.

"*Monsieur?*" answered her frightened voice.

"I thought I could be alone here," said Hampton. "Is there something that you want?"

"Ah, *monsieur,* forgive me!" said the girl. "But when I see how sad you are, I have to come close to you."

In fact, her image in the pool advanced between the head of the green shrub and the tall tracery of the poplar. He could see the white flash of her gesture.

"I am not sad, Julie. I am only a little thoughtful," he stated.

"It is true that *monsieur* is only a little thoughtful," said Julie.

"And I wished to be alone."

"I am gone instantly."

He watched her in the trembling mirror, slowly turning.

"But wait a moment, Julie," he said.

"Ah, yes. I shall wait!"

"After all, there is no good reason why I should be gloomy...."

"No, no, *monsieur.* Too much thinking will make a man thin."

"Whereas it is so easy to be happy!"

"As easy, *monsieur,* as it is for the sky to be blue."

"Julie," he said, "shall I tell you something?"

"Ah, yes, *monsieur.*"

"It is simply this: You are charming!"

As he said this, he was peering down into the pool where he could see his image with that of the girl close by, except that hers was smaller and deeper in the blue so that he barely could make out her smile.

CHAPTER IX

THE LOAN OF A PISTOL

THAT EVENING FOR supper, there were broiled pigeons on the table of John Hampton of Hampton Hill, Virginia. Marceau did not bring them but let Julie carry in the platter proudly and lay it on the table with a smile for the master. She wore a crisp white apron, and her eyes were shining like the mist of a spring morning.

"There's enough here for six men," said Hampton, "and how pretty you are this evening, Julie!"

She touched the glow of her cheek and laughed. "Because I am so happy, *monsieur*. Ah, heaven, I have forgotten the watercress!"

She fled, and Marceau drifted near to sauce the food with his talk.

"Shall I carve the pigeon, *monsieur?* These little birds are complicated by smallness. They need much patience and a sharp knife."

"I do without the knife. In my fingers, you see that I make short work of them."

"Ah, true," said Marceau, laughing. "How it warms me to see a man of full blood at the table!"

"That Burgundy has a good, deep taste," said Hampton.

"It has both fruit and marrow, *monsieur,* like the love which the people of Charlevain begin to bear for you. Poor wretches— they never have had such a master."

He drew back as Julie came again, saying: "Stay, Julie, and pour the wine for *monsieur.*"

She laid the watercress beside the platter of pigeon and then filled the glass of Hampton with Burgundy. He looked from her hands to her face.

"How sweet you are, Julie!" said he. "What a sweet song you are to me!"

"But music is sad, *monsieur;* and it is not my song that makes you sorrowful," said the girl.

"Am I sorrowful?" asked Hampton.

"You fight against it, but your heart is not in the pigeons and the wine," she told him.

"Where is it, then, Julie?"

"Up there—among the violin music—letting it talk for you to Lady Marguerite. Do I dare to say it?"

"There is nothing in the world that you will not say if you please," said Hampton.

"If you permit me to say it, then, is it not true?"

"How great a fool would I be to look so far above me, Julie, so high above my reach?"

"But your reach is longer than your arm, *monsieur.*"

"What makes it longer?"

"Your sword, *monsieur.*"

"Julie, there is something delicious about you that makes me wish to laugh."

"At least you are smiling, *monsieur,* but I can tell why."

"Tell me why, then?"

"Because we are speaking of Lady Marguerite. Ah, if I only had such shining hair and such blue eyes and such a delicate mouth and such a throat like music, and such grace...."

"Well, suppose you had all those things, Julie?"

"I would use them to make you happier when I stand at your table and pour the wine," said the girl. "And tonight above every night I would put on all my graces and shine to make you happy, because tomorrow is to be such a black day for you, *monsieur.*"

"Why shall it be particularly black?" asked Hampton.

"Because Count Duperret comes tomorrow."

"Will he collect taxes from me?"

"He will collect Lady Marguerite."

"He will marry her?" Hampton asked.

"They will be betrothed, *monsieur.* Surely you have heard about it."

"No—ah—no," said Hampton.

"What a sigh!" murmured Julie. "If I could make you happier, I would pour my heart into that wine."

"It would be almost too red and too sweet, dear Julie, if you did that.... This Duperret... tell me about him."

"Does the thought of him roll bitterness over your tongue and into the hollow of your throat, *monsieur?* Is it a dreadful pain?"

"Perhaps.... But tell me about the count."

"He has been here before," said Julie, "and a French village is like a fishing net; it catches even the smallest wriggles of gossip. Besides, we have seen a good deal—Guy de Duperret is a Gascon."

"They fence well, the Gascons," said Hampton, thoughtfully.

"He is a very famous duellist," said the girl.

"Ah?" said Hampton.

She watched him with a strange smile.

"He is extremely wealthy. He has great estates, and a whole fleet of ships sailing out of Bordeaux."

"Wealth is a very good thing," said Hampton, "as long as it is used to keep the heart warm."

"His family is very old and good," said the girl.

"Old families are like old wood," said Hampton. "Often, time has eaten the strength out of them."

"Oh, but the Count Duperret will ride twenty leagues in a

day and drink three bottles of red wine with his supper and then dance till the birds are in the sky the next morning."

"A true man of men," said Hampton.

"He is," said the girl. "Everyone is afraid of him. He has a Gascon nose as long as his sword to smell out an insult."

"I tremble at the thought of meeting him," said Hampton, trimming the leg of a pigeon with his teeth.

"And although he is not beautiful, no woman can resist him," said Julie. "When he goes to Versailles, the wise gentry send their prettiest mistresses to Paris, and when he goes to Paris, they send their lovely ladies into the country until Count Duperret blows over, like a storm. Does he not sound to you like a real hero?"

"Yes," said Hampton, "out of a book—does he kick his servants and beat his valet?"

"How did you guess, *monsieur?*"

"Does he dress like a peacock and talk like a crowing rooster?"

"*Monsieur,* you have known him?"

"How happy the Lady Marguerite will be with him," said Hampton. "She has a pride of her own, I think."

"Marriage means little to the great people," said Julie. "They keep their girls like birds in cages and the only key that unlocks the cage is marriage. After that, how they fly high, and how they fly low!"

"This Count Duperret… he comes tomorrow, Julie?"

"He is on the way now. He uses four horses on his coach and his driver rides a footman with a fowling piece under his arm, loaded with slugs of lead. The count keeps fast horses, and his drivers know how to use the whip. He will be in Charlevain before the moon is two hours older. He will come galloping on the north road. *Monsieur,* there is still wine in the bottle—"

"Drink it yourself, Julie," said John Hampton, and left the dining-room.

HE LEFT the tavern also and went down the street in the darkness.

Few of the villagers were awake, for most of them were in bed shortly after sunset; he had only two greetings from dim figures and passed on towards the clinking anvil of Jacques Cartier with their: "Goodnight; good rest, *monsieur!*" in his ears.

Then he was standing in the doorway of the blacksmith shop watching the hand and the muscular arm of the blacksmith forging a massive lump of iron into a sharp angle.

"Keep on with your work," said Hampton, "while I talk with you."

Jacques Cartier lifted his overshadowing brows with surprise, suspended one stroke of his hammer while he said "... *monsieur!*" and then obediently continued.

"What are you doing with that double-barrelled horse-pistol, Jacques?" asked Hampton.

"I was repairing the lock of it, *monsieur.* But it is yours if it will serve you," said Cartier. "I am yours, also, and everything that I have!"

"I want some of your oldest and most ragged clothes, Jacques—keep on with your work—but have your bay horse tied to a tree north of the village. You know the hollow with the poplars growing thick in it? Have the horses tethered there and the ragged old clothes tied to the saddle in half an hour, and the pistol hitched to the pommel, loaded."

Hampton went back to the tavern and, from his room, looked over the wind-ruffled waters of Lake Charlevain toward the château, seeing through its thick walls, by the faintness of its distant lights, the face of Marguerite. After that, he called himself a fool, but left the tavern by the rear door, softly, crossed the garden, and climbed the garden wall. A few moments later he was in the hollow, filled with poplars just north of the village of Charlevain.

He could hear the horse trampling and sniffing the night air and it whinnied very softly when he came up. The fight they had had together had made them close friends. There in moonlight, thickly-striped with the long, thin, black shadows of the trees,

Hampton stripped off his clothes and dressed himself in the rags and the stale smell of sweated Jacques Cartier. He belted on his sword, pulled on his feet the pair of worn slippers which Cartier had not failed to include, and mounted the bay. After that, he took the north road at a canter.

CHAPTER X

DUEL WITH A GASCON

THE BAY WAS soft, being grass-fed instead of grained for work, and he had to take it from the gallop to a trot, most of the way. Still he went on briskly. The night was very clear, although the moon was young, and from the woods a slanting pattern of shadows ate away the border of the road which ran straight on, after the fashion of French roads, bridging ravines, cleaving through the shoulders of hills, keeping a course as direct as the flight of a bird; for the soldiers of the monarchy were moved rapidly when they were moved at all. In England, such a road would have dipped and swayed like a flycatching swallow in the evening, but in France everything was done with meticulous care, after a rigid pattern, when it came to government work.

For a brisk hour, John Hampton kept on up the road, and not a soul did he pass on the way. It was true of all France that one often could travel league after league, meeting no one, on those magnificent roads which could have borne up half the traffic of the world; peasant labor maintained them faultlessly, even though few wheels or hoofs covered their miles. At the end of an hour, Hampton rode the bay horse into a thicket near the crest of a hill. He tethered it there and returned to the side of the road, where he filled and lighted a pipe.

That pipe was not finished, and the tree shadows had not retracted a yard from the white face of the road when he heard a faint rumbling, and then a slight, chilly jingling noise of small bells; after that he could make out the beating of hoofs, and presently, over the brow of the opposite hill, he saw four galloping horses that drew a gentleman's coach so bright with gilding that even in the moonshine, it flashed like a jewel.

He heard the scream of the brakes as the horses dipped down the farther slope at a trot which swept into a gallop again in the hollow of the valley. Hoofs and wheels rolled thunder across the bridge; then the charge of the horses slackened on the nearer slope. They came up at a trot, then at a walk, their heads nodding with honest effort at their work. On the seat high above them, the driver swung the silk-fine shadow of his whiplash and sang out to encourage them. His companion beside him, swaying with the pitch of the big carriage, held across his knees a heavy fowling piece just as Julie had predicted. And inside the coach might be—how many armed men?

The leading horses gained the top of the slope. Already they were straining unbidden to regain their trot and the coach itself was just reaching the level when John Hampton stepped out of the thick shadows and fired one barrel of the pistol into the air.

"Halt!" he cried, and walked into the moonlight, so that it might show the naked sword in his hand and the folded handkerchief which masked the lower part of his face.

The footman made a vague gesture to lift his fowling piece but the driver beat the gun down again.

"Quiet, fool!" said the driver. "Quiet, or you'll be the death of us both. *That* man means business!"

"Etienne and Pierre, cover the men on the driver's box. Louis, keep your gun on the far side of the coach. Marcel, cover me from this side, and no man show himself. You fellows, climb down from the driver's seat—lively, now!"

THE DOOR of the coach swung slowly open, and the muzzle of a pistol looked out from the shadows, pointing straight at Hampton.

"*Monsieur* the count!" Hampton called. "Be considerate of your own skin. If you fire a single bullet, my men will have the flesh off your bones like so many crows. It is the wrong time to be brave, Duperret!"

The pistol disappeared into the shadows again. The two from the driver's seat already were on the road, where they stood shoulder to shoulder with frightened faces. The fowling piece lay on the seat above.

"Walk yonder," said Hampton to them, "and stand by that rock. If you try to run away or come a step closer, God pity you both, because this pistol does not know how to miss."

They obeyed him.

"Turn your backs," commanded Hampton in a terrible voice.

"Monsieur, will you kill us from behind?" they pleaded.

"Not if you stand as still as that stone," declared Hampton.

He stepped to the door of the coach.

"And now, *monsieur le comte,*" he said, resting the muzzle of the pistol against the lock of the open door.

A slant shaft of the moonlight struck across the face and the shoulder of Guy de Duperret. It showed the angular bigness of his nose and the golden decorations on his coat and turned into a silver mist the fine lace of his standing collar.

"If you will leave the pistol behind you and step into the road, *monsieur,*" said Hampton, "you will honor me…."

"My friend," said the count, "I understand by your language that you are a gentleman of education, and by your accent I take you to be from the south. I am from the south of France myself—"

"My lord," said Hampton, "if you had loved Gascony well enough to stay in it, you never would have met me and left your coach and four behind you."

"I shall step out, *mon ami,* in spite of the dust of the roadway," said the count. "But it is only to argue the point."

HE DISMOUNTED, accordingly, from the coach. He was not as tall as Hampton by two or three inches, but he was a more perfect type of the athlete. In fact, the width of his shoulders and the hanging length of his arms were almost a disfigurement. He had the neck of a bull and a small head mounted upon it; all the features of his face were small except for the great hook of a nose that sat like a handle in the midst of it. He carried in his hand his sheathed sword.

"You need not burden yourself with the sword," said Hampton.

"Robber," said the Gascon, "it is my habit to have it with me constantly, since I serve his Majesty, the King with it."

"In what country, *monsieur?*" asked Hampton.

"In no country at all, but at sea," said the count.

"And on what service at sea?" asked Hampton.

"I sailed with de Grasse," said the count, "when he was sent to make trouble for the English and help the rebel dogs in America."

"Ah," said Hampton, "were they dogs?"

"From the gutter," said the count. "Rascals in homespun. The King of France chose to part them from England, and now their damned democratic ideas have returned to pollute our own land."

"But you fought against the English, my lord?"

"I sat on shipboard and drank my wine and saw luckier people have a chance to fight in the distance," said the count.

"My lord," said Hampton, "I am going to appeal to you to turn out your pockets one by one. I am afraid that I need what is in them."

"My good friend, the robber," said the count, "I see that you are in a desperate way for the lack of money, but a gentleman— I know you are one by your language—needs preferment more than he ever can need hard cash, and I dare say you know that I have power to serve you."

"The trouble is," said Hampton, "that I could not trust your promises the moment I am out of your sight."

"Not trust—"began the count, in an angry voice. But then he

checked himself and said: "You will see when I explain that I am in such a position that I must buy your favor. Release those two cowardly dogs yonder to drive me on my journey—by God, I shall know how to discipline them afterward!—and I shall give into your hand my note to pay you a very handsome sum, indeed. The truth is, *monsieur*, that I am bound on a journey of importance; I must arrive at my destination tonight; and I cannot appear except as a gentleman should. So name your price and make it a handsome one; I write out at once an acknowledgment of indebtedness to you; and the matter is ended."

"*Monsieur* the count," said Hampton, "the acknowledgment of indebtedness which you sign this evening, you can cancel by a fast messenger tomorrow. As for the rest, I have taken a fancy to your clothes, though they would not fit me very well. Doff them at once, if you please."

"My clothes?" said the count. He laughed a little. "Ask for my honor, also. My clothes? Man, do you ask a Count of Duperret to stand naked on the king's highway?"

"I ask him," said Hampton, "to consider the gun I hold in my hand. And I assure him that I would put a bullet through him with no more compunction than he would shoot down one of those American dogs he was speaking of a moment ago."

"Damnation!" groaned the count.

"I hope not," said Hampton. "I shall give five francs to a priest to say a mass for your soul."

"I have fallen into the hands of a savage," murmured the count. "And yet—*monsieur*—if you have remaining to you the last instinct of a gentleman, you will not shame me by the force of your gun."

"I would rather shame you by the force of my sword," said Hampton. "But in that case, we fight for blood, *monsieur*, as well as for the fine clothes, the coach, and everything that is in it!"

"Fight? With swords?" cried the count, overjoyed. "Bright heaven, *monsieur*, will you do me that consummate honor?"

Hampton laid his pistol on the step of the coach.

"Your sword is in your hand. Proceed, my lord!" he said.

Count Duperret gave to the robber one wild glance of bewil-derment and then, with a moan of joy like the growl of a terrier when it sees a chance for a fight, he flung the sheath from his sword and threw himself on guard.

AT THE clash of steel against steel, Hampton saw the two servants twitch their heads to one side, but the orders he had given them and fear of a bullet through the back kept them riveted to their places.

Count Duperret, like a master of his weapon and a true fight-ing Gascon, came in like a wild boar to the attack with a long lunge, a short one, and a pair of rapid thrusts. But he found his sword touched away harmlessly and barely escaped a thrust at the last moment by making a leap that carried him yards away.

After that, he settled himself to his work like the really fine swordsman that he was. His prodigiously long arms gave him an advantage which he tried to use, and which was heightened because the robber used the easily bent arm of the Italian school; yet he possessed all the precision of the French masters and in addition he had the speed of a frightened cat.

Fear restricts the lungs. The count in half a minute began to gasp and sweat and curse, in whispers. He could not help retreat-ing, and yet he was not retreating fast enough when the foot of Hampton slipped on a loose stone and he fell to both knees and on his left hand in the dust.

"Now!" cried the count, and leaped in with a murderous lunge for the body; but the sword of Hampton found a way to rise and deflect the stroke; he rose with an up-thrust that threatened to rip up the face of Duperret and as the count sprang back his body was left open to a counter lunge. For the brief instant of his helplessness, he saw death hanging at a balance in the hand of the robber and shining in his eyes; then that ready lightning deflected and the sword point slid through the right forearm of Duperret.

The count's sword fell from his numbed fingers and he stood

grasping his wound with his other hand, silent, panting heavily, his legs braced far apart, as though he were about to throw himself on Hampton with his bare hands.

"You would have run me through like a poor rat when I was down," said Hampton. "What should I do to you now, *monsieur* the count?"

Count Duperret, being a Gascon, was a man of ready words, but now he found nothing to say.

"Out of your clothes!" commanded Hampton. "Quickly out of them. I have wasted too long a time on you already."

Duperret argued no longer. He pulled off his coat, he drew off his trousers, buckled with diamonds at the knees. He stood in his underclothing and his fine, ruffled shirt.

"The shirt, also, *monsieur*," said Hampton.

"In the name of God!" broke out the voice of Duperret.

But, with groanings, with slow hands, he pulled the shirt over his head and flung it from him.

His two servants remained exactly where they had been standing, their heads turned to the side like two statues; and the moon looked down upon the half-naked body of the count and the cold wind of the night seemed to blow through his very soul.

It was strange that at this instant, the count and John Hampton were seeing in their mind's-eye the face of the same woman.

CHAPTER XI

NO GENTLEMAN

JOHN HAMPTON WAS awakened in the morning by a hand on his shoulder and a repeated shaking.

"*Monsieur,*" said the voice of Julie, "it is your hour!"

"The devil take my hour and eat it," said Hampton. "I want to sleep."

"You always are angry with me if I let you sleep," said Julie. "Here is a hot towel for you to wash your face and hands, and I have fresh strawberries for your breakfast."

"Eat them yourself, Julie."

"And new rolls, exactly as you adore them—"

"I adore nothing but you, Julie. Go away!"

"And frothed chocolate—"

"What?"

"Frothed chocolate, *monsieur.*"

"I don't believe it," Hampton said.

"Here—if you take a deep breath you can tell the fragrance of it."

"True," said Hampton, and sat up in the bed.

He took the hot, wet towel and rubbed his face and hands. He dried them with the other end. Julie piled up his pillows and tied a great napkin around his neck.

"Give me my pipe, Julie," he said.

"*Monsieur,* you cannot smoke before you eat!"

"Fill my pipe and give it to me," said Hampton.

"I shall not!" said Julie. "Only a red Indian savage could do such a thing."

"Julie, you anger me. Give me the pipe!"

"Monsieur, you fill me with despair! The chocolate, also, will grow cold."

"True," said Hampton, yawning. He took the cup of chocolate and began to sip it.

"A great man like you, monsieur," she said, "should never lie so late in bed."

"I have a purpose, my dear."

"What is the purpose, *monsieur?*"

"To have longer dreams of Julie."

"Ah, *monsieur,* what truth is in that?"

"A little, at least," he answered.

"Yes, a little, I hope," she nodded, her head critically held on one side. "I have news to help you begin the day."

"Good news, Julie?"

"Terrible news! There is a robber near Charlevain."

"Frightful," said Hampton. "What sort?"

"A masked robber."

"Is he blond or dark?" asked Hampton.

"Monsieur, with his single hand he stopped the coach of the Count of Duperret, stripped the count to his skin, and rode away with the coach and four horses... a masked robber all in rags who talked like a gentleman and fought like an angel."

"An angel of darkness, Julie, if he was a robber."

"The count went back down the road on foot, five whole miles to Daunay. He entered Daunay in the coat of his footman with the shoes of his coachman on his feet and his sword in his hand. He tried to sneak into the tavern, there, but people happened to see him and he screamed curses at them. It was a dreadful scene!"

"Did he catch cold in the night air, poor fellow?" asked Hampton.

"But you have heard nothing, as yet."

"Is there more?"

"**OH YES!** He drank brandy till he was drunk. He said that a dozen brigands had attacked him, but his two men were getting drunk at the same time and they have let the story out of the bag. One man, *one* man stopped them all, and held them at the point of his pistol, and then—think of it!—fought the count on equal terms, sword to sword, and wounded him after the count had tried to murder him when he was down, and spared the count's life, and stripped him of his clothes—"

"Julie, you are out of breath."

"And Vaullese, the farmer," said Julie, "was down cutting brush this morning early and found in the woods a great coach standing deserted—a huge coach all covered with gilding, and the arms of Duperret on the door of it. And that lucky Pierre Jacques found a wandering horse with carriage harness still on it, and on the back of the horse was bound a great heap of the finest clothes in the world. And a whisper has it that six of our village farmers found another horse with a small casket lashed to *its* back, and in the casket they found whole handfuls of brooches and rings and pendants and necklaces—such as a great, rich count might take as a present to his betrothed."

"Lucky, lucky fellows," said Hampton, crunching a roll between his strong, white teeth. "Tell Marceau that this chocolate would be perfect if only the cook would add a pinch of salt to it."

"But who could have done such a thing?" demanded Julie.

"What thing?" asked Hampton.

"*Monsieur,* have you listened to me?"

"The truth is, Julie, that you talk so fast that I cannot understand a word you say, and your eyes are so bright and your smiling is so delightful that I can do nothing but watch you, while the words fly away over my head."

She sat on the foot of the bed and laughed at him.

"Ah, *monsieur,*" she said, "you are so calm that you are a little *too* calm.... But try to think of what manner of robber, in rags,

*Hampton's blade was red when it came away, and he
stepped back to watch the Frenchman stumble down*

would rob three men at the risk of his life, fight with a great duellist for the exercise, carry off a whole fortune in rich plunder, and then cast the plunder away on the backs of wandering horses?"

"I hope the poor count will recover everything," said Hampton.

She laughed again.

"From our peasants? Not even the holy saints could get the prizes from their hands!"

"Ah, but that's a pity," said Hampton.

"But the man! The robber! What sort of a person could he be?" insisted Julie.

"The kind God knows, and perhaps He will tell us, if we pray," said Hampton.

"It could not be," said the girl, "a man who wished to make the great Count Duperret suddenly appear as a fool before the entire world, could it? It surely could not be that, do you think?"

"But, Julie, how can any blue-blooded count be made to appear a fool? Heaven would not permit it, I'm sure."

"A man, monsieur, who knew that tomorrow was the day of the bethrothal—a clever, dangerous, wicked man who had put his own eye on the bright hair and the blue eyes and the lovely face of Lady Marguerite? It could not be such a man, could it?"

"Julie, how cleverly you talk! How your children will adore you when you tell them stories!" said Hampton.

"It could not be," she whispered, leaning suddenly forward, "it could not possibly be an American, *monsieur?*"

"Julie, you should not let yourself dream like this in the open light of the day."

"Ah," said the girl, "whatever I dream, trust me I shall not speak of the visions again—but how much, how much, how *much* you must love her!"

IT HAPPENED that the noble Marquis d'Alenton at that very moment was receiving news while his valet combed his hair, but the news came to him through a letter which had been brought post-haste by a special messenger. And the letter read:

"My noble friend,

"I salute you and give you to know that last night, when my coach was well inside your domains, I was set upon by villainous robbers, in particular a tall man with long legs and wide shoulders and a mask over the lower part of his face. I was stripped of my coach and all that was in it, and my very clothes were torn from my back, to my shame, the shame of my entire blood, and above all to the shame of the Marquis d'Alenton, on whose estate this outrage occurred.

"As for the loss of the coach, it now has been found, and the horses also, but the clothes are gone, including two sets of diamond buckles. Above all, there was a casket filled with jewels to be presented to Mademoiselle Marguerite. I note you the contents.

"Item: A golden brooch, curiously worked by Oriental artists, and set with clear, unflawed sapphires to the number of seven to the value of 300 Louis d'Or.

"Item: A good golden ring set with one diamond, value of 55 louis.

"Item: A bracelet of woven gold with a clasp enriched with one large emerald, slightly flawed but of the purest color: 150 louis.

"Item: A necklace of matched pearls, over fifty in number: 1,100 louis.

"Item: A pendant consisting of a fine golden chain to support a large diamond set around with a pattern of rubies: 400 louis.

"Some smaller trinkets of less value but all esteemed by connoisseurs I shall not mention, but the list above totals the sum of two thousand and five Louis d'Or, stolen from me on your estate.

"What construction your honor as a gentleman may place upon this occurrence, I cannot tell, but trust to the future and your known magnificence.

"In the meantime, I regret that I could not attend half-naked upon Lady Marguerite, and the negotiations for the marriage will be necessarily postponed until I have further word from you.

"If, in the meantime, you apprehend a suspect, I shall be pleased to make a hasty trip to attempt to identify him, which I think I could do by his voice. The scoundrel spoke with the vocabulary and the accent of a gentleman. God forgive me if I do not strip off his gentility and his skin together.

"And so farewell, with every compliment to you and to the charming Lady Marguerite and her esteemed father, the Count de Fréron...."

The marquis, when he had read this far, dropped the paper. It fell not upon the table but upon the floor, where a gust skidded it into a far corner, but the marquis did not turn his eyes after it. His own expression had not altered in the slightest and his face was still calm when Count de Fréron was admitted into the room.

"It was a message from Duperret, was is not?" asked Fréron.

"My dear friend," said the marquis, "it was a letter from a merchant or a moneylender, or some such creature. I did not read to the signature, but the letter lies yonder. You may see for yourself."

Fréron went to the corner and picked up the letter in haste. He glanced through the contents; he noted the signature; and gasped.

"It is the letter of a man in a great passion!" he said.

"True," said the marquis. "A letter from a *man* in a great passion, but not a letter from a *gentle*man. Let him lie there for a while."

"Ah, my dear friend," said Fréron, distressed, "is this high hope to be cast away forever?"

"It will soon be forgotten," said the marquis, "for there is one precious essence in time which people value too little, and that is the dust which falls from it softly and covers the face of the past."

CHAPTER XII

RETURN OF A DEAD MAN

IT WAS LATER on this same morning that half the village gathered in the street listening to the reading of the last little pamphlet which the Count de Mirabeau had printed to describe the proceedings of the States General. It was Jacques Cartier, the blacksmith, who did the reading, for he was one of the few learned men in Charlevain. Cartier, sweating behind the glasses which he had put on his nose, followed the words with a soiled forefinger and uttered them one by one, a booming reverberation in his voice, and the villagers listened with a hushed eagerness, regardless of the heat of the June day.

To listen to that news from Paris they had forgotten their own troubles. For a long time there had been something more than village quarrels to argue about, for the price of white bread had risen until the wages of a day's labor bought only a single pound.

John Hampton, from the storehouse, had been distributing grain at the old price but even their own good fortune could not keep the peasants from hearing eagerly about starvation in the rest of France.

Famine walked abroad even in their own neighborhood. The men of Charlevain, knowing their good fortune, fought with fists and clubs to keep away the residents of the other little towns on d'Alenton's estate, when they came begging for food. But they were receiving on this morning something more than food from the words which Cartier spelled out to them.

Hampton, lounging under the tree of justice, heard little of the pamphlet, for he was using his eyes more than his ears. He thought of the château across the lake as of a sun-lit hill-top and of the village as the dark valley where winter remains all year in the shadow.

And he still was full of that thought when he heard the rumbling of wheels, the padding hoofs of horses in the thick dust of the street, and looked up to see the diligence arriving. Cartier's audience refused to budge for it. When the driver cracked his whip, a long, humming murmur lived on the air for a moment and not a man gave place. The diligence had to crawl with difficulty between the edge of the crowd and the wall. It paused in front of the tavern as Hampton turned his head to his four old judges.

"Antoine, tell me," he said. "What is happening to our people? They forget their quarrels; they forget their bread to listen to news from Paris."

Antoine looked up at Hampton and then past him at the green branches of the tree.

"Is it revolution, *monsieur?*" he asked.

"Revolution?" exclaimed Hampton. "No, no! It simply means a great deal of talk is going on in Paris and Versailles."

"There may be something more than talk, *monsieur*," said Phillipe. "People who have been hungry for a long time even when they are fed are afraid that they may be hungry again."

HERE THE crowd which was listening to Cartier, suddenly broke up with a clamor and swept around the diligence, shouting. Hampton started up to stop the riot, and at the same time he was issuing from the open door of the coach a slender, sprightly, handsome Frenchman with a narrow bandage wrapped around his head. The face was that of Jean-Pierre, Viscount of Charlevain!

He brushed away the hands that stretched out to greet him, for it was plain that he was a favorite with the villagers, and came hastily through the crowd toward Hampton, calling out: "Ah, ha, *monsieur* the American!"

A voice from the middle of the street called the first English word that Hampton had heard in all those weeks: "Hello, Hugh! *Hai!* I can taste Madeira wine and see Virginia foxes again when I look at you!"

Jean-Pierre came on waving his hand, laughing; now he was looking up at Hampton and clapping him on the shoulder.

"My God, how big you Americans are!" he cried. "How many millions of acres of brawn and bone! Ah, Phillipe... Antoine... how happy I am to see you all once more! God bless Charlevain! God bless you all!... There is something in this purse, Antoine. Make it into bits small enough so that everyone may have a little portion."

The whole throng down the street was pouring up around their former master, shouting. Jean-Pierre, bright and lean as a swordblade, leaped onto a chair and waved them away. He called: "My friends, I love you all. But go to the driver of the diligence. He is packed full of news from Paris. Make him tell it. If he tries to keep silence, wash his mouth open with wine which I'll pay for."

On this tide of words he swept the people away, even to the four elders who had been sitting under the tree.

Old Antoine alone lingered a moment to say: "God bless you, *Monsieur* Jean-Pierre, for giving us a master like *Monsieur* Massey!" Then he hurried along to join the rest of the throng.

The viscount, staring an instant at Hampton, suddenly bowed to him.

"Are you Hugh Massey?" he asked. "The last time I saw Hugh, he was wearing a different face."

Hampton glanced across the lake at the white face of the château. In another moment it might become an irrecoverable part of his past, never to be approached again.

"*Monsieur* the viscount," he said, "my name is John Hampton."

"*Monsieur* Hampton," said the viscount, "the last time I saw you, you were walking like an angel through the guard of that damned scar-faced buccaneer in Le Havre; that was just before one of the rascals cracked me over the head with a chair, and the next thing I knew I was being dropped over the side of a boat into the harbor water, But I managed to swim ashore and so at last here I am. But Massey—you were going to his rescue. Where is he, man?"

"Dead," said Hampton.

"God have mercy on his soul!" said the viscount, in a half-whispering voice.

"The scar-faced devil did for him just before you dropped," said Hampton. "The whole four of them ran out. I went into the street and got two of the police. By the time they came, Massey's body was gone. You were gone, also, and I thought you were dead. Massey gave me, as he died, the letter to your father. I brought it here. A devilish combination of circumstances forced the name of Massey on me—and I haven't thrown it off yet—but you can say three words and I'll take a fast horse and start for the harbor."

Instead, Jean-Pierre held him by the arm; and with a downward head, the viscount muttered: "Poor Massey! Poor Hugh! If only he could have locked up his tongue that day… but God knows that he's in heaven if good, dull men can get there. *Monsieur* Hampton, what do you think of Charlevain? Do you love it? I know the people love you; I saw them look at you like an annuity. Have you argued with Fréron? Have you been frosted to the marrow by the marquis? Have you fallen in love with Marguerite?"

THIS FELLOW no more remained on one subject than a swallow could remain in one part of the sky.

"What is it to be?" asked Hampton. "A fast horse for the border?"

"*Monsieur* Hampton," asked the viscount, with his amazing frankness, "are you an honest man or a rascal?"

"*Monsieur* the viscount," said Hampton, "I think I am half one and half the other."

"You mean that you're a human being, like me," said the viscount. "*Monsieur* Hampton, I saw you come in with your sword smiling like a dancer on a stage. If you've been wearing the name of poor Hugh, I believe that you've done no shame to it. What have you been doing since you came here?"

"I have to have wine to go with the talk," said Hampton.

"We shall have it," said Jean-Pierre, "even before I present myself at the château."

"If you present yourself at the château," said Hampton, "you'll find a father who forbids your name to be mentioned in his house."

"Because of what, for God's sake?" asked Jean-Pierre.

"Because you sold your rights to Charlevain for twenty-five years."

"And he forbids my name to be mentioned?"

"He does."

"How my purse aches because of that!" sighed the viscount. "Wine, wine!…"

They were in the tavern, now.

"Marceau—wine!" shouted the viscount. "And that pretty little Julie to serve it. Julie—wine and your sweet smile in the glass along with it."

They got into the tap-room where Julie met them, curtsying. Jean-Pierre kissed her, and held her off at arm's length.

"Why, Julie," he said, "you are no longer little. And why do you blush like a little fool and look askance at *Monsieur* Massey? Oh ho, is that the story? Out of my sight, wench! You have broken my heart! Out of my sight—or is there anything you wish to say to me?"

She stood before him, laughing, avoiding the eye of Hampton.

"I only wonder, *Monsieur* Jean-Pierre," she said, "how many wonderful things you have seen in America."

"I have seen the inauguration of General Washington and heard part of his solemn talk. He's an Indian chief with a white skin, Julie. He talks as though he sees the future. Witchcraft or pipe-smoke. And at the same time I saw the most delicate, exquisite, charming, adorable—"

"I know," said Julie. "But how many times have you been in love since you saw her?"

"Not twice, Julie. And then only after I had spent the last of the money that your uncle loaned me on new clothes, horses, a carriage; for this delightful girl, Julie, had a fortune as big as her wrist was small. She had a hand, Julie, that was a miracle of dantiness, and seven thousand acres of tobacco in... ah, well, she's lost in the arms of a damned fellow as big as a Caroline pine tree who never spoke a word in his life except: 'Beer!' Yet there was one night when I saw the stars in her eyes and held her as close as a prayerbook. And now that you know that, Julie, you know everything that I learned in America. Wine, wine, my dear, and nothing but the best Burgundy for old friends should drink nothing else."

HE ADDED, as the girl disappeared and they sat down: "Not old friends, Hampton, but good ones, I think we shall be. Now tell me what you have done in Charlevain."

"Shall I confess?" asked Hampton.

"As to a priest," said Jean-Pierre, somewhere between a smile and sharp curiosity.

"I have played the part of an open-handed American, with another man's money," said Hampton. "I have forgiven some of the poor devils of peasants their back rent, failed to collect half the taxes, smiled with Julie, drunk with Marceau, and—seen Lady Marguerite."

Jean-Pierre drew himself up suddenly and stared. Hampton met him with a grim eye.

Suddenly the viscount laughed.

"Ah, well, to the devil with family pride!" he said. "She's only a cousin at that, and she's as sure as death to break the heart of any man who looks at her twice! What have you done about her?

"The noble Count Duperret—"

"I know that Gascon fox. I know the length of his teeth, too."

"He came with a coach and four, by night, with two servants, his best clothes, a sword at his side and a box of jewels in his hand, to be betrothed to Mademoiselle Marguerite today. But last night, a masked ruffian held up the coach, robbed the count of every stitch of clothes and every jewel in the box; and today, this very morning, the lucky peasants found the horses of the count wandering in the forest with the jewels and the clothes tied to their harness. A very mysterious matter!"

"By God," whispered the viscount, "did you do that?"

"*Monsieur*, you are my father-confessor," said Hampton.

"You *are* honest!" said Jean-Pierre. "I swear by the blue in the sky and the wine on the table that I love you already—but ah, my God, don't let me die of this laughter!"

He laughed, in fact, until he almost rolled from his chair.

At last he was able to say: "Does anyone know about this?"

"No one," said Hampton, "but Julie has a busy little devil in her brain that allows her to guess anything and everything."

"She is safe, however," said the viscount, "if I judge by the eye she rested on you a moment ago. Now we forget all this. We talk of other things, of how I shall make my peace with my father or of whatever you will. What shall it be, *Monsieur* Massey? Only let me know, first of all, why these hardy fellows of Charlevain seem to love you so much?"

"Because I love *them*," said Hampton.

"Nonsense! Love an entire village?"

"I know it's nonsense," said Hampton. "And from day to day I expect this silly passion of mine to disappear. What? Bother my head about a scattering of unwashed peasants? I can't believe it of myself. I have heard Mr. Jefferson talk about loving our fellow countrymen, but what countrymen of mine are these men of Charlevain? And yet they are in my heart, Jean-Pierre."

"Do you mean it?" asked the young viscount.

"They *are* in my heart," said Hampton. "I can't tell how or why. But when they open their hands like fish out of water, I have to put money, or least good advice, into their grasp. Are you laughing at me, *monsieur* the viscount?"

"I do not laugh. Will you recover, or is this an incurable disease?"

"It's an incurable disease, I'm afraid," said Hampton. "Tell me the last news from Paris. All we hear is stale when it reaches Charlevain."

"But you've heard, of course—the oath on the tennis court and all that?" the viscount said.

"Not a word, I think."

"THINK? A man doesn't think about such news. It blasts him apart and puts him together again in a new way. All in three days there is a new France prepared under our feet and a new sky over our heads....

"Our good, fat king sends word that he will meet the three orders on Monday; when the states go to assemble in the hall they are turned out by soldiers and bayonets. Why? Because the hall must be cleaned and prepared before the coming of the king? Think, eh?

"The deputies stand around twiddling their thumbs. How can hens hatch eggs unless they have nests to sit on. Then that devil of a Mirabeau begins to thunder. The whole crowd gathers in the *jeu de paume;* the deputies swear never to be dissolved but by their own consent and declare themselves the National Assembly. They send off expresses to Nantes to hunt for new quarters and safe quarters. Paris buzzes; the Palais Royal is full of clattering all day long."

"I've heard something about all this," said Hampton.

"Heard something? How can you be so damned cool? Perhaps

France is being reborn under your eyes! Louis the Fat sits in Marly, yawning and trying to think and having another bottle of champagne to cool off his brain. He stills eats and sleeps as though every day were Sunday—and that with the Long Parliament of Charles First under his nose. Yesterday at ten in the morning the streets are lined with troops. Why? To guard our king from his people? Swiss regiments. The crowd begins to hate them. At last in the great hall the king comes in before his States General. The Third Estate sits in silence. Some of the clergy, a few of the nobles, shout: '*Vive le roi!*'

"Our poor king! Even through the fat of his greasy eyes he can see that his throne is trembling. He commands the three orders to retire to separate chambers. The clergy and the nobles go. The Third Estate remains like stone. 'Gentlemen, you understand the wishes of the king?' say the Marquis de Breze. But that's no good. Every head turns to Mirabeau. What a great man he seems as he stands up to speak for them all!

"The Third Estate, he says, has sworn not to be removed. Is it the voice of all France? I think it may be. Here the king, there Mirabeau; equals and opposites. Today, all Paris is talking at the Palais Royal. The cafes are stuffed full of speeches. Every good Frenchman is trying to be a jewel on the forefinger of this great time…. I myself am only here to be reconciled to my father; then I gallop back to join the chatter. Will you come with me, Hampton?"

"After you are reconciled with your father? Yes, after that!"

"Do you mean that he won't forgive me?"

"Jean-Pierre, he hates me for what I've done with the village."

"What *have* you done?"

"He wants to buy me out; I refuse to sell and so long as I have authority in Charlevain, the marquis will sleep little at night. You'll be blamed for everything, I suppose."

The viscount said gloomily: "But what shall I do about my father? Walk up to fall into his arms and be received with a *lettre de cachet?*"

"What the devil is a *lettre de cachet?*" asked Hampton.

"You don't know that? What have you been doing with yourself in France, my dear John Hampton?"

"I have sunk into the dark pool of Charlevain and never come to the surface."

"A *lettre de cachet*, dear boy, is a warrant signed by the gracious hand of our lord and sovereign majesty, the king. He sends 'em around as presents to his favorites or to the older branches of the nobility. A fellow like my father is sure to have a few of them at hand. It is a warrant for an arrest and confinement for an indefinite period. The name of the criminal is left blank."

"If I were you," said Hampton, "I'd lie low for a time."

"Lie where?"

"Here at the tavern."

"If he decides to have me, he'll tear the tavern apart the way a wolf tears a chicken."

"He will *not* tear the tavern apart," said Hampton.

"Why, man, he could bring more than fifty armed men at his back, if he chose," said the viscount, staring.

"There are more than fifty men in Charlevain," said Hampton.

"What?" cried Jean-Pierre. "Arm the rabble against their masters? It's only the heat of your mind, John. You've cooped yourself up too much with your thoughts. You'll addle your brain before long, at this rate. But after all I might risk a letter to my father and ask permission to lay myself at his feet, so to speak, eh?"

"If that seems the proper thing to you," said Hampton.

"You hate the marquis?"

"No, not hate. He is your father, Jean-Pierre."

"Ah, John, what a friend you will be! When I think of your friendship it enlarges my soul more than the greatest cathedral can do. But I'll write the letter and then we'll see what happens."

"Jean-Pierre, I am remembering one thing with all my might.

When you write to your father you could make your peace with him by simply revealing the real name of the false Hugh Massey in the village. If you expose me, he'll love you for it.... Particularly since the strange robber attacked the count on the highway, the other evening. He'll forgive you anything, if you show him a way to put the law like a wildcat on my back and send me howling to the frontier, and slide me forever into some dark, quiet little prison cell."

"I think you're right," said Jean-Pierre. "I think he would forgive me; but I swear to you now, monsieur, that so long as I have a heart and a brain, I shall never forget the gallant way in which you came to the rescue of Massey and me in that damned tavern. What were we to you? But you came in with your single hand like a troop of His Majesty's horse to aid a couple of princes of the blood royal.... And if I ever open my lips against you, whatever happens—if I ever reveal so much as a word—may I be blasted by black hell-fire!"

CHAPTER XIII

MARGUERITE'S LETTER

THE MARQUIS, AN hour after he had opened the letter, remained still in the same chair. Sometimes he drummed his pale fingers on the arm of the chair; sometimes he looked calmly into space; and for the most part nothing about him stirred except the deep lace at his wrists and his throat.

At last he said: "You may retire, Marguerite."

She had been keeping up a pretense of a murmured conversation with the marquis but on the whole she had been aware of nothing except the frightened face of her father, for whenever trouble entered the château he, like a true dependent, took the entire care of it upon his shoulders. So disgust and pity had been working in her so long that she was eager to escape from the scene. The moment she was in her room she said to her maid: "Victoire, go back to the red salon and haunt the doors. Poor Jean-Pierre has written a letter to his father and the marquis has been sharpening a hate in his eyes ever since. Go quickly. Hear everything. If you dare to fail, never look me in the face again! I'll undress myself. Quick! Quick!"

In the salon, the marquis said: "There are three of us, all reasonably well-bred and reasonably experienced in the world. Give me your attention while I read you this letter from my son and heir."

He continued, spreading out the sheet of paper carefully:

" 'My dear father and most honored lord,

" 'At this moment I find myself so close to the château that

I can smell the capons turning on the long spit of that noble Martory, that excellent Pichon. For I can conceive everything up to the estate of blessedness, but not that you would give up Martory Pichon as chef....

"'Alas, sir, I begin with speech of my stomach but it is from my heart that I would talk.

"'I am near the château. I am near you. And still I hestitate to go forward. I have done things which, I know, may have angered you. The alienation of the village of Charlevain, I fear, is a mortal stroke to you.

"'You will be annoyed again when you know that I have not more than three francs in my pocket, because when I reached Paris, I saw that it would be as well to arrive at home completely bankrupt as to come with a few Louis d'Or in my pocket. For in Paris, as you once so wisely told me, my dear father, even good talk is not to be had for nothing. I could not afford to ask our friend, the bishop, to dine but I have seen Fourcroix, Anville, Brioud, and many others capable of knowing a part of the truth and of repeating it discreetly. I yearn, sir, to unburden myself of everything I have learned. I wait in the tavern in Charlevain merely to learn from your own pleasure whether your love is greater than your anger. I try to trust in the former but I dare not face the latter.

"'With devoted respect and loving obedience,

Your son,

Jean-Pierre.'

"And so," said the marquis, "I ask for comments."

"He's frightened out of his wits; and that's clear," said de Poncey.

The marquis considered the young man for a moment and then turned his head slowly to Count de Fréron.

THE COUNT gradually rallied himself, seeing that he would have to make another of those desperate gambles which he was continually forced into by his position in the household. He was an intelligent and courageous man who feared only one disgrace—poverty. This terror had unnerved him, and the marquis kept him on such a babis as the eagle keeps the fish-hawk. Gathering his faculties as he saw that the appeal was made to him to decide between the marquis and his son, he discerned at once an attitude of compromise.

He said: "I see at first glance two facts of importance. The first is the influence of wine."

"Every gentleman," said the marquis, "understands perfectly how to keep wine and his mistress in the proper place. Let me have your second fact. The first is worthless."

"In the second place," said the count, "he plainly is under the influence of the American."

De Poncey picked up his eyes from the floor which he had been studying.

"Give me your reasons for saying that," said the marquis.

"He formed a friendship with *Monsieur* Massey in America. He is staying in the tavern owned by Massey. And a certain lightness of phrase in his letter, which might almost be taken for insolence, is exactly the sort of license which one might inherit from the free speech of a man like the American."

"My dear Armand," said the marquis, "I listen to you with delight. Nothing is more surprising and nothing is more grati-fying than to hear intelligent speech in one's own house."

He added: "Perhaps you can suggest what attitude I should take toward *Monsieur* Massey?"

De Poncey said: "Every peasant in every village on your estate now wishes—"

He stopped himself short, but the marquis encouraged him with a smile. He concluded for De Poncey: "Now wishes that I were dead and he in the hands of the American."

De Poncey made a gesture of despair.

"That, also, is the truth!" he said. "What can the poor fools understand? They think that Massey is an angel from heaven! He has dismissed that Chaumont, his bailiff. He says that he does not need a spur to stick in the sides of his friends the villagers. They will not cheat him, says *Monsieur* Massey. Chaumont has been sent away, poor devil. And your own bailiffs, on the other hand, are met by nothing but sneers and snarls when they go collecting what is your due."

"The picture seems to be perfectly clear," said the marquis. "In the one hand the American corrupts my family and turns my son against me. On the other hand, he undermines my authority over my peasants and in way directly threatens the bread we put in our mouths. If the picture is accurate, there is only one thing to do about it. Armand, do you see what the solution is?"

"Solution? The law must be brought against him!" said the count.

"Do you say the same, Georges?" asked the marquis.

De Poncey answered: "He must die! I shall call him out tomorrow!"

Here Count de Fréron stood up suddenly from his chair; he turned pale.

"These extreme measures are an affront to a gentle soul like my dear cousin," said the marquis. "In time of war, turn to the warriors. Like you, de Poncey. However, the second part of your idea is not so well conceived. When you and my son last had a turn at the foils, how did you come off?"

"Well, he is not classical in his style," said de Poncey, "but when he grows warm, he is a devil in the attack. No, I have never been able to match him."

"The American has, however," said the marquis. "And let us learn one thing from his own country. The Red Indians teach us to strike at our enemies with impunity to ourselves. But the thought of a challenge is not bad. We only must be sure that the man who challenges him will win. For instance, there are now at Epinfort one Contrecoeur with his assistant cutthroat, one Hans von Hildesheim, a German villain. This Contrecoeur cares for nothing except to attach his services to the man with larger purse. You will ride down to Epinfort tomorrow, de Poncey, to have conversation with Contrecoeur."

VICTOIRE, WHEN she came to her mistress, had the look of a cat that has stolen cream and still is tasting it. She found Marguerite de Fréron combing the golden, weighty masses of her hair, with her image smiling before her in a mirror.

"Ah, Victoire, it was worthwhile, then?" she asked.

"But it is only the American rascal, after all," said Victoire.

"How much of a rascal is he?" asked the girl.

"At least he is not a gentleman, *mademoiselle.*"

"And why not?"

"Because he is an American," said Victoire. "So it really doesn't matter that he is to be put out of the way."

Marguerite stopped the combing of her hair.

"Put out of the way?" she asked.

"He inconveniences the marquis," said Victoire. "A certain Contrecoeur will challenge him to a duel tomorrow. I have heard about this Contrecoeur. Not a big man. But he slides in under the guard and when he steps out again his sword is always red."

Marguerite had started up from her chair.

"But, *mademoiselle,* do you care?" cried the maid.

"For the American? Nothing!" said Marguerite. "Where are your wits, Victoire? How could the Fréron blood be stirred by an American? But a cowardly murder—*that* I care about."

She went to the window and, drawing the curtain a little, looked over lake Charlevain toward the village lights. They were few and dim, faintly suggesting the length of the street, and even as she watched one of them went out.

She turned suddenly and commanded: "Bring me something to write with. Then put on shoes that you can walk to the village inn."

"Mademoiselle! The village? At this time of night?"

"Do as I order," said Marguerite.

Afterward she wrote:

"My dear Monsieur Massey,

"It is rumored that a certain practised duellist, one Contrecoeur, will challenge you. Monsieur, avoid the man. He is not large, but he is deadly with a sword. There is no question of defending honor against a hired man. I cannot sign this letter but it comes from one who abhors even a polite murder."

By this time Victoire had appeared again, with a cloak thrown over her arm.

"Take this letter to the tavern," said Marguerite. "There always are loiterers around its door. Pull the hood of your cloak down over your face so that you will not be recognized. Give the letter and a few sous to one of the men at the door. Tell him to take it to *Monsieur* Massey—and here are some francs which will help you to enjoy the night air more, Victoire. We all should walk more, anyway. It's a healthful exercise."

VICTOIRE, WHEN she had the letter in one hand and the money in the other, left her mistress at once. Her dress contained a small pocket, excellent for thread, pins and other utensils, and she managed to fit the letter into it, exactly. The moment it was completely out of sight, all sense of guilt left her; she was smiling as she took her way through the upper hall, feeling certain that she would meet no one on the way. In fact, its mirrors showed her nothing but herself until she was almost at the farther end and about to enter the semi-round of the vestibule at the head of the stairs.

Then the marquis opened a door at her left and appeared so suddenly that she started; and conscience almost made her cry out.

The marquis said: "Am I a ghost, Victoire? Have I frightened you?"

"It was unexpected; I beg ten thousand pardons!" breathed Victoire.

"Why should you beg ten thousand pardons?" asked the marquis, giving his mind freely to this small problem of the maid and her terror. "What is it that troubles you, Victoire? Have you been stealing something from Lady Marguerite again?

What is it, Victoire? A length of old lace? A silk scarf? Or a few francs out of her purse?"

"Steal?" cried Victoire, holding up her hands. "Ah, my good lord!"

"Come, come!" said the marquis. "All maids steal, and I have known about you for a long time. A household like this is filled with voluntary spies, you see, and just as you spy on others, so they spy on you. I even know the Paris shop to which you send your odds and ends of plunder. But all maids steal, and you have kept your thefts within reason, therefore nothing has been said. But simply from curiosity, what is it that frightens you when you see the master of the house? What is in your hands, Victoire?"

The calmness of his assured voice terrified her more and more because she felt that she was in the grasp of a resistless power and his eyes, which remained young and bright, seemed to be opening the doors of her mind.

"My lord," she panted, "I swear that I have stolen nothing. Nothing in the world!"

"Why do you cover that pocket, then?" asked the marquis.

"It was only a gesture," said poor Victoire, shrinking.

"Why do you sneak back away from me?" persisted the marquis. He felt not the slightest anger but suddenly he poured thunder into his tone.

"Give me whatever is in that pocket!" he commanded.

If it had been her own life, Victoire would not have been able to refuse obedience. The letter was instantly in the hand of the marquis. He made to tear it open. But the moment he began this gesture, Victoire protested bitterly. For she remembered that this belonged to Lady Marguerite, and the memory roused all the fighting instinct in her.

She cried out: "You have no right to open it! It is hers, and it must not be touched, my lord!"

"Is it Marguerite?" asked the marquis. And instantly he ripped the envelope open.

THE MAID groaned as though a knife had entered her and even the marquis broke into a small sweat that caused his handsome face to glisten, as he realized that his impulse had caused him to perform an action in the highest degree dishonorable. However, now that the seal was broken and the writing of Marguerite lay exposed before him, he could not help reading what was written.

He put the letter into his pocket and drew out his purse.

"You have taken the letter to the tavern, Victoire," he said. "You have delivered it to *Monsieur* Massey. And that is all. He will not complain about the failure to deliver it. Not a word. Walk out into the night, therefore, and see that you get dust on your shoes and on the hem of your skirt. In fact, walk as far as the village. You can carry something better than a letter with you. Here is a Louis d'Or; and here is its brother. You carry this gold with you, Victoire, and also my favor, which will end the moment your lips mention this matter."

Victoire had seen the sudden perspiration on the face of the nobleman. She could not understand what had caused it. She could not realize that the merest whisper of this story, repeated in the Palais Royal, for instance, would set a thousand tongues wagging and cause a mountain of scorn to be heaped on the head of the marquis.

She only knew that by a blessed chance she had been linked to the marquis through the mutual possession of a secret. And though Marguerite was important, what was she compared with a peer of France?

Victoire bowed to the floor. When she straightened again, the marquis had turned his back and was disappearing through the door.

CHAPTER XIV

CROSSED SWORDS

THE QUARREL BEGAN in the simplest and most direct manner possible. Hampton stood in the hall of the tavern as a diligence load of travelers came dusty and hot into the hostelry. He was speaking with the viscount and with only a vacant eye regarded the new arrivals.

Among them walked a man whose waxed and twisted moustache was like two black pins stuck in his upper lip, He wore a linen dustcoat carefully tailored in at the waist to accentuate the spread of his wide shoulders, and the tail of his wig also passed inside the collar of the coat to keep it from the dirt of the journey. He had rather a strange face, big at the base of the jaw and pinched out forward so that he gave an effect of leanness though in fact he was a solid piece of rubbery muscle.

As he came to Hampton with his quick, light, athlete's step, he paused and looked back towards the rest of the passengers who were entering, and at the same moment he freed the queue of his wig from his coat collar in such a way that it flicked right into the face of Hampton.

In spite of the way it had been sheltered, the pigtail was dusty and contained a slightly rancid odor of oil. Hampton instinctively put out his big hands and pushed the man away from him, exclaiming: "Not in my face, if you please!"

The other whirled upon him in a deadly and sudden fury.

"Did you put your hands on me? On me?" he shouted. "Ignorant, clumsy, stupid yokel, did you dare to touch me? I touch you, then, like this!"

And he flicked a glove right across the face of Hampton. Hampton caught him by the wrists. He struggled, but the grasp of the big man held him easily.

"What's to be done with this sort of a thing, Jean-Pierre?" asked Hampton.

"If I have found a gentleman who is a man of honor—there is only one thing to be done!" said the stranger. "I am Captain Etienne Contrecoeur.... You may loose my hands, *monsieur.* You have done quite enough! You need not insult me further. My friend shall wait upon you. Quite enough! You have done quite enough!"

"Well, then, my name is Hugh Massey—at your service," he answered.

Contrecoeur bowed, smirked with great satisfaction, and turned on his heel.

"What the devil have you done, John?" asked the viscount. "Are you going to fight a duel with a man you never saw before?"

"If I hadn't accepted, he would have pulled my nose in front of the whole village," observed Hampton.

"Damn the opinion of the village; what will the opinion of your liver be when there's a rapier-blade sliding through it?"

"I fence well enough," said Hampton.

"Well enough—for a gentleman. But there is too much man in you and not enough cat; and that Contrecoeur looks to me like a professional."

"Professional?" queried Massey.

"Ah, John, those who are born innocent never will grow up! Professional—yes! He looks to me like one of those adventurers who go through Europe looking for trouble to keep themselves in good practice with their swords. What fencing does a gentleman do? Perhaps an hour three times a week for exercise! But these scoundrels work half of every day at their retreats and feigned advances and trick lunges and stop-thrusts and all the rest. They are dancing masters and they dance the life out of an ordinary man in no time at all. We'll look into this Contrecoeur."

A MAN in a plum-colored coat came up to them. He had a featureless slab of a face with a pair of bright little eyes set close together in it. His mouth was hardly discernible until he began to speak. He introduced himself as Monsieur Von Hildesheim, a friend of Contrecoeur, for whom he was acting. Since his friend was leaving the village very shorty, Von Hildesheim could not help pointing out that the village was surrounded by those charming woodlands which would guarantee to gentlemen so many places of privacy. The sword of Contrecoeur, he said would be at the service of the American at once.

"Are you better with pistols than swords?" asked the viscount.

"I've rarely used them," said Hampton.

"Swords it is, then," said Jean-Pierre.

The little eyes of Von Hildesheim shone with gratification.

"The hour, *monsieur?*" he asked.

"In ten minutes, in that group of chestnuts behind Charlevain. You can see them from here," said Hampton.

"It's indecent to hurry the thing on like this!" protested the viscount. "There's not even a doctor. You can't stir before tomorrow morning."

"In ten minutes," repeated Hampton.

"It's murder!" said the viscount.

But Von Hildesheim already had turned his back and was hurrying away.

"The whole thing's arranged. It's a trick to finish you off," said Jean-Pierre. "Hugh, I forbid you! My father has jurisdiction over affairs like this in his district—"

"Tell me one thing right out of your heart," said Hampton.

"I open the book," answered Jean-Pierre. "Name the page to me and I'll read aloud."

"Well, if someone challenged you like this, no matter how the thing might be out of order, would you fight or would you not?"

"John, turn to another page, will you? Yes, I'd fight, I suppose."

"You've given my own answer. This thing has to go ahead," said Hampton.

The entire affair was almost totally irregular but irregularity did not trouble Monsieur Contrecoeur. When Hampton and the viscount approached through the chestnut trees, they had sight of Contrecoeur engaged in a little practice bout with Von Hildesheim. The German fenced very well, though in a rather stiff, precise manner; but Contrecoeur flashed back and forth, in and out, gliding close to the ground, and springing back again as though he were drawn by a cord.

Jean-Pierre stepped short and gripped the arm of his friend.

"Do you see, John?" he whispered. "What did I say of the dancers? That devil moves so fast that I can't follow his hand in the air. His sword-point will find the way to your heart before your blades have touched three times. That Von Hildesheim is good enough but before Contrecoeur he is a baby! Look—see it!—and again!"

Hampton tried to draw a deep breath but the muscles across his stomach had stiffened so that he could not get enough air into his lungs, it seemed.

"I think you're right," he said. "But I'm in the middle of a bog and have to flounder my way forward and try to get to the farther side. Oh, Claude Epivant, this is the time for me to remember our hours with the foils. The only brain I can use now is in my legs and my right arm."

"The damned murderers!" raged the viscount. "They catch us about the throat with the silken thread of that word: Honor. With the one thing that they lack, they force us to face them with swords. And we are lost! I forbid the duel, Hugh. I will not permit it!"

"Think again," said Hampton.

"Ay. True. When I think again, I know there is nothing for it except the fight. John, he has been hired. Who in France could have set him on you? Or it is simply that he wants to see if his sword is still sharp at the point!"

THEY CAME up with the other pair who left off their practice at once. The whole air of Contrecoeur was perfectly casual. He was sweating a bit with the exercise and walking about to regain his breath until he set eyes on Hampton at close range. Then his face contracted to a hawklike attention which never relaxed; but every instant he seemed to be killing the big man in his thought.

Hampton looked about him as Von Hildesheim and the viscount arranged the details. There was enough wind in the sky to draw out the clouds in blue-white combings but in the hollow only occasional bright rufflings ran over the grass. Dusty streaks of sunshine fell through the trees; in the open it was very warm, a place of sleeping peace away from which all the events of his life whirled back, receding into long perspectives. A miniature cry of hounds trailed somewhere on the horizon of his mind with a miniature John Hampton riding behind it through a Virginia countryside. He had thought of life as a long, fat book; for him most of the pages might now remain blank forever.

Then he was aware of the black glistening of the eyes of Contrecoeur, hungry, impatient, now choosing the head, now the body as the better target; or was the man trying to break him down by mere force of will?

Then Jean-Pierre, stone-grey of face, tight-lipped, was saying: "His sword is an inch shorter than yours. He prefers a light blade, I suppose."

He added, more loudly: "Gentlemen, I suppose this wretched business must begin. We presume it to be all honor, all honor. If it is anything else, by God, I'll have you followed to the ends of—"

"Be silent, Jean-Pierre," said Hampton.

"If *Monsieur* the viscount has any meaning," said Contrecoeur, "after my little engagement with *Monsieur* Hampton, I shall be glad to—"

"*Schweigen Sie!*" growled Hans Von Hildesheim, and muttered some other words in German that caused his friend to shrug his shoulders.

Hampton faced Contrecoeur and their swords crossed; in a moment he knew that a new book of fencing was opening before him. He was accustomed to finding a firm blade against his, but Contrecoeur's weapon yielded like a feather. And Contrecoeur himself, always in continual, gentle motion, drifted around Massey. He tried, automatically, a thrust, a lunge, another lunge, a swift, brief attack according to that mode which old Epivent had taught him so thoroughly. The soft blade of Contrecoeur still touched his with the most delicate parries which did not beat his thrusts aside but caused them to glance harmlessly off, inches from the target. Once or twice he assured himself that his blade actually was entering the flesh—it was only passing close to the flank of Contrecoeur.

With that he gathered himself to an effort that would contain the full danger of his attack. He had fought so many times that he could not believe he was entirely overmastered in this manner, and he roused his heart as if with a silent voice calling within him. Instantly he was in at Contrecoeur with a cold, swift fury of onslaught.

THE PROFESSIONAL'S smile vanished. He gave ground rapidly. The dismayed voice of Von Hildesheim shouted in the background. Contrecoeur was grinning with desperate effort and fear.

For that one magnificent moment it seemed to Hampton that he was winning by sheer sword-cunning and fire.

Then a time thrust flashed at the eyes of Hampton, a movement so swift that he never could have parried it. Only a violent backward leap saved him. Contrecoeur followed softly in. The glance of Hampton found a twitching smile of greed on the face of Hans Von Hildesheim and then Jean-Pierre all turned to stone with dread. Hampton made up his mind that he would look no more except into the hawk eyes of Contrecoeur and that glistening of light on the point of his sword, like a drop of concentrated brilliance, about to fall.

He attacked again. Again those delicate touches put his blade aside; again he sprang back from the little snake-like dartings of the rapier.

Contrecoeur said in an even voice, undisturbed by panting: "The meadow here is very pleasantly smooth, *monsieur*. Do not force me to follow you into the rough ground!"

"Don't listen to him!" shouted the viscount, suddenly. "He's trying to drive you back into the mud!"

"Monsieur, you help your friend with advice? It is not honorable!" called Von Hildesheim.

"You poison-faced German toad, I'm for you if you'll draw your sword!" cried Jean-Pierre.

"Leave him, Hans!" ordered Contrecoeur. "I'll see him after I've finished this!"

Hampton, sweating at his work, damning the unruffled calm of his enemy, tried to circle to the left. The subtle danger of Contrecoeur's attack stopped him and drove him back again. He remembered, now, the little run of water that darkened the grass in a part of the meadow; the damp smell of it was just behind him.

Of course the tactics of Contrecoeur were clear enough. He had been baffled more than once by the long, active legs of the American. In soft ground the edge would be taken from that speed.

AND IT seemed to Hampton, as he fought, that with his leaps and prancings he was like some gaunt puppet yanked about on the strings by the hands of a child, made absurd, gamboling like a witless thing before the smooth, insistent attack of Contrecoeur.

If he could let the thrust enter his body and then pin Contrecoeur with his own lunges... but he knew that when that point entered it would sting him to the heart.

He tried again to circle back onto the dry ground—and almost impaled himself on a lunge as Contrecoeur extended his body suddenly, stretching out close to the ground. Only another backward spring, so violent that it knocked a red mist across the eyes of Hampton saved him from that deadly stroke. He saw Contrecoeur gathering with a smooth, swiftly effortless flexion. The lunge came again, and again, and again. He saw mere flashings, not the full sword. He parried by guesswork, and thanked God when steel touched steel in the dizzy air. In the middle of that attack his foot touched the first of the wet ground behind him. He could not venture to spring back and away from the next thrust; all the hot blood of courage rushed to his heart and he flung himself forward in a counter attack. His right foot, slipping in spite of himself on that treacherous surface, staggered his body to the side and he felt the side of Contrecoeur's blade glide against the skin of his throat. That involuntary wavering had caused the Frenchman to miss by the least fraction or else Hampton would now be gasping and choking on the ground; instead, for the least instant he was inside the guard of Contrecoeur, inside, but falling forward toward the ground. But as he fell he risked the upward thrust, instead of trying to save himself with his hands.

He saw Contrecoeur's face contract in a sudden agony of apprehension. There was only a tenth part of a second for the whole maneuver. Then his sword-point passed into the Frenchman's body, and he struck the grass with his face.

In the instant that it took him to rise, it seemed to Hampton that he could see Contrecoeur poising his weapon to plunge it again and again through the back of the helpless body at his feet, but he reached his feet unharmed. It was only then that he heard the wild cry of Hans Von Hildesheim and saw Contrecoeur grasping at the left side of his body with his right hand. The rapier sparkled half-seen in the short grass. Jean-Pierre, in the distance, had thrown up his arms in a gesture of thanksgiving.

The German ran in and caught Contrecoeur under the armpits, lowering him to the ground.

Contrecoeur said: "I think it's not the lung; I don't think it touched the lung."

And Von Hildesheim was snarling: "How, *mein freund?* How, how could you miss?"

Contrecoeur laughed. The man was wonderfully cool. "I aimed at his smile," he said. "I forgot that a smile is also a thing of the spirit, which is invisible."

He kept on laughing, softly, so that the tremors of the laughter might not give him greater pain. The viscount, wringing the hand of Hampton, kept whispering words which were inaudible; then the two of them went over to the fallen man. Blood was running lazily over the breast of Contrecoeur. Already Von Hildesheim was cutting away the shirt. The flesh looked white as stone with the purple-red of the blood welling from it.

Contrecoeur said: "Pay no attention to me. My dear Von Hildesheim is a good surgeon. This is a nothing. No more than a week in bed."

"Well, in the château they have soft beds, don't they?" asked Hampton. "But will they take you in?"

"What do you mean?" asked Jean-Pierre.

"Never mind," answered Hampton.

"I've got to know what's in your mind!" declared the viscount.

"Why, Jean-Pierre, it's plain enough that your father hired the pair of them."

"Listen to the man!" said Contrecoeur. "Words run out of him faster than blood runs out of me!"

Von Hildesheim spoke not at all but slowly lifted the animal brightness of his eyes.

"From here it's a long cry to the château," suggested Hampton. "Will you let me send you a litter and bring you back to the inn? Besides, you know, in the château they may not wish to acknowledge you."

Contrecoeur answered: "No matter what I have had to pay for the introduction, I am enriched by knowing you, *Monsieur*

Massey.... To tell the truth, the best thing in the world that I can think of is to be near that excellent wine in your tavern."

"I'll send some people immediately," declared Hampton, and walked off with the viscount.

AS THEY got among the trees, he said: "What's the matter, Jean-Pierre? Your back is as straight as a poker. You walk like a soldier!"

The Vicomte de Charlevain halted, took a step back, and drew himself up.

"Monsieur," he said, "today you have offered a public insult to the man nearest my blood."

"If your father's a rascal, I can't help saying so."

"Then I must tell you that the honor of my father is safe in my hands."

"Put his honor in your pocket, then," said Hampton. "There's not very much of it."

"Monsieur, you are too generous! One insult is enough!"

"Are we to fight?"

"If you will honor me so much."

"Name your weapons," said Hampton.

"Monsieur Hampton, I am your man with any weapon you name!"

"Monsieur le Vicomte, I'll be damned before I name a weapon!"

"Monsieur Hampton," said the pale Frenchman, "I demand an explanation!"

"Monsieur le Vicomte, the explanation is simple. You are an idiot!"

The viscount rubbed his eyes and stared.

"True," said Hampton, "it was only a silly dream. We have not been standing here wrangling."

Jean-Pierre sat down on a tree stump and covered his face with his hands.

"My God, how my heart aches!" he said.

Hampton dropped to one knee and put his big arm around the slender Frenchman.

"Jean-Pierre," he said, "we will wash this away with a single bottle of wine!"

"But murder, murder!" groaned the viscount. "Dirty murder that's bought and paid for!"

"In every family there has to be a black sheep," said Hampton.

"I would have fought you, John. God forgive me! You'll never trust me again."

"Fought me? Bah! The sword would have dropped out of your hand."

"Do you think so?" asked the viscount, lifting his unhappy face from his hands.

"I think it and know it."

"It's true. Yes," said Jean-Pierre. "The sword would have dropped out my hand." He started up to his feet and gripped the hand of Hampton, exclaiming: "In the whole world I have only one friend. Everyone else is nothing. There is only one who understands and bears with me. But I'm going to front him now!"

"Front whom?"

"My father. I'll stand to him and make him confess. I'll find a way to wring his heart."

"You'll only break your hands trying. Wait a moment, Jean-Pierre."

"I'll not wait! Take your hands from me! They were to murder *you!*"

He rushed off at a run through the woods.

HAMPTON THREW up his hands and went back to the inn.

He found Marceau sweating with industry as he attended the wishes of three travellers by post who had stopped at the tavern for a meal.

He said to the inn-keeper: "Send three or four fellows over to the chestnut grove behind Charlevain. I think they'll find there a man who may need help. A little accident."

He left the sword in his room after he had wiped the blade and went down to the garden, where he walked up and down beside the still face of the pool and tried to think matters through to a proper end.

He decided that he must leave the village at once. The firmness of that decision caused him to lift his head so that he saw above the garden wall the distant heights of the château, softly golden now in a golden sky. And then he knew, as he watched, that he could not leave Charlevain.

When he came into the tavern from the garden, he passed Julie in the dark of a hall.

"Julie!" he called.

She made several steps before she turned towards him, slowly. In the dim light her face was done in black and grey, like a drawing, but the beauty remained in it, though darkened.

"Have they brought in the injured man?" he asked. "The fellow who was out in the chestnut grove?"

"They did not find all of him, *monsieur.*"

"What do you mean?"

"They only found his blood."

"Do you mean to say that he disappeared?"

"Almost as cleanly as the blood from your sword, *monsieur.*"

"Julie, I have to tell you something."

"Yes, *monsieur.*"

"You must give up this habit of prying into matters that don't concern you. As for the sword, there may be a little rust on it."

"But nothing to speak of, *monsieur?*"

"Julie, I don't want you to talk like this, and I don't want you to be gossiping through the village."

"All the rest are blind and deaf, *monsieur.* They would not be able to guess at anything."

She slipped up to him with a sudden rattle of words: "Ah,

my God, do you think that we don't know the marquis? Are we
such fools that we can't see how you stay here for our sakes? Or
is it for the girl in the castle? Is it for her that you are staying?
Is she the bait?"

"Julie, go about your business," he commanded. "You are a
very silly girl."

There was the flutter of her skirts as she hurried down the hall.

Another thought touched him, then, like a knife and he found
out Marceau.

"Has the viscount returned from the château?" he asked.

Marceau kept shaking his head while he lifted his glance
from the floor to the ceiling.

"What do you mean, Marceau?"

"Nothing, *monsieur*. When a whisper comes to us from the
château, we are wise enough to be silent."

"Has the marquis…?"

"*Monsieur*, my lord the marquis has bolts and chain that know
more than a poor tavern-keeper can guess about his secrets."

Hampton went down to the wide quiet of the lake and got
into one of the small fishing boats which he reserved for his own
use. A good wind soon had his boat leaning and leaping, washing
the bow waves over the images of the sunset sky and the great
white towers of the château which sank into it.

CHAPTER XVI

THE ISLAND

THERE WAS NO word about Jean-Pierre, Viscount of Charlevain, the next day, or the next, or the next. When Hampton sailed on the lake, the thought of his friend looked up to him from among the drowned images in the water; and at night the image of the viscount followed him.

One day he walked down the street with old Antoine Honat, who was as sour as vinegar and had as sharp an edge.

"Antoine," he said, "the marquises of Alenton... a pretty hard lot, eh? Proud and all that?"

"All of that, *monsieur.*"

"But inside their own family? Kindness there, I suppose?"

"Monsieur, there never is any trouble that the world knows about. Now and then someone disappears. That is all."

A groan formed with an ache in the throat of Hampton.

"For instance?" he said.

"The grandfather of the present marquis—he had a pretty daughter named Anne who displeased him. *Mais oui!* She favored the wrong suitor, they say. And Anne disappeared. In a convent? In the castle prison? Who can say? A long time ago there was the Marquis Raoul. His son rebelled against him and was beaten in a battle. The marquis had a saddle strapped on the back of his son and made him crawl on all fours around the field of the fight."

"And afterwards?"

"I think he stabbed his father, one night. I'm not sure of the story."

Hampton went gloomily from the village and into the woods. He walked blindly, glad of the heat, glad of the sweat that poured out on his body, for every irritation of the flesh helped to drive away the thoughts of Jean-Pierre. He had been out for some time when he had a glimpse of a man armed with an old musket who stole through the woods behind him. When he was about to call out to this hunter, he was aware of another figure half hidden in the brush just ahead of him.

The second form disappeared instantly and the hot, close silence settled down around him. It was not a well-kept forest and clouds of green brush made an ambush on every side. He waited until he could hear the humming of the insects grow louder.

The whole absurdity of his situation in Charlevain was clear to him at last, for the moment he stepped out of the village he was exposed to the danger of the marquis and this lonely country was ideally suited to secret strokes. In his own Virginia woods he would have set about hunting the hunters, no doubt, but here the pride of the seigneur seemed more important than such a temporary trifle as life and death.

HE HAD a feeling that he was being reduced to an absurdity, above all by that position of fatherhood which he had stepped into by accident. The village insisted on looking up to him. They placed him at such a height above them that he felt an obligation like a heavy weight. When he considered the reality of their devotion, his heart was sickened a little by the realization that they would awaken, one day, and understand that he had been no more than a happy dream in their lives. In fact, he was constrained in a nightmare existence. Whatever he accomplished was nothing. But the thought of Marguerite de Fréron bound him like a golden chain.

He called out suddenly, in a great voice: "Who's there?"

He swooped her off the ground with grace and strength

"It is only I, *monsieur*," said Jacques Cartier, the blacksmith, stepping out with a fowling piece under his arm.

"You have work in your shop," said Hampton. "You have the wagon to repair for old Philippe. Why aren't you at your business?"

"*Monsieur*, my business is also to be in the woods and bring fresh meat home."

"I have not heard your gun and yet the birds are everywhere. You are hunting *me*, Cartier. And what the devil do you mean by that? Am I a part of your business?"

"You are the best part of it, *monsieur*. I have three children and a wife. You are the bread I put in their mouths and the clothes I place on their backs…. The other day you went into the woods with certain men and one of them failed to return. Suppose that *you* had failed to return, *monsieur?* The happy days in Charlevain would end. So now we try to keep you from accidents. *Oui!* It may not be healthy to walk too much alone in the fields and the woods. There is talk of werewolves in the village."

"So I am to be trailed like a stray dog every time I leave the village?"

"You are our father; we have a right to be troubled about you."

"Jacques, I shall not be angry if you will tell me one thing. The whisper about it has gone through the village already, I know. What has happened to Jean-Pierre?"

"Nothing but good, I trust and pray, *monsieur,* since he is your friend. God knows he was never a friend to the village. For he never had time to see us. He knew the faces of his horses but not our faces."

"I ask you a simple question. What has come of the viscount?"

"I answer simply: Nothing but good, I trust and pray, since he is your friend. But if I knew of an evil thing that had come to him, it would be hard to tell you, *monsieur.*"

"Jacques, why would it be hard to tell me?"

"You have two strong hands, and they do what your heart tells them. Suppose that your heart said to you: 'Jean-Pierre is in trouble in the château!' Would you not throw yourself into danger for his sake?"

"Is that it?" asked Hampton. "Has the marquis placed his own son…?"

"*Monsieur,* I know nothing. None of us know."

"What does rumor say?"

"*Monsieur* knows that only wicked men and old women listen to rumor."

Hampton went back toward the village in darker thought than before; and again he knew that someone walked before him through the woods, and someone followed after. He was close to the town when the bent figure of a woman started up on a hillside near him and cried: "*Monsieur* Hampton! May I come to you safely?"

"Come, of course," answered Hampton.

The voice of Cartier bawled out angry words from a thicket behind, but the woman came scuttling down the slope. When she reached Hampton she threw herself on her knees and began to beg: "For the sweet name of the Virgin, for the sake of the saints who love you, have pity on me; have mercy, kind *monsieur!*"

She gripped his legs and wept against them. Her hands were sharp claws, the nails black and broken as though she had been digging in the soil.

Hampton lifted her to her feet. He had a glimpse of the scowling face of Jacques Cartier as the blacksmith came out of the thicket.

"Don't listen to her, my lord," said Cartier. "She's a bad woman; she's not one of your people."

"I am not bad!" she screamed. "I am a mother of ten and seven of them still live; I am not an evil woman. *Monsieur,* will you listen to me?"

"I shall listen," said Hampton. "I shall hear every word. Tell me who you are?"

CARTIER GROWLED like an angry dog in the background. But the woman, for a moment, was unable to speak except to gasp: "Praise be to God! If you speak to me, I know you will save me."

Her gray hair, stuck together in greasy locks, she pulled back from the dirt and wrinkles of her face and grinned at him. Joy set her mouth gaping so that he saw the toothless gums.

"I am Marie Cressey," she said. "I come from the village of Arlette. My husband lies with a curse twisting his legs so that he can't walk. There's no work done except what I do. And the famine has sucked the marrow out of my bones till I can't work with a hoe. No one will hire me. No one...."

"You have seven children, friend," said Hampton. "The older ones can work for you."

"The oldest is only ten, Monsieur."

Hampton, with sickness in his heart, looked at her again and guessed at the horrible truth; but he made sure of it.

"How old are you, Marie?" he asked.

"I am twenty-eight, *monsieur*," she said.

It was youth, therefore, as well as starvation, that flashed like a new penny in her eyes.

Hampton said: "Jacques, you are a man of sense with children of your own. What do you bid me to do?"

"I only beg you to remember that your granary will not be full of grain forever; you cannot be a father to the whole of France."

The woman howled out something in a new panic. Hampton said hastily: "Here are ten francs. When they are gone, come to me again."

She gripped the coins without a word of thanks. The dread of the future was all that she could think of now.

"I have tried to come to you before, *monsieur*," she said, "as I would try to come to the feet of the good God; but your people have beaten me away."

"Cartier," said Hampton, "when she comes again, you will bring her to me?"

"Yes, *monsieur*," said Cartier, hating the woman with his eyes.

"And wash yourself, Marie," said Hampton.

"My lord, I shall spend a few sous for soap and we all shall be as clean as stones in the rain."

Hampton went on toward the village. He could hear the dour rumble of Cartier behind him, saying: "Tell all the beggars in Arlette. Tell them about our lord. Let them all come. He can refuse no one. Presently Charlevain will starve and you with us. But tell everyone. Be sure to talk!"

"Don't worry about that. If I had a treasure," cried Marie Cressey, "do you think I would give the key of it to strangers?"

A DILIGENCE load of news from Paris had arrived when he reached the tavern again, but it had been taken apart and scattered into rumor. Only one thing was certain: the poor king played the tyrant today, the coward tomorrow, and the whole city was talking of a "new constitution," which meant some form of republic. Nobles and clergy were swallowed in the voice of the Third Estate.

Cartier... Louis the cripple... Marie Cressey... these were members of the Third Estate; Hampton remembered that Danton was a member, also!

Before sunset Hampton was again in his small sailboat, trying to lose in the deep reflections of the lake the thoughts which had tormented him all day long; for he felt like a child that was making a gesture to uphold a falling house. The wind over his shoulder, the sail swelling before him, restored to him a false sense of progress to which he clung, blinding himself to facts.

He had visited the granary that afternoon and knew from his own eyes that Cartier's warning was true enough. The bread supplies would not last long in Charlevain; and when they failed, what mind could foresee the future?

In these thoughts, he found himself suddenly beyond the white image of the Château de Charlevain and in the quiet upper reaches of the lake where most of the wind was stolen from his sail by the lee of an island.

When he looked up, a little bewildered by this flight of time, he saw Lady Marguerite on the shore of the small island waving and calling to him. She had turned from the easel at which she had been working. Her boat nuzzled the white sand on the shore of the island.

Hampton brought his own craft out of the wind and dropped the sail. There was still enough momentum to carry the prow steadily in towards the cove, spreading about it silent waves that ran as though in oil.

"Do I intrude if I land?" he called.

"Ah, but *monsieur*... this is your own island!" she cried back to him, laughing.

The boat ran on until it nudged the beach. The hull sprang uneasily beneath his step as he walked forward and stepped

ashore. To find her here in the lonely end of the day, unaccom-
panied, when night was about to stretch out all the distances
with danger, and mystery, made him feel as though the boat had
carried him over the boundary of reality into the shining margin
of legend and romance. He walked on toward the girl, enclos-
ing himself, as he knew, in one of the great moments of his life.

CHAPTER XVII

HAMPTON'S PROPOSAL

SHE SAID: "THE château's lovely from any point of view; but from the island it's really romantic. Do you think I have any of that in my drawing?"

"I think the drawing is charming," said Hampton.

"No, but to speak with honesty."

"Well, if you were drawing a horse I could tell you whether or not it was good."

"Art does not interest you, *monsieur?*"

"You know how it is?" answered Hampton. "We are interested in things we understood. To some people, foxes are sly little beasts that steal chickens. To me they are the reason for the hounds, the horses, and the hunters, but… I know nothing about pictures."

"So?" said the girl. She smiled at him with an expectant friendliness for a moment. Then she said: "Still, I want to know what you think."

"I'll tell you, then," said Hampton, frowning as he made an earnest effort. "I think you've been a little too tender with it."

"Tender, *monsieur?*"

"You know the château so well that you want to let all your knowledge appear; but from this place what I feel is the age of the walls and the way the towers jump into the sky."

"That's good. I like that," nodded the girl.

"But your picture is too faint. If I saw it in a book, I would not think of Charlevain but of something pretty, and rather dim."

She made a slight moaning sound and smiled at him.

"You are a truth-teller, I see," she said.

"Am I too blunt?" asked Hampton.

"When a man fits himself out with manners like court dress, it's too silly," she answered.

He would have liked to say something clever but his brain was empty.

"When a man appears to take his ease in the world—that should be good manners," he said at last, "but not French manners, perhaps."

"I think I know what you mean," she said. "In France, manners are taught by the dancing master; they should be taught by the priest."

"That's very neat," he said.

"Not as neat as a sword-thrust," she answered.

"Doesn't that depend on who receives it?" he asked, watching her for secondary meanings.

"Say it's received by a worthless adventurer who lives by his fencing. Say that it goes through the body of a Contrecoeur?" she suggested.

He was mute before her.

"*Monsieur* Hampton, could you not be warned from a brawl with a common cutthroat?" she demanded.

"How can one be warned?" he asked. "An insult is an insult. Particularly in a public place."

SHE BEGAN to look at him with something between amusement and concern until he asked her with a sudden frankness: "Since we're speaking of names—the Vicomte de Charlevain has disappeared from my eyes. Can you tell me where he is?"

"Is he a very dear friend?" asked the girl.

"He is," said Hampton.

"But a foreigner? A Frenchman, *monsieur*? And he was not long in America."

"He is quickly known. He opens everything to the world,

including his purse. The way he laughs over a glass of wine is enough to teach every man to love him."

"I think you *do* love him," said the girl.

"With all my heart," said Hampton, solemnly. "If you could tell me a word about him, you would be doing a great thing for me."

She said: "He is perfectly safe. He eats three times a day. I have heard him singing."

"He is in the château, then?"

"I should not have said so," answered the girl. "But—well, you can make up your own mind and I won't deny it. I love poor Jean-Pierre, also."

"Will he be kept there long?" asked Hampton. "Is his father enraged with him? Do you think that if I sold the village back to the marquis, Jean-Pierre would be forgiven?"

She held up her hand and shook her head, smiling.

"I've talked too much already," she said. "But don't you see that I'd like to tell you everything?"

"Which means that we must talk of something else?"

"Yes, of you, for instance. You know, it is *something* to have here in Charlevain a man from another world."

"Like a ghost, *mademoiselle?*"

"Someone who makes the rest of us seem ghosts; someone who can pay no attention to history and begin a great experiment on the people."

"What experiment, if you please?"

"What you are doing with the villagers."

"I am doing nothing but trying to let them live."

"Do you know what happens when they live as they please?"

"Tell me."

"When they feel their strength, they rise. Did you ever read the history of a jacquerie? When they rise and pull down castles and murder everyone?"

"Well, I've read about those things. They were centuries ago."

"In France, time hardly matters because the French people are always the same."

"I find them very polite."

"That is what they have been taught—by the dancing masters," said the girl. "We are quite good at schoolwork. That is all."

"And underneath?"

"Well, every post from Paris makes my father say that another jacquerie is about to begin. The poor king!"

"Consider it in this way," said Hampton. "In the streets of the village there were a great many hungry people when I arrived. Also, there was a great deal of grain in my granary. Now the people are better in flesh and I have less grain. Isn't that a good thing?"

She replied with another question: "Is it true that this very day you gave ten francs to a poor wretch of a woman?"

"Well?" he asked. "She was a pitiful thing."

"But *ten* francs!"

"If you had seen...."

"The marquis said, when he heard: 'There are ten cannon pointed at the walls of the château!'"

Hampton was silent, shaking his head.

"Suppose that you were a keeper of lions," she went on, "and you had for them only cages of wood, with nothing but black paint to make the beasts think that they were enclosed by iron bars. Would you feed them a great deal of raw meat every day, or would you give them the sort of a diet that would keep their spirit down a little? Not to save the cost of the meat but to keep them from breaking out and butchering you and then slaughtering one another."

"Do you believe all this, or were you taught these things?" he asked.

"We do not have to be taught. We see the truth when we're children. We understand that no one can think for himself except the king.... If the marquis is angry with you, it is because he knows you are doing dangerous things."

"Mademoiselle, I may be dangerous to others, but they are equally dangerous to me."

She parted her lips to answer but checked her words while she watched him narrowly. "That is why you must leave Charlevain!"

He said: "If the marquis were the devil, I would not leave the village on account of him."

She looked away from Hampton at the gold of the sunset that began to waver over the lake. The anger went out of him.

"I'm sorry," said Hampton. "I see that you love him."

"It's not even a matter of love," said the girl. "It's merely knowing that none of us can do what one pleases. Here is my hand, you see, but I can't give even that where I please."

"Monsieur le marquis disposes of you, of course," said Hampton.

"I am talking and talking when it's past time for me to return," she said.

THE SUNSET color was now deepening through the sky, so that the waves of the lake were golden ridges of fire between little valleys of cool violets. Hampton watched it and found no meaning in all that beauty.

"I must go," she decided.

He picked up the easel and the drawing board and put them in her boat. Then he handed her in and pushed the boat clear of the beach. She picked up the oars.

"Au revoir," she said.

"Farewell, *mademoiselle,*" answered Hampton.

"Ah, but I shall see you again."

"Never, I think," he replied.

The wind had drifted her out a little. She made a half-stroke, pushing against the oars so that the boat glided close to the sand once more.

"And why?" she asked.

"When I see you, I shall think of your husband-to-be."

"The Count of Duperret is not an ogre, *monsieur.*"

"It sickens me," he answered. "What will he take from you?"

He made a gesture that indicated the entire sky and the girl, glancing down at her hands on the oars, flushed as she looked up to Hampton again.

"Well?" he insisted.

"It isn't romance," she said. "The founding of a family isn't that. It's an alliance."

Here Hampton made a long stride into the water until he was knee-deep in it. He put his hand on the gunwale of the skiff.

"You'll have children, won't you?" he asked.

"If it is the will of God, *monsieur.*"

"When you see the look of their father in them will it be a happiness to you?" he asked.

"Monsieur!..."

"I'm not what angers you. It's the picture in your own mind," said Hampton.

"I am missed at the château, *monsieur.*"

He kept his grip on the boat, nevertheless.

"The château be damned," said Hampton. "You're already missing out of my life. Do you know, when I saw you, what happened?"

"No, *monsieur,*" said the girl.

"Why, all the horses and hounds galloped out of my head. Virginia turned into a ghost. I was picked up by a wind that blew me into a new country. Do you know what it was?"

He was so deep in the water that they were at an even height, staring at one another.

"Tell me, *monsieur,*" said she.

"I think you understand. Don't you? Love, eh? I mean, doors opening and your soul walking through into bigger rooms. D'you know anything about that?"

"I suppose we're born knowing something about it," she said.

"I could kiss you for saying that," said Hampton. "No, like a brother, I mean. Almost like a brother—well, shall I go on talking?"

Over his fist on the gunwale she put her hand suddenly. "Yes," she said.

"My God, how beautiful you are, and how near!" said Hampton.

"You are only to give me advice, Hugh?" she said.

"I'll try to do it. What's the trouble with these women in France? You can see it in their eyes when they're old. They've thought that love is something for the bed, only. By God, it's more than that... it's gold... and you can't pick it up... not with your hands. It has to be given—the way that color is given to the lake."

"I wonder if I'll remember any of this when I go back to my own life."

He said: "You think as far as the wedding day, the music, and the fine clothes. And then you skip a step, don't you? You skip all that comes between that day and the babies all fresh from heaven. Bah! It curdles my blood. I could do a murder. I think I could do a murder with my bare hands, and taste every drop of it, and love it like meat. For the good of the world. For the good of my soul. D'you understand me? Well, I could say more... but that's enough—goodbye!"

He took his hand from the edge of the skiff.

It was drifting away when she reached out and caught his sleeve.

"Suppose that you *are* right; but what could I do?"

"Why, tell your father and the marquis... no, you couldn't do that. They'd have you on bread and water and starve you as white as a bone."

"What *is* there that I can do?" she asked.

"Do I hear you asking me that?" demanded Hampton. "Why you can do this, if you have the heart for it: you can say, 'There is some place in the world where I can be safe from the beastly marriage. Hugh Massey will take me there.' Say that, will you?"

"There *is* a place," said the girl. "There is my aunt in Calais."

"Do you mean it?"

"Do I dare to mean it?" whispered the girl.

"Why, that's right. Look up!" said Hampton. "You'll see some sort of a sign up there to tell you that this is right."

"Well, I've seen the sign," she said.

"You won't change your mind?"

"Not even when I'm back in the château playing cards with the marquis and my father; not even when I'm in my room. I'll look out the window at the village lights and remember you."

"Tomorrow night?" Hampton said.

"Can it be done so soon?"

"Every minute you wait will rot away your purpose. Tomorrow night. I feel us already on the road, and the horses running… I could sing a song that would shake the castle down. I'm drunk with this!… a dozen more bottles, garçon, and lay another dozen on the ice…. But now let me see… I send tomorrow up the northern road, a messenger who arranges two good horses at every post. Two excellent horses or there will be the devil to pay. That arranged, how shall I take you? Where shall I find you?"

"I can leave the château and walk in the garden on the island. A little after sunset. I often do. But it would be hard to leave the château in a riding cloak and a hat."

"Can you wear the cheap stuff that is sold in the village?"

"I can."

"Then here's the final word," he hurried on. "I take this boat of mine out from the shore at sunset time, as I often do. I sail up the lake. With the darkness I come down to the château. Where the steps go down to the water, I wait. I hear you coming. I take you on board; and the wind carries us both away."

"Hugh, you forget one important thing. This is not a story out of a book and bound to have a happy ending."

"No, not out of a book. It's out of the heart of France, if France has a heart."

"If the marquis has schemed against you before, why, when he knows that you've done such a thing as this with me, he'll pile up mountains to fall on you. You never can stay in France."

"Tell me this: You've begged the marquis not to force you into this marriage?"

"Well?" she asked, strangely quiet and watchful.

"And since he insists, and since he has means of forcing you to comply with his wish while you're in his hands… what is there to do except to run from him? Why do you talk to me of difficulties? The thing's already as good as done; and damn all that comes after."

"Do you know how you make me feel?" said Marguerite de Fréron. "Tell me, then."

"Like a queen, with a great, great kingdom!"

CHAPTER XVIII

HORSES FOR CALAIS

LADY MARGUERITE DE FRÉRON, when she reached the château again, had Victoire put out the lamps in her boudoir and sat for a time in front of a window that overlooked the lake. A few dim stars and one golden planet shone in the upper sky but the sunset banded the horizon still with green. While she still was there, her father came into the room and asked: "Are you gloomy, Marguerite? I used the glass from an upper window and saw you with him. Was it very difficult?"

"I just want to sit here without thinking," said the girl.

"The marquis will wish to hear how everything went," said Count Fréron.

"I couldn't endure talking with him; I couldn't look at his stone face," she answered.

"Marguerite, my dear!" protested her father.

"Is that treason?" she asked.

"You've had a bad time of it, eh?"

"Rather bad. Oh, it was easy enough to wave him in from the boat. He seemed to take it for granted when he found me clear up at the end of the lake sketching the château. It didn't seem at all improper or unchaperoned to him. I dare say the women in America go roaming in the twilight—or at midnight, for that matter."

"But you could do anything with him; that's why you're depressed?"

"No, that's not the reason. It was perfectly easy. Tomorrow

134

evening is the time. The poor fellow is coming with his boat to rescue me from the danger of André Hyppolite."

"My dear, rash girl, you didn't actually use the name of Count Duperret?"

"You know, father, when one talks with a man like this Hugh Massey, the use of names doesn't matter. He's not a chatterer.... Tell me something. Was my mother a clever, scheming, hard woman?"

"Your mother..." began the count, in an altered voice.

"Was a saint," concluded the girl, dryly. "But as a woman who lived on this earth for a while, was she a practical, keen, shrewd, unfeminine creature like me?"

Her father sat down beside her and took her hand.

"The life we lead is the knife that shapes us," he said. "It has been hard for me to watch you here in the château, always in danger of the frown of our cousin the marquis. But what could I do? How can a gentleman find money? And without the help of the marquis, where would I discover a marriage portion for you? And without a marriage portion, who could you marry except some nameless merchant, some middle-class fellow with wealth and no background? A hideous thought, Marguerite!

"The alternative has kept us here scheming, devising, planning, enduring, to continue the favor of the marquis. It has been a long battle, God knows, and whatever we win, we have had to pay with shame. But it soon ends. Your marriage with Duperret concludes the struggle. Your poor mother must weep in heaven when she sees the devices to which we are condemned. But even she, even in heaven, must wonder what else we can do!"

IT WAS the first time in the life of the girl that her father had spoken to her with such open frankness. She felt older, and less guilty. Suddenly she despised him less and pitied him more. She had understood his problem before but she never had known how his soul revolted against the solution of it. So she pressed his hand and smiled on him. Instantly their common misery united them.

He broke out: "But this is the worst of all. This is degradation, Marguerite, to use you as a bait in order to entrap the American, to permit you to go alone with him, and at night…. Is there any manhood and fatherhood in me if I permit the marquis to use you as a tool?"

"After all, the marquis is the head of the family; and we are bound to serve him," she answered. "But when I take him up the road to the trap, he won't be harmed—not really harmed, will he?"

"Ah, certainly not!" cried the count.

"He's a strong, quick man," she answered. "He would not surrender to numbers, I think; particularly if he thought that he was fighting for me. That's the bitter part of it, father. That he will think it was on my behalf—"

"They will swarm him in a moment," said the count, more cheerfully. "About that don't have the least fear. That moment doesn't bother me in the slightest. He will not have time to lift his hands. Numbers will stifle him, no matter how strong he is. And after that, he will be hurried at once to Le Havre, put on the ship for the East Indies—and so goodbye to *Monsieur* Massey and troubles with him for a few years, at least. It is true that we are bound to aid the marquis. It is also true that the American is undermining his authority throughout his estate. We deal with an economic necessity. No, no, it is not the safe handling of Massey; it is you that I think of, alone on the road with him…."

She lifted a finger.

"There is no fear for that," she said. "I could control him as easily as this."

"He finds himself in the middle of a romance?" asked the count, glad to bring this gloomy conference to a more common conversational basis.

"I think he loves me. I don't know," said the girl. "It may be that he only loves the danger from which he intends to save me. But what a man of men! What a great heart! What words burst out of him!"

"Marguerite, has he touched you as deeply as this?" asked the count. "Do you begin to grow a little fond of him?"

At this she was able to laugh, quite heartily and naturally.

"Are you suspecting me, father?" she asked. "With a poor nameless colonial? With an—American?"

"Of course not," he answered, relaxing. "It was not the brain or the judgment that was speaking in me. It was only the father."

IT WAS a dark day, the upper sky a grey roof, and under it blew, through windows of the northwest, lower clouds as black as peat-smoke. It was so dark a day that the fire at the forge of Cartier cast rays into the gloom. Into the thick obscurity of the shop and that sweet pungency of burning charcoal, Hampton went to the blacksmith.

"It is *monsieur!*" cried the boy who worked the bellows.

Cartier jumped around and pulled off his cap.

"Command me!" said the big smith.

"Come to the door with me," said Hampton.

Cartier followed him out of the dingy shop. He still carried an eight-pound, short-handled sledge, and dangled and played with it while he talked.

"Cartier, you are my best friend in the village," said Hampton.

"Monsieur, there is I, and there is the girl, Julie. But it is true that she is only a girl."

"The truth is, Cartier, that I want you to do something for me that will take you from here to Calais. I want you to start at once."

Cartier untied his leather apron and dropped it on the ground.

"I am ready," he said.

Hampton gave him a purse.

"You will find plenty of money in it," he said. "Go by post from here to Calais. At every station, stop and order two horses to be ready for me and a companion. We start tonight just after dark from Charlevain."

"Monsieur?" said Cartier, turning pale behind his soot.

"But I shall return," said Hampton. "I shall not leave the village in the lurch."

"God bless you, *monsieur*."

"Be certain of one thing: that the horses ready for me will be the finest that the post can offer. You know horses, Cartier."

"I shall select them myself."

"One thing more. One of each pair must be gentle enough for a woman to ride."

Cartier stared.

"Julie!" he whispered, then clapped a hand over his mouth, while his big, frightened eyes stared at the master.

"No, not Julie," smiled Hampton.

He went to the tailor and found ready made what he wanted. The stuff of the riding cloak was rough but it would turn the rain that now was falling in sheets over Charlevain. As for the hat, he got that in the big shop across the street, and picked out a red feather to stick in the side of it.

When this was done, he returned to the tavern, his purchases folded under his arm and a certain sense of shame accompanying him when he thought of such cheap goods on Marguerite de Fréron.

BY THIS time the sun was westering rapidly and he went up to his room to get the riding cloak and the hat. Julie was there making a pretence of dusting the furniture. He was going out again with his packet when she said: *"Bon voyage, monsieur!"* He turned at the door.

"Why do you say that, Julie?" he asked.

"Because I wish a happy journey to you both," she answered.

"What sort of talk is this?"

"It is only *my* talk, *monsieur*. And I shall not whisper a word in Charlevain."

The slant light from the west poured its golden dust over her and he saw her cheek glistening with wet. He lifted his package and examined the way it was tied.

"You have opened this," he declared.

"No, *monsieur.*"

"You actually have opened it and spied on me."

"*Monsieur,* no matter what my hands may have done, my heart—*mon coeur*—never has sinned against you."

Here her head fell suddenly and she began to weep. Hampton closed the door.

"Now, Julie, look up at me," he commanded.

She raised her face but kept one hand over it. He drew her fingers away. Her chin was trembling.

"I am *not* a child!" she cried at him. There was such a blaze of anger in her that he was frightened, as a man always is by a woman's passion.

"Certainly not a child," said Hampton. "But why are you in such a fury, Julie?"

"Because I know she will not keep you long. What are you to her, really, except a little amusement?"

"To whom, Julie?"

"Because she has golden hair and blue eyes, do you think that she hasn't a cruel, cold, treacherous heart? Do you think she's not a Fréron?"

Hampton stared at her.

"Ah, *monsieur,* I know! There's no other woman near Charlevain who could make you so blind to me... and I was in the stable and saw the horses saddled. I saw old Phillipe lead them away behind the village. I saw the saddle for a woman... and there is her cloak and her hat! And oh, the kind God give me comfort!"

She interlaced her hands across her breast.

"Julie," he muttered, "will you be still? Will you stop crying out?"

"No one has heard me, *monsieur.* I have shown my wretchedness to you, but do you think I would let the others guess at it?... Saint Catherine give me her patience and keep me from hating you!"

"But what have I done, my dear?"

"There it is again… 'my dear!'… Or else it is: 'Julie, how pretty you are this morning!'… or again: 'Julie, when you sing you make my whole day happy!'… or again: 'Julie, the damned rain has sunk me in the mud. Smile for me, my dear. Bring back the summer for me, Julie!' How could I keep from loving you when you talked so?… And now you go off with her and ride to some sort of wretchedness. Oh, she'll despise you and laugh in your face, before the end. You'll stand in the crowd and watch her walk into the church with my lord of What-not; and then you'll eat your heart like bread, as I'm eating mine!"

She ran suddenly from the room. He could hear the clatter of her shoes down the hall. Then a door slammed.

He listened to the dying echo and tried to lift from his heart the heavy presentiment that she was in fact a prophetess. When he went down the stairs, he walked very slowly. To tell the truth, the picture of Lady Marguerite de Fréron had grown a little dim for he could not help feeling that he had been living like a blind man, with an unknown treasure ready at hand all the while.

It was not until he stepped from the door of the tavern that Julie was for him lost in the shadows that thickened behind him as he faced the brilliance of the outer day.

CHAPTER XIX

MUSKET AMBUSCADE

A CHANGING WIND had cleared the sky, rolling the rain clouds back into the horizon from which they had been pouring, so that the end of the day was brilliant on the wet of the leaves, and the grass was gilded with brightness.

Hampton put out in his small boat at the same time that three sails of fishermen drifted slowly in towards the shore. He could hear them singing as the breeze gradually blew him up the lake, under the face of the Château de Charlevain. He saw the small waves, dark in the shadow of the island, lapping at the steps down which his lady might come with the dark of the evening. Their emptiness now seemed as cold as the unending winter.

The sun was down when he reached the small island in the upper lake where he had talked with her the evening before; the two ghosts were there still, he felt.

He waited with the sail down beside the island until the color had died out of the sky. Only a dull green remained in the west and as the stars began to shine through this, glimmering faintly, he raised the sail once more. The wind being well forward of the beam, he had to tack twice to bring the craft close to the island part of the château. The night was so warm that the windows of the great salon were open and from them came a music of violins as thin as a song of the wind, at first, but deepening to the full voice, as the boat slipped up to the landing steps.

Something flashed close to Hampton's eye, bright as metal. That was a single ray of light striking the white of the sail, so he lowered it, with the bigness of his hands trying to stifle the small, squeaking noises. Afterwards he made himself small in the little craft. With one hand he gripped the lowest step. The slop of the waves drenched his sleeve.

Shame began to make him colder than the damp wind of the night as the music ended and a murmur of laughing voices drifted out through the window. Perhaps she was telling them now about her *chevalier* who was waiting for her in the darkness. The moment the black of the night began she had promised to be there but now for a long time the stars had been shining in the west. Of course Julie had been right; she knew that a Fréron could only use the American barbarian for a gesture, an amusement.

Shame had begun to chill him when a light slid across the garden shrubbery, glistening on the leaves, throwing a tangle of shadows before it. The light went out. A door closed with a noise like a muffled drum-stroke. Then the music sprang out on the night again. He heard the stir and small grinding of footfalls on the gravel, then she came to him down the steps. He stood up, one foot on the step, one foot in the middle of the boat as he took her hand. Her satin dress kept whispering in the small wind.

"It isn't too late," she was saying. "I can go back into the old life. If you take me away, there never may be an end of trouble for you."

He heard the words with a very small part of his mind for with the rest he was peering at the starlight on her face, watching her eyes and the movement of her lips.

"Hush!" said Hampton, and handed her into the boat. He swept the cloak around her before she sat down. "It was the best I could find in the village," he told her as he raised the sail.

THE WIND was carrying them smoothly away. They crossed pale beams of light, broken on the water; and now they were away from the leaning presence of the château, nearing the village shore.

The quartering breeze bore them on a long slant, the waves barely rustling under the keel. He dropped the sail. They passed soundlessly through the lee of a projecting bank; the shelving beach stopped them with a soft, strong hand. He was helping her ashore; he was drawing the boat half its length from the water; he was taking her arm and guiding her through the deep darkness of the trees. How long it had been since a word was spoken!

"Phillipe!" he called softly.

He had no answer. His heart stopped.

"Phillipe!" he called again.

"Monsieur!" said the voice of the old man, broken by his age.

Just beyond the next screening of brush they reached the horses.

The silk of the grey mare gleamed faintly under the starlight.

Hampton explained: "Her name is Dorade. She goes with a good deal of spirit but just keep her neck straight and you'll have no trouble."

The girl said quietly, clearly: "I understand." Hampton helped her into the saddle.

He swung onto the bay and held out money to old Phillipe.

The villager took off his cap. *"Monsieur,* give yourself happiness and it will be more than gold to me."

"Well..." said Hampton. "The boat is there on the shore. Sail it back and beach it, Phillipe. Are you strong enough to work it out of the water onto the shore?"

"Monsieur, I have been a sailor!"

"Adieu, Phillipe."

"God give you happiness, my *seigneur,* and return you to us quickly."

The bay horse had begun to dance; Hampton guided it carefully out to the road. He paused there a moment as the girl came out beside him. Small pools dotted the highway, silver in the open, tarnished beneath the trees. In the east a pale hand above the horizon promised them early moonrise and more light for their journey. In the warmth of the June night the horses already were sweating and rank but the sweetness of the open fields kept its breath in their faces. He turned the bay at a walk up the hill; the mare followed.

"Did you know me, Hugh?" asked the girl. "Did old Phillipe know me?"

"Here in France everyone knows everything," answered Hampton. "But does it matter what everyone will know tomorrow?"

"What the peasants know is different," she answered. "They can look at one with horrible eyes; they know filthy words that will cling like tar, for centuries."

They reached the top of the hill, where she drew rein to look back. The moon, like a big golden shield embossed with mysterious figures, was lifting out of the eastern forest. Its light did not touch the village of Charlevain in the hollow but already it struck the château pale so that the lights in the windows were yellow blurs that cast no rays.

"Let's gallop!" cried out the girl, and instantly gave the mare its head. Down the long slope she raced as though she were in flight from him until the easy stroke of the bay's gallop carried him up with her. They passed under the dark of trees. Water crashed under hoof, flying as high as his face.

THEY PASSED the village of Mareuil, so deep in its hollow that only the top of its church reached into the moonshine.

"For a person afraid, that would be a nice place," said Marguerite de Fréron. "A good place to hide in. Was that why Rousseau wrote so much about the country quiet? Was he afraid, also?"

"I don't know very much about him," answered Hampton.

"You don't read a great deal?"

"No."

"What is your life at home?"

"A good many horses and hounds; a good deal of Madeira wine."

In the moonlight he saw her smile a little as she looked away. Up to that moment she had been watching him from time to time with what seemed to Hampton a touch of pity and concern. This preoccupation now vanished. She seemed at ease with the world and her smiling never ended, as though from this instant she forgot fear and gave herself to the beauty of the June night.

So a singular distance grew up between them. He had felt in his heart that they would come to one destination together but he was reduced now to a mere escort.

He had to make mere conversation, from time to time.

"Tell me about your aunt?" he asked.

"Aunt Diane? She is very rich. She has such a wicked tongue that she says at the very moment the thing, that the rest of us think of the next day. She's never kept awake wishing that she had made a different reposte. I've heard Tallyrand-Périgord swear that she has the only mind in the world that he envies. Have you heard of Tallyrand?"

"No," said Hampton.

"You will, some day," she answered, and laughed a little. "He's all edge and point. I never saw such a man!"

They climbed a hill from which the whole world fell away, rolling towards the horizon in the faint checkerwork of cultivated fields and the shadow of extending woods. The grey mare reared suddenly as a rabbit scudded across the road, making its spy-hop before it was well into the next field. The girl, flung half from the saddle, spilled out of it at the next spring of the mare. She fell sprawling but with a good grip on the reins which she held as the grey backed off, snorting, dragging his rider till Hampton got to them. He hooked the two pairs of reins over his arm and lifted her to her feet. Neither of them spoke. She was dusting herself off, breathing hard, while Hampton looked her over with an anxious eye.

"The damned mare has torn your dress," said Hampton at last. "Are you all right?"

She lifted her head and watched him for a moment, as strange to him in her composure as a night animal is strange to the creatures of day.

"I'm glad it happened," she said.

He waited for her to explain.

"Say something!" she exclaimed. "And keep me from feeling like such a clumsy fool."

"There's no quick French on my tongue," said Hampton.

"You wouldn't have it, would you?" she demanded, rather angrily.

"I'd rather be a backwoodsman in a coonskin cap with a cold in the nose all the year round than one of your whining, fawning, lying Frenchmen," said Hampton.

She frowned.

"Because you think you're free, you think you're a nation of kings," said Marguerite. "But you're not free. You're never free from homespun and muddy roads and three thousand miles of distance from a decent city."

He said nothing.

"I really don't mean to silence you," said the girl.

"No one but a governess could answer you," said Hampton. "She'd take you over her knee and spank you. You're French, that's all."

"*Monsieur,* do you realize that the French are the greatest nation under God's heaven?"

"The greatest nation of cats," said Hampton. "You tear your dress and get a fall, so you scratch and spit."

"Well, I think we *are* beasts, rather," said Marguerite.

"Except when you choose to be charming," he said.

"I've chosen to be, but it did not a bit of good with you, Hugh. Don't you remember how humble I was when the ride began, very winning and simple, and all that? And then I was chatty; and then I was proud; but all of that made no difference to the big American rock. What did he care for France and a French woman? Ha! He is a man!"

"Marguerite!"

"Don't talk to me! The moon could break its heart shining, and the rivers could keep their fingers at their lips for fear of disturbing, and the kind French wind could know exactly what to whisper, but what devil of difference does it make to the American? Give him a tomahawk in one hand and a red scalp in the other before he wakes up!"

"Marguerite, you are delicious and a devil; and that is all."

"I was a cat, a moment ago."

"Cats and devils change their skins all the time. Any child knows that."

She sighed.

"*Monsieur* Hugh, will you let the road bore me all the way to Calais without saying once that you love me?"

"*Mademoiselle* Marguerite, you are alone on this road with me."

"And therefore sacred, eh?"

"Entirely sacred," said he.

"Perfect gentlemen can be perfectly dull."

"French girls in tantrums can have very sharp claws."

"Hugh, how easy it would be to adore you!"

"Marguerite, I've shown you already that I love you to the tips of your eyelashes."

"My memory is a wretched thing."

"I shall write letters to you when you are in the house of your Aunt Diane."

"I shall burn the letters," said she.

"The smoke will be incense."

"Where did you read that clever thing?"

"I read it in an old book."

"About what?"

"About a proud, spoiled hawk of a wild girl. I forget her name."

HE WAS silent. She whispered: "We've been making such a chatter that we haven't heard...."

The music came to him dimly out of the next shadowy hollow. A nightingale was singing.

"What does it say, Hugh?"

"It is such a stupid bird that it says only one word, over and over."

"What is the word, *monsieur?*"

"Marguerite, Marguerite, Marguerite!"

"Listen! He is changing the song."

"He says: 'I love her, I love her, love, love, love....'"

He put an arm around her and took both her wrists in his hand. She let her head fall back on his shoulder. He kissed her.

"So..." she said. "Till the bird stops singing, *monsieur.*"

The song at that instant ended and the silence moved outward in soft waves.

"That is all."

"No, *mademoiselle.* He is too well trained to be rude. He is a French bird, Marguerite."

"Yes," said the girl. "Do you hear?"

For the song had commenced again, but at such a distance that it was only half heard.

"Is that still the music," she whispered, "or only a memory?"

The singing vanished.

"There! That is the end!" she said. "God and the kind saints, how sad this is... like death!"

He kissed her again.

She said, with her lips moving against his: "It is ended, Hugh!"

"These French girls, they *are* well trained!" he said.

"Monsieur!"

"Mademoiselle?"

"It is the first time that a man has touched me."

"Marguerite, I beg you to pardon me."

She made no answer but went to her horse. Then, as he held the head of the mare, she turned and kissed her hand to the moonlight on the open road.

"Adieu!" she murmured, and mounted at once.

They went on silently for some time, the girl watching the road and Hampton watching her.

He said: "Will there be a future to put with this evening...?"

"Why not?" she asked. "You could be a taverner, at least, and I could carry the drinks to the drunken young men...."

"Sweetheart, what a smiling face you put on everything!" said Hampton. "But suppose there were no American fortune behind me, no thousands of tobacco acres, no loaded ships laboring on the sea, and even the possession of little Charlevain no more real than a dream?"

"If it were all gone? If there were only you and your sword? I think I should like you better, Hugh," she said.

Astonishment stopped his breath.

A LITTLE after this they came to a forking of the road where the right hand branch rose over a moonlit highland, but towards the left the way dipped into a darkness of trees.

Marguerite de Fréron had fallen a little behind. She called out with a sudden sharpness of voice that Hampton was to remember afterwards: "The right fork... take the right hand way, Hugh!"

"That's not the main road," he called over his shoulder, letting the bay stride down under the shadows of the trees.

She called after him with a wordless cry, high and tingling.

He could remember the place afterwards in every detail, from the moon-whitened hayfield with its big shocks of hay to the flash of the creek that paralleled the road and then the little spots of moonlight that fell on the highway, one of them burning on the face of a pool. To the left a dense thicket made a shadow within a shadow, a wall of black. A touch of wind at this moment rattled the leaves of the trees and knocked a scattering rain over him, as though the horse had carried him at three strides from a clear sky into a storm. Figures crowded out onto the road from the thicket. One finger of moonlight ran over the barrel of a musket.

"Marguerite, turn, turn!" he shouted, reining his horse.

Then he heard the voice of the Marquis d'Alenton, unmistakably clear and ringing: "Fire at the horse! Bring him down! Halt, Massey!"

He never could pass through the moonlit field on the right, he knew. The guns would be sure to find him. To the left there was the black wall of the thicket. At this he drove the bay gelding. Long flashes spat from the muzzles of the muskets; the explosions smacked like enormous handclaps at his ears. He only had time to throw himself forward along the neck of the horse as the bay struck the thicket and rifled through it like a projectile.

Beyond, an obscure mass of woodland threatened him with crowding trunks and sweeping branches; the gelding bolted through it. Men shouted behind him. The thin cry of a woman ran like a flame through the confused brain of Hampton.

Then he was out in the open of a field, his whole body on fire from the whip-strokes it had received in bursting through the entangled brush. His hat was gone, his face bleeding, his clothes rent in a hundred places; and the voice of Julie pressed on his brain again: *You'll eat your heart like bread!—Cold, treacherous, and cruel—a Fréron!*

He struck Marguerite de Fréron out of his mind and left in it only a black, faceless anger.

CHAPTER XX

HOW USEFUL—FRENCH WOMEN

THE FIRST THIN grey of the dawn moved out of the east before Hampton reached the hill above Charlevain. He paused there without motion until the sunrise colors were pouring through the sky and streaking Lake Charlevain with faint rose and gold. The beauty of the scene was to him like an acrid taste on the tongue and in the throat, for it made him remember how he had talked of love to Marguerite de Fréron; and as he watched the color flush the white face of the château, his jaw set hard.

Then he went down into the village.

The children of André the tailor saw him first. They had their breakfast bread and cheese in their hands as they came dancing and shouting around the seigneur.

A wordless growl from Hampton scattered them. He left them with stupefied faces and with open mouths; then they scattered through the village to whisper news of the storm to come. The American seigneur at last enraged!

When he reached the tavern, the kitchen life had commenced to stir, with gong-notes from the great copper pans and obscure rattlings of crockery. Hampton thrust open the swing-door. The cook, her helper, and the kitchen lout who turned the spit, held up their hands as they gaped at the tattered clothes of the master and the long, red weals on his face. From a corner Louis the cripple stood up with his crutch and pointed.

"The whip!" he gasped. "The whip!"

"Send food to my room. Anything at hand," commanded

Hampton. And in fact he felt no shame as they stared at him for his real wounds were in the soul.

In his chamber the morning light showed him Julie lying crumpled on his bed with a pillow crushed by both arms against her face. His step roused her. She sat up, blinking at the ghost, some of her draggled hair stuck to her face by perspiration. As she sprang from the bed she could only say: *"Monsieur… monsieur…* ah, the cruel, wicked, treacherous devils!"

Afterwards, when she saw him clearly, she shrank suddenly from the room.

Some of the dark of the night still clung to the walls, making the room smaller as he walked up and down. His mind and his memory closed over him like a grave until he looked out the window at the face of the château with the fire of the rising sun poured on every window of the eastern wall. Then anger began to burst his heart. The kitchen maid came softly in with a tray of cold meat, fresh bread, fruit, white wine from Bordeaux. She lifted the napkins from the dishes, inviting him with frightened smiles to inspect the breakfast. Afterwards, like Julie, she fled from his silence.

He could not eat.

His gorge had risen too high. At last he sank into a chair by the window. Now and then he put out a hand and grasped the air in his capacious fist but he could not find a plan. The marquis was too old to be challenged.

Justice, then, for a midnight attack?

The judges were sure to be old friends of d'Alenton. And even if the score with the marquis could be settled, there remained Marguerite de Fréron laughing among her friends. He could remember that at the last moment she had warned him with a cry; that merely showed how perfectly she knew the scheme, though a last touch of conscience remained in her. If a hired duellist could not remove the American from Charlevain, a woman of the household could bait the trap that would catch him. The French women—how useful they are, really!

He shut his eyes, overwhelmed and choked with self-loathing.

JULIE APPEARED before him holding a plate of buttered bread, cut into thin strips, and white chicken-meat laid over the butter. In her right hand was a glass of the golden Bordeaux.

"I want nothing, Julie," he said, and closed his eyes again.

Against the dark of the mind he still saw her. She had put on a fresh dress, gathered her hair into careful order, washed the sleep from her face, and fastened around her throat the thin necklace which was her only ornament.

When he opened his eyes again, he saw her standing as before.

"Julie…" he began, angrily.

"Monsieur, they would be happy if they knew that you were in a rage and also starving yourself."

A hand relaxed from his throat. He took a morsel of the food and hunger returned with the taste of it. A moment later he was eating with appetite from the tray which she laid on a small table beside the chair. He seemed to have lost blood which the wine replaced.

Afterwards he lay back in the chair and stared at the Château de Charlevain. He could see all their faces; the smiling mockery of the marquis, Fréron lean and dry as a stick, and lovely Marguerite. The three faces, like three reiterated words, prevented thought.

The slender brown hands of Julie carried the tray away. He closed his eyes again but sleep could not approach him because of the quick tapping of the pulse in his brain. At last he turned his head, blindly, towards a thin fragrance of violets, and his face touched the dress of Julie.

"Julie…" he said, without opening his eyes.

"Monsieur, you must sleep," answered the soft voice of the girl.

She passed her hand slowly over his head.

"I wish to be alone," said Hampton

"Certainly, *monsieur,*" replied the girl, but she did not move.

His head sank deeper on her breast. Her touch was more soothing than the noise of quiet rain at night.

"Julie, you must go," he said, but the perfume of the violets breathed a darkness into his mind and his voice was half-stifled by the warmth which pressed against his lips.

When he wakened, his shirt was loosened at the throat, his shoes were off, a small pillow had been placed under his head. He stood up and saw that the shadows had shrunk back to the feet of the walls across the street. He had slept until noon.

CHAPTER XXI

SOLDIERS OF THE KING

THAT AFTERNOON, NEWS came from Paris that sent Marceau scurrying up to the room of his master. Already an excited humming ran up and down the village street and when the fist of Marceau had rattled at the door he hardly waited for Hampton's permission before he burst in. The little man could not stand still. He had to dance.

"*Monsieur*, do you know the day?"

"Wednesday, July fifteenth, Marceau."

"The whole world will remember yesterday!" cried the tavern-keeper. "All of the my-lords and my-ladys, all the princes and the dukes and the marquises, too. Every king in Europe has lost his appetite; the people—the people—ah, my God, *monsieur*, the people have *risen* in Paris! They have ripped open the Bastille and let the sunshine and the crowd pour into it!"

"The Bastille?" shouted Hampton. "What do you say they have done?"

"Gone in a crowd to the Invalides, *monsieur*, taken thirty thousand muskets and twenty cannon—rushed to the Bastille! The Swiss guards shoot them down by hundreds. They laugh at death! The French Guard turn to the cause of the mob; they batter open the drawbridge! The people sweep in—the governor dies—the cowardly beasts of Swiss surrender! Now will the king attack the city with his armies in revenge? The barricades are thrown up in the street; there is nothing anywhere but the making of ammunition, and pikes. *Monsieur*, is it the beginning of a new world? Is the king's army now charging on the barricades? Or do the troops fraternize with the people? Ah, for a glimpse of *Monsieur* Danton! Where he lives in the district of the Cordeliers, everything that is for the people has its beginning. My God, how much he will have to tell us when he comes!"

Afterward, Hampton looked out the window and saw in the street the people knotted in clusters, all gaping with a silent laughter, as if though the air they breathed had a new quality, sweeter than wine. Yet even the exciting tidings from Paris could not take his mind from his own problem. When he fell asleep that night, strange thoughts roused him half a dozen times.

Once, being warm with the heat of the still air, he went to the window to cool himself and was astonished to see the figure of a man skulking into a house across the street. He was half-minded to give the alarm as he watched the stealthy opening and shutting of the door but now he saw other forms moving soundlessly through the street, disappearing right and left; last of all came Louis, the cripple, swinging on his crutches.

In a moment the street was empty again.

But a faint chill of old legend remained in the blood of Hampton. Like great, prowling cats, the villagers had slipped back to their homes from what expedition? The dawn commenced to turn the moonlight gray as he stood at the window, watching. When he lay down again, his sleep had ended.

MORE NEWS from Paris the next day.

The huge diligence-driver said to Hampton:

"The stone has begun to roll. The hill is long. The slope is steep… And the king is a fool!"

"Tell me everything," urged Hampton.

"Talking won't tell you. But you'll see it in the faces of the people. They're crawling out of cellars and looking up at the sky for the first time in a thousand years. I saw Danton on a table in the library of the Cordeliers staring down at the crowd. Hungry devils, Brother Hugh. Gaping for food. And he fed them."

"What did he say to them?"

*Flintlocks, knives, spears,
scythes, all were in the
hands of the Third Estate*

"Do you wish to know?"

"I want to know."

"He said... what did he say? He said that only the people could be trusted. He told them to be ready to do their thinking with their hands; and to carry in those hands something that would make their thoughts felt. When a man has so much as a stone in his grip, he's closer to nature and more ready for a fight. Those fellows were the color of frog-bellies. Some of them had no more flesh on their bodies than I have on my thumb. But every one of them could fire one shot or manage one stroke with a club, a stone, a knife, a sword, a pike. One stroke is enough, if it reaches the head, said Danton."

"Does there have to be blood?"

"It's the only solvent," answered the driver. "It's the only liquid that will cleanse wounds a thousand years old."

Here a horse galloped down the street, paused at the inn, and at once a rattling murmur of voices began, spread, and broke out the garden door in the person of Marceau. His feet stumbled as he ran towards them, his eyes blindly fixed upon a terrible future.

"The marquis—he is coming with soldiers!" cried Marceau. "A company of soldiers marching for Paris! He has drawn them away to his own uses and now he comes with them to murder us! *Monsieur*, what shall we do? The Count de Fréron has been found dead in the woods near the lake!"

"De Fréron?" cried Hampton. "The father of—who has killed him?"

"*Monsieur*, his throat was cut from ear to ear; and a bloody scythe lay on the ground near his body."

"A peasant?" said Hampton. "Who, Marceau?"

"Only God can tell! The people will not accuse one another."

"How many soldiers are coming on us?" demanded the huge voice of the driver.

"Eighty or five score! *Monsieur* Massey, what shall we do?"

"*There* is your answer," said Hampton. "There's no time to do anything."

For the rhythmical treading of men marching in step was audible now at the farther end of the street, a pulsing weight upon the mind rather than a sound at the ear. "Fréron? Who murdered Fréron?" demanded the driver.

"Who can tell, *Monsieur* Hampton," groaned Marceau.

A voice barked an order in the street. The marching feet stamped heavily and were still. Gun butts thudded on the ground in one briefly rolling drum-beat.

Between a whisper and a cry, someone called from a rear window: "Marceau, *monsieur le marquis* wishes to speak with you."

"To speak with me? To speak with me?" murmured Marceau. Then, as though remembering who it was that summoned him, he threw up his arms and ran back through the tavern.

"This is going to be something," said the driver. "Shall we go together?"

HAMPTON WENT with him to the door of the tavern. It seemed to him at first that four score generals were standing at ease in a long column of fours that stretched down the street, the uniforms were so brilliantly new. A captain and lieutenant controlled the scene from horseback and with them rode the marquis.

Marceau, at this moment, was guarded before him by a pair of soldiers, and the marquis said: "Marceau, you know everyone in the village, and you know everything that happens. Who murdered the Count de Fréron?"

"By my lord, consider that here in Charlevain we are not murderers; we have enough to eat; we have clothes to cover us. There are other villages on the estates of your lordship. They are hungry, discontented men, my lord. Why should you look towards Charlevain?"

The smile of the marquis turned from Marceau up and down the street where the villagers peered out from every door.

At last his glance found Hampton at the entrance to the tavern and dwelt upon him still as he answered: "Dogs that are fed raw meat soon will be using their teeth. The other villages are in *my* hand, and the people know better than to lift their heads. Marceau, tell me your secret. Who murdered Fréron?"

"Monsieur le marquis, in the name of God and all that is sacred—"

"Will you speak, or will you not?"

"How can I tell lies?"

"How can you be a tavern-keeper, then? Put the fellow in the stocks and we'll soon have his tongue rattling," directed the marquis.

"Monsieur Massey!" screamed Marceau. *"Monsieur* Massey! They are seizing one of your people!"

Hampton strode from the doorway.

"I have the jurisdiction in Charlevain,' he said. "You have no authority to make arrests here."

"Is that true?" asked the captain of the marquis.

D'Alenton answered with his smile. "This is in your own hands, captain. Naturally a gentleman and a soldier like you wishes to look into the cause of the death of a fellow officer."

"Ah, but was the count an officer?' asked the captain. He was quite young, with a plump, good-natured look which might be wine-bloat.

"Naturally he was an officer," said the marquis. "An officer, retired."

"Marceau, stop whining," said Hampton. "This will come out perfectly well. Captain, as I told you before, Charlevain belongs to me, and any action—"

"Ah, damn what belongs to you!" said the captain. "The Count de Fréron belongs to the army, or used to belong to it, which amounts to the same thing. And he's been murdered. That's obvious, isn't it?"

"What has that to do with my village and Marceau?" demanded Hampton.

"Why, if Fréron was murdered, someone is guilty. Isn't that a fact?" answered the captain. "And why not one of your people? The marquis will answer for the rest of the peasants, it seems."

"And I'll answer for Charlevain," said Hampton.

"It comes to this," said the captain, "that I am to take against the assertion of my lord the marquis the words of an—American! *Monsieur,* I beg you to retain your sense of humor along with your tavern and your village."

"If I were you," said the marquis, "I'd keep the fellow in hand until we're through with this business. A violent type, as you see for yourself."

"Then it's my duty to restrain him," said the captain. "Sergeant, put the American under guard."

The sergeant's order brought a grinning squad of soldiers around Hampton.

"Shall we truss him up?" asked the corporal.

"Let him have his hands," answered the marquis. "He may wish to use them. And what a pity if a free man should be too much constrained, eh?"

The sergeant looked upon Hampton with a smile of possession.

"These guns are loaded, *monsieur,*" he said. "Having said that, I shall warn you no farther."

Here the voice of Louis the cripple cried out from some hidden place: "They have taken our *seigneur!* They have put hands en *Monsieur* Massey! Shall we endure it, friends?"

A booming murmur ran down the street of Charlevain. The right hand of every villager was filled with a weapon of some sort, a stone at least; and they began to throng along the edges of the street towards the soldiery.

Hampton shouted: "Be quiet, my friends, there is nothing you can do. There are guns against you, here, and people who are ready to use them. Cartier, I trust you to keep order."

"You see what a father he is to them?" asked the marquis of the captain. "They're ready to die for him if he asks them to. Suppose we get our tavern-keeper forward to the stocks. But carefully. The devil may be to pay!"

Shouted orders from the captain started his column of infantry forward; they marched in good order to the little square and halted beside the stocks.

CHAPTER XXII

DEATH OF MARCEAU

THE ENTIRE MASS of the villagers was gathering rapidly; word had spread to those who worked in the field and they came in every moment, panting. From the sides of the street, from the windows of the houses, voices called out continually: *"Monsieur* Massey, what will they do with you? *Monsieur, monsieur,* what shall we do? Give us orders!"

A purposeful, angry bustling began on all sides, a wasp-like eagerness among the villagers, until the captain said to the marquis, close to Hampton: "My lord, these people of Charlevain may make trouble. If they start a rush, we have no room to stop them with volleys. They'll be all among my men in no time at all!"

"A firm front is better than a thousand guns, with the low rabble," said the marquis. "Remember that a nobleman has died at the hands of just such a mob. Examples must be made, my captain."

"I'll do what I can, but I don't like it," protested the captain.

They had come out now in front of the church, where the street widened into a sort of square or plaza which had a touch of architectural dignity, for the best houses had been built at this point and the little church possessed an old, somber beauty of its own.

The marquis rode close at the side of Hampton.

"Monsieur Massey," he said, "it is very strange that all your efforts have brought nothing but trouble to your village. But

162

have you had troubles of your own? It seems to me that I see marks on your face."

"I recognized your voice the other night," answered Hampton.

In spite of the frozen smile of the marquis, he could see his words take effect. But d'Alenton answered: "My voice? In a dream, perhaps?"

"A dream on horseback. Before I woke up, the horse was dead."

"Even in beautiful France? Even in June? Can there be death?" said the smiling marquis.

"Even ambuscades by moonlight," said Hampton, as the column halted; and he felt the eyes of the marquis, retouching, one by one, the marks on his face.

"Every moment we reach a better understanding," said d'Alenton. "You and the people of the château."

"Yes," said Hampton, "I understand better both the men and the ladies of the château."

"Shall I tell her that you remember her?" asked the marquis.

"With all my heart," answered Hampton.

UNDER THE direction of the captain, the ankles of Marceau had been lodged in the holes of the stocks. His strength of mind maintained all the burden until this moment. Now, however, he began to writhe on the hench and beat his head, while he wailed: "What have I done? My God, have mercy on me! What is my crime? What have I done?"

Hampton looked away from the crowd to the green hills that rolled back from Charlevain, to the shining face of the château, and then to the villagers who ringed the square. They seemed to feel for Marceau no more pity than the flock of sheep feels for the lamb at the slaughter-block. The huge figure of the diligence driver stood forward from the rest, his arms folded, a deeper shadow on the grotesque ugliness of his face. Around the stocks ranged the soldiers in a hollow square.

The marquis was answering the wail of Marceau.

"Your crime is in knowing too much of everything that goes on, Marceau. My poor fellow, no one asks anything from you except a little talk. There has been a murder of a man worth you and all your village. Talk just a little about the killing, my friend. Open your mind to us. Let us hear the truth."

"What will you have me do?" screamed Marceau. "I know nothing. There is nothing that I can tell you. I swear before God—"

"Do you hear the howling?" asked the marquis, turning to the captain.

To this the captain answered: "Is it a Frenchman? To beg and yell like this, can it be a Frenchman?"

"How can you tell until the skin is broken?" asked the marquis.

"What do you mean, my lord?" asked the captain.

"Why, he's in the stocks, isn't he?" said d'Alenton. "And that makes him anyone's game, doesn't it? *Monsieur,* do I have to point out that there are stones on the ground, and that your soldiers may enjoy a little sport? Ten sous to any man who hits the head. But keep them in their ranks, captain!"

The officer rubbed the red bloat of his cheek for a moment but afterwards he laughed.

"After all, you are the law, here," he said. He called out to his men: "Do you see the game, my boys? Ten sous from the noble marquis every time a stone hits his head! But no breaking of the ranks, there; every man pick up what he can. Sergeant, keep an eye on the villagers...."

This speech from the officer roused a deep, humming murmur from the soldiers and passed beyond them into a shrill outcry from the people of Charlevain. Then the huge voice of the diligence driver roared:

"Charlevain! Up, Charlevain! Are you beasts or are you men?"

He shook his enormous fist at the villagers. They stirred, a staggering and swaying motion which left them huddled closer together. They had the will to interfere but not the leadership they could trust.

"This diligence driver, this huge hogshead of a man, this fat fool of a cannon stuffed with powder and no ball," said the marquis, his tone as gentle as his words were fierce, "it would be very wise to handle him, before long. What do you say, *monsieur* my captain?"

The captain, at that moment, had turned on his soldiers and rode along the inside of the square which they formed, striking his riding whip against his boot. Only two or three of them had picked up stones from the ground.

Now he sang out to them: "Do you hear me, you rascals? And did you hear the noble marquis? Ten sous to the fellow who first strikes the head. Ten sous to the one who shows us the first blood. And a good taste of my whip to any sullen villain who fails to throw a stone. What! You'll fraternize with the damned, greasy, onion-eating peasants, will you?"

After this threat, the soldiers began to throw the stones but they threw them awkwardly, as though they were women stiff in the shoulder-joints, and not one of the rocks came close to Marceau.

The captain, however, was a man of action and without fear. He fetched some good whip strokes at the nearest half dozen of his soldiers, shouting: "I'll warn you, you dogs! I'll teach you to eat when there's meat in front of you! You lack a master, do you? I'll master you, damn you!"

HALF A dozen stones were flung in good earnest, after this. One of them hit Marceau solidly and brought from him a screech that jagged like lightning across the brain of Hampton, who lurched forward, dragging the men who held him, and shouting a wordless protest. A whip stroke fell on his head and shoulder. At the same moment the whole squad of soldiers flung themselves on him. They could not bring him underfoot as they wished but they stopped him short.

Hampton looked up to the smiling face and the raised whip of the marquis.

"What? Treason?" said the marquis. "Lieutenant, can't your whole company handle a single American? A half-breed American, I take it, because he has the look of a red Indian under his skin. *Monsieur* Massey, you learn that you must bow to the ways of an older culture."

The cut of the whip burned into the flesh of Hampton. Through the uproar of his brain he could hear the sergeant saying: "See, my lord! He has a look as though his teeth were in your flesh at this moment!"

"Come, come! Answer me," said the marquis. "You are not all brute, I take it. You have the gift of speech, *monsieur*."

In fact, a groan broke from the throat of Hampton, but there was no word in it.

Then he forgot himself because of Marceau. For the soldiers, after they had hit their victim once, were turned to beasts, shouting to one another as they snatched up new stones, laughing, bending their bodies far back to give impetus to every throw.

The marquis, smiling on his horse, tossed coins right and left towards those who reached the target. In the distance the villagers, so far as Hampton could see, showed no emotion except curiosity. The tailor's wife was holding up her youngest boy so that he could look over the heads of those in front; Louis, the cripple, kept getting himself to tiptoe with his crutches and then losing his balance.

Marceau, as the stones whizzed at him, screeched without drawing breath while he defended his head with hands and arms.

"Now, Marceau, will you talk?" called the marquis.

"I talk! I talk!" yelled Marceau. "Cartier and the diligence driver—they murdered the count!"

He could not get on to other names for, at this moment, a heavy stone struck him fairly on the side of the head so that he fell backwards from the bench, a limply hanging body.

"You have your names!" shouted the marquis. "Captain, you have your names! That is Cartier—the big fellow with the dark face, there; and yonder is the driver."

Cartier, close at hand, was instantly in the grip of the soldiers; but around the driver a wave of the villagers curled. Hampton could see their hands trying to push him into flight. He swept those hands away. His huge voice exclaimed through the outcry: "I'm too big to run like a rabbit. France, France, it is for you!"

And he flung up one hand towards the sky. Hampton, cold to the heart with nausea, kept his eyes after that on the face of the marquis. It was perfectly calm.

The captain was saying: "Shall we turn these people over to you, my lord?"

"Why not deal with them at once?" answered the marquis. "Take the other rat out of the stocks."

WHEN THE legs of Marceau were freed, he did not rise. The blood from his head soaked into the dust, black on the ground and red in his wig. And here the sergeant called: "Dead, I think, or dying, this one. They've broken the shell of this egg and the life's running out of it."

"Monsieur!" cried Marceau, faintly. *"Monsieur* Massey."

This voice could be heard because a silence had come over the villagers and the soldiers. The only sounds were those of movement around Jacques Cartier.

The marquis commanded: "He's about to accuse Massey. Take the American to him. Let him see the American's face!"

The soldiers accordingly took Hampton to the side of the innkeeper, where their hands freed him involuntarily, as they stared down at Marceau. Hampton crouched beside him.

The blue lips, the half opened eyes, already looked like death but there was audible breathing.

"Marceau, I am here," he said.

"Monsieur..." panted Marceau. "A sword struck me through the brain.... God struck me because I lied."

"Do you hear, sergeant?" asked Hampton. "And you—and you, are you hearing? *Monsieur le marquis,* will you listen?"

"Speak up clearly, Marceau," said the marquis. "You won't make me dismount to listen, will you?"

"Poor fellow," said Hampton, his eyes fixed on the horror of the wound, "how is it with you, Marceau?"

"God have pity!" groaned Marceau. "And the new Burgundy just laid in the cellar! And all the Paris trouble bringing travel our way!"

"Marceau, you have put two men in danger," said Hampton. "Do you know, truly, a single word against Carrier or the driver?"

"*Monsieur,* in God's name what could a poor man do? I could only pick out the two biggest that I saw. They were killing me!"

"Do you hear?" called Hampton, looking up to the marquis.

"One lie on top of another," said the marquis. "I suppose they cancel out. You can set the two prisoners free, captain. At any rate we teach the peasants that there is such a thing as blood for blood in the world. But let them never think that the matter ends here. There were days when a village would have been razed to the ground for the sake of a Fréron. Those days may come again."

"*Monsieur,* I cannot breathe," whimpered Marceau. "Now that I've unsaid the lie, God will not send me to hell for it, will He? Where is the doctor? Where is the priest?… *Monsieur,* with your big hands, hold in my life until…."

A convulsion dragged his mouth open as if for screaming, but not a sound came. His body arched up. His head, twisting suddenly, dragged the gaping wound into the dust. He relaxed.

He was already dead, *it* seemed to Hampton, when he whispered: "Julie… the napkins…."

With that, the last breath left him.

"**SO WE** go on from day to day, and, in the end, time tells," said the marquis to Hampton, as he turned his horse.

The lieutenant was shouting orders. The company formed. It

went off at a quickstep, the tall, plumed hats nodding at every stride. They seemed to be hurrying and only the officers were at ease, loitering on their fine horses beside the marquis while little Marceau lay dead on the ground.

Julie sat cross-legged with the head of her uncle in her lap. She had a cloth wrapped around the wounds, so that the face appeared as white and clean as a stone. Hampton stood close to her. The villagers kept in a dense circle but at a little distance, and as she looked around, her glance skipped Hampton as though he were a bit of thinnest atmosphere.

"Monsieur," she said to the diligence driver. Her quiet voice sounded through the silence like words spoken in a small room. "Will you tell me why he is dead?"

The big driver dropped heavily to one knee and picked up the lifeless right hand of Marceau.

He said from that enormous throat: "Now I want you to think about the hawk in the sky, my friends. When it is hungry, it looks at the chickens in the barnyard. It doesn't wait to pick and choose. It folds its wings and stoops at the first one that offers to its talons.... What do the other chickens do? They run into the barn, screaming. Or else they stand in a huddle, and hope that the hawk had been fed and will not return. They stand as you and I are standing now, huddled together. Some of our blood has gone to our masters. Perhaps it is the will of God. Ask your own hearts as the men of Paris are asking theirs. Perhaps it is the will of God. But be sure of one thing. The hawk that has been fed will return to feed again."

How the villagers turned then and looked towards the château across the lake was the picture that remained in the brain of Hampton.

Afterwards he walked back with the driver, who let his coach stand all day. Others were carrying the dead man with Julie stepping before them, her head high and her step light. Word had been sent to the church that the burial was to take place at once, for that was Julie's wish, and the bell of the church was tolling.

When someone said to her: "Why, Julie, we must make your uncle clean for his grave!" she answered: "Well, God has seen him, I suppose. God doesn't blind Himself today so that He can smile tomorrow. Clean clothes don't make such a difference to Him. And I want God to see him with the murder freshly done upon him!"

The great hand of the driver closed on the arm of Hampton, as he saw at the tavern the diligence which would take him back to Paris.

"Come with me to Paris, *monsieur*," he said. "Out here in the open country, you are too big. The devil can see you too easily. He will put his hand out for you first of all. But back in Paris, there is a crowd that will swallow you. You won't be noticed."

Hampton answered: "Perhaps I want to be seen?"

"As you will, then," said the driver.

Hampton watched the huge man climb into the diligence. Then the wheels turned up feathers of dust like helmet plumes until the big wagon turned the bend of the street.

Afterwards Hampton went on the burial of Marceau. He did not enter the church for the service. In fact, the little place of worship could not hold half of the village, which had flocked to it. Instead, he walked up and down in the burial ground until the coffin was borne out and lowered into the hastily dug grave.

No one shed any tears. He noticed that first of all, and beyond the rest the placid face of Julie as the priest intoned his last words and crumbled soil into the grave, and while the heavy shovel loads of earth thumped down upon the wooden box. She had an air of uplifted sorrow, which is almost the face of happiness. But all the other villagers were staring darkling at the ground.

When they looked up, it was towards the shining front of the château across the lake.

CHAPTER XXIII

THE RABBLE MEETS

THE NIGHT CAME on very warm and still with Hampton buried alive in his room at the tavern. He wanted to be out in the open but he felt that he could not face the villagers so he sat at his window as he had done often enough before this and looked at the lighted château windows and their ghosts in the quiet water of the lake.

From the village street the acrid smell of dust came to him; afterwards he found himself straining his ears towards the voices that passed up and down. Their murmuring seemed more hushed than usual; he told himself that he could turn those sounds into words. Then a light, quick step went along the hall and he heard a voice singing very softly.

"Julie!" he called.

She came into the open door of his room and waited on the threshold. "Yes, *monsieur?*" she said, and by the lightness of her voice he knew that she was smiling. He would not turn to make sure.

"Did I hear you singing?" he asked.

"Yes, *monsieur.*"

He took a breath.

"Do you mean that I should not be singing so soon?" she asked.

"I simply wonder a little. It is *not* very long, is it?"

"I have other things to do than to grieve. The whole burden

of the tavern falls on me, until my lord gives the place to some man."

"Why should I give it to a man when you know all about the running of it, my dear?"

"Ah, do you mean it? That I should rule the entire tavern?" demanded the girl. She came before him, keeping a proper distance but standing close to the window where he was bound to see her.

"Well, you understand how to keep accounts, don't you? And the prices of everything?"

"I have been very well educated, *monsieur*. I was in a convent school for four years."

"Why, then, you're the one to take charge of the tavern. Besides, you know how to put a smile in every man's glass of wine."

"I thank God and you, sir, for this wonderful great fortune."

"Stop bowing and scraping, Julie. Stand up on your feet and keep your back straight when you're talking to me."

"Certainly, *monsieur*."

"Poor Marceau… it seems that you were not very fond of him?"

"Uncle Camille? Well, it is our duty to love our relations and you see that I am dressed all in black."

"But as for your heart, there's no shadow there, I imagine?"

"He was a practical man, *monsieur*, and therefore he would be perfectly satisfied to see me in black, rather than to have me scant the business of the tavern by moping in a corner. He paid me very little money, and therefore I don't need to pay him very much love."

"Like your uncle, you have a practical nature, Julie."

"You would not have me one of these sentimental creatures with the eyes of a calf?"

"No, I suppose not. To be the mistress of the tavern makes you happy, does it not?"

"*Monsieur*, in all the history of Charlevain, when did a woman have such power in the village?"

"That may be true."

"You are very dark and unhappy, *monsieur*."

"I have reason to be, Julie, considering what is in the hearts of the villagers tonight."

"Ah? What have they in their hearts?"

"Bitterness and grief, Julie. They had been telling themselves that their American *seigneur* was a fellow who would fight for them and for their interests, but now their village has been invaded and one of them has been tortured to death. So they have reason to despise me."

"*Nom d'un nom!* Do you think so?"

"I know it is true, Julie."

"May I speak?"

"Whatever is the truth."

"Well, this is the truth: The *seigneur* of Charlevain is above ordinary men, but the marquis d'Alenton is above even you, *monsieur*. Is not that the truth? *N'est-ce pas?*"

"I dare say that it is."

"And when the marquis comes with an entire army at his back, what could you do?"

"Nothing. You could see that. Everyone could see it. Nothing! I could do nothing!"

The thought made him groan. "I could only stand and take the whip-lash over my head and shoulders!" he ended.

"Yes, that was a bad thing," agreed Julie. "On the one hand it makes the people of Charlevain love you because you suffered for our sakes. On the other hand, your great grandson after you will blush when he knows that his ancestor was beaten with a whip."

"You keep things in a nice balance, Julie."

"Managing accounts teaches one to think of everything," she said. "And every day has its own future and its own past."

"Julie, what a clever girl you are!"

"I am not a very big book, but there are some good things written in me."

He dropped the big square of his chin on his fist and fell into thought. When he was aware that she still was standing before him, he said: "As you were saying, you have all the affairs of the inn to attend to; you had better be about them."

"*Monsieur,* you are the largest affair of the tavern."

"There is nothing you can do for me, Julie."

"I could beg you not to be unhappy about small things."

"Small things?" he cried. "Small things, Julie? Murder in the street? Murder of my own people? Is that small? Murder—and my damned hands tied together, helpless?"

"All of Charlevain is a small place and my lord comes from the great world. We love you all the more for what you did or tried to do, today."

"This morning I was a friend and a protector for these people. Now I am nothing. They see that they are naked."

"Do you think that is what they feel?"

"That is what they must feel."

She linked her hands together before her and looked for a moment at the ceiling. Her thought made her smile a little.

"Suppose that I should show you the minds of these people?" she asked.

"Can you do that?"

"It might be that you would find in them things that would make you wish to leave Charlevain forever."

"What do you mean by that, Julie?"

"Beyond the village, half-way up the hill, there is a path that turns to the right into the woods. If you were to meet me there in a few minutes, I could take you into the minds of your people."

"Well, a moon will be shining before long. I'll meet you there, if you say so."

"If you wish to think of us as you think now, as a father thinks of his children, you should not go, *monsieur.*"

"I shall be waiting for you at the path."

CHAPTER XXIV

DEATH FOR A DEATH

VICTOIRE, DRESSED IN black and sitting on a low stool by the couch, said: "Are you nauseated still, *mademoiselle?* Will you take this drink? It will be good for you."

"I need nothing," said the girl. "I am well. But what have they found, Victoire?"

"They made that Marceau do some talking."

"Marceau? That poor mouse of a man? He never would have lifted his hand to—"

"Mademoiselle, he did nothing. *Seulement* the noble marquis thought that he might know the man who was guilty."

"And did he know?"

"He named the blacksmith—but alas, he recanted the name before he died."

"Before he died?" cried the girl.

"It was rather unlucky," said Victoire. "They had put their hands on Marceau and on the American—"

"Did they suspect *him?*"

"Only to see that he did not rouse the villagers against the soldiers. And then they put Marceau in the stocks and the marquis had him stoned just a little."

"Good God, what are you telling me, Victoire?"

"To make Marceau's tongue wag more freely. And he *did* start to talk, just as one of the stones cracked his head for him. A mere bad chance, *mademoiselle.* So he recanted the names of

176

the driver and Cartier. And so far the guilty man has not been found. And the American went free, also."

"Their hands are not large enough to hold him!" exclaimed Marguerite. "They've only given murder for murder!"

"Hush, my dear!" said Victoire.

Marguerite dropped her head back on the pillow. She lay so still that after a moment Victoire thought she must be asleep, but then she discovered wide eyes that stared at the ceiling. The silence became to Victoire a pregnant thing, swelling towards an outburst that still did not come. An unhappy, sick suspension of life.

THE MOON got up above the trees and turned the road into the white of marble before Hampton saw, on his right, the dim beginning of the path among the trees. Before he entered it, he looked over the brightness of Lake Charlevain with the dark shadows of the hills poured over the eastern side of it, then he turned into the trees. He took a few steps. As soon as the forest closed behind him, he halted.

Bits of moonlight glistened here and there like living creatures; but the big trees closed almost solidly above him. The warmth of the night kept a smell of resin in the air together with the damp odor of decaying wood, half sour, half sweet. He had to wait long enough to hear intimate, secret noises begin among the trees, all ending when the wind carried a long wave of whispering overhead.

Then the voice of Julie said, dose to him: *"Monsieur?"*

"How long have you been watching me, Julie?"

"Hush, *monsieur*. We must only whisper. I have not been waiting. I have come at this moment."

"I heard nothing."

"Every child in Charlevain knows how to go through the forest silently. Give me your hand. Can you see the way?"

"I'll find it presently. I've been in the woods enough to have eyes in my feet."

"That is good. Follow me."

They slanted across the shoulder of the hill, Hampton feeling his way dexterously; but in spite of his care a twig snapped underfoot now and then while the girl moved soundlessly before him. The way dipped down a sharp descent. What he took for a murmur of voices turned into the rapid babbling of water, then a stroke of moonlight showed him the stream running around boulders that offered natural stepping-stones across the creek. The girl went over them lightly. In the shaft of light she turned an instant to smile at him and then went on.

That was the French of it, he thought. They know how to use every opportunity, decorate every moment, with only a slight sense of unreality left at the end.

On the farther side of the stream she was waiting for him.

"Now the place is close," she said. "We'll go on softly. *Monsieur*, if anything should happen to separate us, wait where you are until the morning begins."

"What in the world are you talking about, Julie?"

"*Monsieur*, if they were to find you wandering alone, so near to them—will you promise?"

"We'll see! We'll see!" said Hampton. "Go on, Julie."

They entered a section of the forest so overclouded with foliage that not a ray of light entered. She moved very slowly. Once she paused to whisper to him: "Tell me the strongest man, the most important man in Charlevain?"

"That good fellow, Jacques Cartier."

"And who is the weakest, *monsieur?*"

"Well, who could be weaker than poor Louis, with his stump of a leg?"

"That seems true. We shall see," said the girl, and went on again.

They came to the unmistakable sound of voices again, the quiet, controlled voices of men. Moonlight appeared among the tree-trunks; and Julie stopped behind a great tree around the side of which Hampton looked out into a circular clearing where five or six score peasants had gathered. Most of them kept inside the shadow which slanted down on one side of the clearing, but a few sat on a fallen tree in the middle of the open space. Louis the cripple was one of these.

Someone was saying: "Is there anyone from Pont-le-Vair?"

"Pont-le-Vair!" said a general murmur.

"Here is Jacques Fournier from Pont-le-Vair," said another voice. "I went all the three leagues to the village and fetched back this man in my cart. Stand up, Jacques. You can tell us a few things. Stand up on the tree, will you, so that we can see your face while you talk."

JACQUES FOURNIER stood up on the trunk of the tree. He had a drooping face for his head was stuck on the end of a forward sloping neck that grew out of a pair of bent, thick, powerful shoulders. One could say that nature, after thousands of years of effort, at last had shaped a man perfectly for the hoe. He took off his cap and pushed back his hair, which hung almost as thick over his face as down the back of his head.

Big Cartier said: "Now here we've got a man all the way from Pont-le-Vair who can tell us just what has happened over there. Talk right out to us, Jacques. I guess we look like friends to you."

Fournier began to rub his hands together as though for warmth. The place was so quiet, the night was so still, that Hampton faintly heard the rasping of the calloused skin.

"Well, we just all went out from the village. That's all we did," said Jacques Fournier. "We just got together and we just all went out."

He laughed a little, throwing up his head to let out a brief gust of mirth.

"I can't make any speech," he said. "We just went out together."

"No! Talk to us. Tell us everything!"

Cartier said: "Be patient, everybody. Now, Jacques, tell us how many of you there were?"

"There were ten twenties of us and more," said Jacques. "We all went out together."

"Yes, and where did you go?" asked Cartier.

"Why, we went up the hill. I never had gone up the hill before. There were plenty of us that never had gone up the hill before."

"And what was on the hill, Jacques Fournier?"

"Why, the castle was on the hill, of course. It was standing up there on the hill—"

He waved his hand two or three times at the moon. Hampton was able to see the castle, suddenly.

"Did you go all the way to the castle?" asked Cartier.

"Yes. We went all the way to the castle. Some of us went all the way to the castle."

"Why didn't all of you go to the castle?" asked Cartier.

"Well, some of us stayed behind. They stayed behind on the hill."

"Why did they stay behind, Jacques?"

"They were dead," said Fournier. "Or else they were hurt and screaming. Some of the ones that were hurt and scream-ing started to crawl back down the hill. Some of them kept on crawling towards the castle. I could feel them screaming. I could feel it in the top of my brain. It's still up here high in my head. The screaming is, I mean."

"Why were they screaming?" asked Cartier.

"Because the bullets had hit them," said Fournier.

"Who fired the bullets, Jacques?"

"The men of the count. They stood on the walls and fired."

"Some of you got to the castle?"

"Oh, yes, some of us got there."

"What did you do when you got there?"

"We tied bags of powder to the gate. They went off with a big bang, when fire was put to them. That killed a lot of people."

"What people were killed?" demanded Cartier.

"What people? Why, our people. Some of us were standing

too close. Some of us were blown to pieces. Somebody's arm hit me across the face and knocked me down."

"What happened to the gate?"

"That was blown to pieces, too. It all smashed and fell in."

"What did you do then?" asked Cartier.

"Well, then we went inside. That was all."

"You just went inside?"

"Yes, we just went inside."

"And what happened in the court of the castle?"

"Well, a lot of the men of the count came running out at us with guns and bayonets. One of them was a big man with a sword. I had a scythe tied on to the end of a straight stick. I hit the big man across the belly with the scythe and all his insides came rolling out and fell down around his shoes."

Jacques Fournier laughed again, tossing his head to let the laughter out.

"What happened after that?"

"Well, then we went on into the castle. We went all through the castle."

"That was all?"

"Yes, that was all. There was a big picture made of cloth in the hall of the castle. It showed a lot of dogs running after a deer, and behind the dogs came the riders. They rode all down one side of the hall and they didn't make any noise because they were made of cloth."

"Did you meet any people in the castle?"

"Yes, we met a lot of people."

"What did you do to them?"

"We killed them all. We killed the count and his oldest son. We killed the countess and the wife of my lord, and we killed the grandchildren, too. It was no good to kill the old people and leave the young foxes."

"What did you do then?"

"Then we took everything out of the castle and carried it down to the village. That was all."

"Who led you?"

"Nobody led us. We just all went up the hill together."

"What made you go?"

"A man came from Paris and told us what to do. In Paris, they have made the Bastille all empty. There is nobody in the Bastille any more. And the king is so afraid that he sits in a corner and cries all day long."

BY DEGREES, everyone had drawn out from the shadows at the edges of the clearing and gathered in a compact body around the speaker from Pont-le-Vair. Their upturned faces were whitened by the moonlight, and as moonlight shadows and whirls and shifts on the surface of water, so it seemed to move on the grinning faces of the villagers as they listened to the account of Jacques Fournier.

He now stepped down from the tree trunk which had been his rostrum. Cartier stood up on the tree in his place. The deep-throated murmuring began among the people he hushed by lifting his big arm.

He said: "Now you see what I've told you before. A word comes from Paris. The people go crazy. They attack castles. They murder everybody. They lose many of their own lives while they are attacking and afterwards they crawl back to their village and wait for what is sure to come—soldiers! You know what the soldiers are. You saw them stone Marceau to death today. It is always that way. Now I say, let us all go home to bed. No matter what is happening in Paris, we must wait a while. Maybe there will be a new constitution. Maybe there will be a new army. Maybe everything will change, but we had better wait. Do you want to wash your hands to the elbows with blood? No, you don't want to be murderers. Murderers end on the gibbet. Now, everybody go home to bed."

He waved them away. The crowd slowly huddled off from him, forming into groups before it dispersed. Someone said:

"Let us hear Louis. Louis always has something to say. Louis, stand up on the tree and talk to us."

The voice of Louis answered, lost in the crowd: "No, I'm nobody to talk. I'm not even a whole man. I can't say anything to big, strong people like you. If the marquis would give me back the leg he took away from me, if he would make me a strong man, then I might have something to say."

Here he suddenly appeared, thrust up onto the tree by many hands.

"You talk to us, Louis," they told him. "Talk right out. They cut off one of your legs, but they didn't steal any of your brain."

Louis hung on his crutches like a half-filled sack.

"I cannot talk very well, my dear friends," he said. "I keep seeing poor Marceau as the stones smashed his head, and I can't talk very well. I'm afraid. It makes me sick at the stomach. And that's why I can't talk."

"Talk out, Louis," called several voices. "We want to hear you."

"I can't talk," said Louis. "I keep seeing Marceau dying. He was good to me. He used to let me sit in the warmth of his kitchen. Sometimes he would drop some stale bread into a bit of soup and give me that to eat. I don't know what I'll do; I don't know how I'll live, now that Marceau is gone. That's why I can't talk. I can only see the picture of the marquis throwing his money to the soldiers when they threw their stones very straight and hit Marceau. I see our poor American *seigneur* struggling in the hands of the soldiers. And I see the marquis strike him with the whip. That is why I cannot talk. I simply see the pictures and how all of us made ourselves small and shuddered for fear the marquis might become angry with one of *us*."

"Louis, you have talked enough!"

"No, Cartier. No, no! Let him talk!" cried the villagers. "Talk to us, Louis. We want to hear you talk—the dog of a marquis! The beast with his whip and his money!"

"It isn't good to talk," said Louis. "I can't say anything. You've already heard Jacques Fournier.... They must have stronger men at Pont-le-Vair, if they would charge all the way up that hill of theirs and blow open the gates of the castle. But perhaps the count of Pont-le-Vair had not used his whip so much as our marquis. Perhaps he had not beaten the hearts out of his people and turned them into dogs. Over in Pont-le-Vair, perhaps there are *real* men!"

The crowd had drawn back around the speaker on the tree and now they growled, in fact, like a big pack of hounds.

"We would not have to charge up such a long hill," said Louis. "There would be the woods to shelter us until the last moment, almost. And we have plenty of powder in the village, too. The American is not very clever. We could buy more powder from his stores, if we wanted it. Also, the soldiers are going away from the château. They have marched off this evening. But we are not like the men of Pont-le-Vair. The first gun that bangs, and we would run away."

"That is a lie!" shouted a voice.

"A lie! A lie!" cried others.

"Oh, dear friends, don't be angry with me!" called Louis. "I am only the poor cripple, but *I* would not run away from bullets, I hope and pray. But then I have a reason for not loving the marquis. He owes me a leg, and I would like to have it back from him. The rest of you never lost a leg to him. You know how great he is and what fine horses he rides and I suppose all of you love him as though he were your father. But I… God, see me stand here in your moonlight with Edmond on my left and Phillipe on my right, and hear me say that peace will never come to Charlevain until the marquis is as dead in his castle as Marceau is dead in his grave!"

One brief, deep shout answered the violent appeal. The voice of Cartier began protesting. He was shouted down to silence. Then the hand of the girl pulled at the sleeve of Hampton.

"It is time to go!" she whispered.

"No. It is time for me to speak to them," muttered Hampton.

"*Monsieur,* for the love of God, believe me! If you appeared and they thought you had been spying on them—"

He looked again at the contorted faces that waited to gape in further words from Louis and he knew that she was right. He turned with the girl to pass back through the woods.

"There must be a death for a death!" he could hear Louis screeching behind him.

"A death! A death!" rumbled the men of Charlevain.

CHAPTER XXV

"FOR FREEDOM!"

WHEN THEY GOT out of the woods into the open road again, Hampton was still working with his doubts. He could not solve them.

"Tell me what you think of it, Julie?" he asked.

She answered him with a perfect assurance, saying: "Well, what can *monsieur* do? He loves his new people in Charlevain but he loves them a little less since he saw them drinking in ideas of murder from the hand of Louis. That is true, is it not?"

"Well, go on," muttered Hampton.

"In such a time, *monsieur* must either lead or be forgotten. He cannot keep the people of Charlevain from attacking the château; therefore he must lead the charge. Is he willing to do that?"

"Continue, Julie," said Hampton, for the clear, cold mind of the girl entranced him with its conclusions.

"Consider the people of the château. *Monsieur* detests the marquis but he loves the son of the marquis. He detests the marquis and he despised the Count de Fréron; but just as the old wines in the cellar were always in the mind of my uncle, Camille, so the Lady Marguerite is always in the mind of *monsieur*. So there is nothing for him to do. Two dogs are about to fight. If he comes between them, they will tear him to pieces first, and then they will fight one another."

"And therefore, Julie—?"

186

"Therefore, *monsieur* should go away to Paris, where there is so much to be seen. He should go by the morning diligence."

"And leave Charlevain and the château completely behind him?"

"*Monsieur* cannot help it when business calls him away. Besides, he might take with him a memento of Charlevain."

"What memento, Julie?"

"The first soul in Charlevain to understand the goodness of our master."

"I should take you with me, Julie?"

"Certainly, *monsieur.*"

"You know, Julie, that I am not rich."

"Well, that is a pity," said Julie, shaking her head and frowning. "But I have a pair of hands that could make you at home in a ship's cabin or in a tent."

"If you went with me, you would have to give up the inn."

She stopped short and stamped her foot in the dust. She struck her hands together, also.

"What a devil of luck that that should be true!" she said.

"You would not carry about the keys to the wine cellars."

"No, alas!" said Julie.

"You would not have all the servants to order about."

"That is true, also," moaned Julie.

"You would not receive all the interesting and the great people who stop at the tavern; and how they all would wonder when they saw such a young girl, such a charming girl, with so much responsibility!"

"Please do not talk, *monsieur!*"

"Then there would be the money to count up every day, silver and even gold; and presently all the villagers take off their hats when they see *Mademoiselle* Julie pass by. Moreover, presently comes the young merchant, rich, traveled, who sees at a single glance what a treasure is locked up in the mind of Julie more than all the wines in the tavern cellars. He marries you, and

afterwards you have a splendid home and the keys to all the
fortunes of the wise young man who—"

"*Monsieur!*"

"Julie?"

"Do you see the moon on the lake?"

"Certainly."

"If those were all diamonds and I could have them, I would
not stay in Charlevain if you would take me with you!"

"You are a very foolish and unpractical girl, Julie!"

"*Tiens!*" said Julie. "Will you look at me?—So!—Now, at this
very moment, you are about to love me. Is it not true?"

"Yes, it is true," said Hampton.

"If it's the color of my hair that is wrong, it can be changed."

"Julie, be still."

"Yes, *monsieur*. Only this word… You will leave Charlevain
in the morning, will you not?"

"I shall not," said Hampton.

"You will not go?"

"I shall not go."

She walked closer to him and touched the bend of his arm
with her fingers.

"Then everything must end in a wretchedness," she said. "But
I knew this in the beginning. When my heart first opened for
you, it was a sad music that entered me. And I am so sad now
that I hardly can draw a deep breath. There is nothing but sorrow
in everything. The moonlight on the village is not beautiful; it
is like something I remember, far away…. When I remember
you, also, shall I see the bigness of your feet, and the greatness
of your knee or shall I think of the huge, ugly kindness of your
face? Will you tell me one thing?"

"Yes, Julie."

"Is it mostly for the village or mostly for Lady Marguerite
that you are staying in Charlevain?"

"For something else, more than the rest."

"But what other thing can there be?"

"There is a sense of duty that is rather blind."

"But duty to what, *monsieur?*"

"To my dear friend, Jean-Pierre."

"To a mere man? *Tiens!* But why?"

"I don't know. I don't reason as cleverly as you, Julie."

A THUNDERSTORM brought in the morning, roared on the roof, rattled on the windows, filled the air with the pungent odor of dust that still was still drinking deeply. John Hampton hardly lifted his eyes from the paper on which he was writing, scratching out, scribbling again. Then with the document stuffed in his pocket he went down to have breakfast.

Julie came to serve him, all in black except for the crisp white of her apron. She had a sullen look with heavy, shadowed eyes, and all the bright grace and the smiling was gone from her lips.

"What have they decided to do, and when?" asked Hampton.

"I know nothing, *monsieur*," said Julie.

"Could you stir about and learn?"

"I have my work in your tavern, *monsieur*, and your chocolate soon will be cold."

He looked away from her out the window which showed him the front of the carpenter shop and gave a narrow glimpse of the yard behind it, where a number of long staves rested against a hurdle. To one of these the carpenter was affixing the crooked blade of a scythe, like a twisted lance-head.

When he glanced back at the girl, she was as dark, as unmovable as ever.

"Send Cartier to me, if you please," he directed.

He had not finished the chocolate when Cartier returned with her. He had washed his hands clean of the surface dirt but not of the black, oily ingrainings; he had combed the forepart of his hair, also, before appearing before the *seigneur* of the village.

"Sit down, Cartier," said Hampton.

"*Monsieur*, I am not tired, thank you."

"I've heard a whisper out of the village. What is the truth in it?"

"A whisper, *monsieur?*"

"A whisper that says that all the old guns and pistols in the village are being cleaned and that powder is being bought at the store. The whisper tells me that scythes are being fixed on staves to make lances."

"There is no truth in this, *monsieur,*" said Cartier.

Hampton pointed out the window and Cartier found so much worth seeing that it was a long moment before he could face the master again.

"Well, Cartier?"

Cartier parted his stiff lips but his eyes wandered without finding words.

"The château?" asked Hampton. He added: "Have a glass of wine. It will help you to talk."

Cartier dragged the back of his hand across his mouth as though he already had drunk. *"Monsieur,"* he said, "you have been a father to us, but our other overlords have not been so kind."

"In one word," said Hampton, "the village is up. Does it want new rights, or must it have old blood? Would it be contented with a free gift of the lands for which the men now pay a rental? If all the rights of the *seigneur* are removed, except those of his private domain—"

"Monsieur, as for your rights over this village, we are better with you than without you as every man knows. But there are other villages on the estate of the marquis."

"How long would it take you to find representative men of those villages and bring them here?"

"By noon they could be here, *monsieur.* And I shall tell them...."

Voices began to call out down the street and Julie appeared in the doorway, saying calmly: "There will be no trouble, after all. The wise marquis is leaving you nothing but empty hands."

"What do you mean by that?" demanded Hampton.

"The picture of it will tell you, *monsieur*. It is in the street."

HAMPTON WALKED to the tavern entrance. At the bend of the street he saw a large cart manned by a dozen men who wore the red and blue feathers of the marquis in their hats. Some of them were coming out from the shop of the tailor at that moment, carrying with them an old blunderbus, a pistol, and a scythe. Other weapons of a similar nature stuck their noses above the edge of the cart. A crowd of villagers stood by at watch, sullen, restless, but unable to interfere because some of the servants of the marquis continually pointed loaded guns at their heads.

"And now, *monsieur*…?" demanded Julie.

He watched for an instant longer, then ran up the street at full speed, with a walking stick in his hand. When he arrived, he found the same gamekeeper who had testified against Louis now pointing a musket over the tail of the cart at his breast.

"All in peace, *Monsieur* the American," said the man. "But if there has to be trouble, we will have a hand in the making of it."

"What claim has the marquis on the weapons he takes from Charlevain?" cried Hampton.

"He keeps the peace of our royal king, God save him!" said the gamekeeper. "Keep back! Keep back, all of you! If we have to fire into you, there will be some new graves in the churchyard."

For the villagers had crowded close to the cart the moment Hampton appeared.

"Do you hear me, friend?" said Hampton. "Pass out every tool you've taken from the village and you can leave the place in peace."

"*Monsieur*," sneered the gamekeeper, "the noble marquis is not here to argue with you, and I can only perform his orders until—"

He found such a satisfaction in the words he was speaking that he lowered the muzzle of the musket a little and let it sag to the side. Hampton caught the barrel instantly and by the help of a strong pull on it sprang up into the cart. The gun went off, the barrel shuddering against the grip of his hand; but he had the gamekeeper pinioned at once.

Not another shot was fired.

The men of Charlevain poured into the cart behind him like water through a vent and mastered the weapons of the rest of the searching party. There would have been a multiple murder in another moment except for the voice of Hampton thundering: "Peace! Peace! It is over! Pierre, let him be! Jacques!—Cartier!—do you hear me?"

The yelling of the crowd, that had broken out suddenly like that of a pack when it finds a hot scent, died out suddenly and left a single voice that screeched: "It is war with the marquis, now! War! War! There can be no back-steps now! He'll come down on us with all his men!"

Hampton, turning, distinguished the face of Louis as the cripple yelled out the last words. The truth that was in them he could not deny. Whether right or wrong was with the marquis, he could not endure such an affront as this and hope to keep the respect of the countryside.

And there was the savage murmur of the gamekeeper close to his ear, saying: "Whether I die for it or not, I'll die happy, *Monsieur l'américain!* how you'll pay for this pretty work!"

HAMPTON, IN desperation, looked up and down the street. The cart stood at the curve of it so that he could see through to each end, and he thought, as he had thought before, how like a close-walled gorge the street was, with house fitting against house for mutual support. If the ends of the chasm were closed, it would be highly defensible in every military sense. He remembered, then, what he had heard of the barricades in the streets of Paris.

"Jacques!" he called out.

"Here, *monsieur!*" answered the big blacksmith.

"Take charge of these fellows from the château," commanded

Hampton. "The moment that one of them gets back to his master, we'll have fifty or sixty men with guns charging on horseback up the street of Charlevain, as fast as the marquis can get them into the saddle and down here to plague us.... The rest of you, block the ends of the street. Pile up benches and tables. Some of you sharpen stakes and drive them into the ground. Incline them outwards and sharpen the upper ends, also. Barricade the streets and then we can hold off the marquis until the law of the land decides between us. If it means fighting, do you stand with me, Charlevain?"

"With *monsieur!* With *monsieur,* for freedom!" screeched the voice of Louis the cripple, first of all; and then the whole street burst into such an uproar that it seemed to Hampton the sky rang with it.

CHAPTER XXVI

REVOLT!

HAMPTON SAT UNDER the old judgment tree across from the inn all during this day. He had become a formal enemy of the marquis and perhaps the king of France, worthy of hanging by the neck, or of torture first and drawing and quartering afterwards. He kept beside him the four old men who had given an air of traditional law to his decisions since he came to the village. Today they were as mute as stones most of the time. It seemed to Hampton that the centuries were crashing about him as he gave his instructions to Charlevain.

First, all work in the fields ended; all the laborers were forbidden to leave the village.

Second, at either end of the village street a barricade was erected of sharpened poles which pointed outwards. These fences were strong enough to break any charge of mounted men.

Third, from the stores of the village fifteen fowling pieces and ten muskets were produced, cleaned and oiled. Another forty firearms appeared in the hands of the villagers, some of them old blunderbusses of uncertain date, worthless from a distance but carrying double handfuls of death at close range.

Fourth, every man in Charlevain, without or with firearms, was given a weapon of some sort. A few cutlasses were distributed. Sickles straightened and placed on the ends of sticks made excellent short spikes. Scythe blades, terrible and clumsy, made spear points for others. A few had nothing but knives and clubs.

In two hours the crowds of workers had erected at either end of the street barricades capable of repelling a cavalry charge. Accordingly, Hampton turned loose the dozen retainers of the marquis, giving to the gamekeeper a letter to his master which, after due salutations, ran:

"The people of Charlevain desire to inform you that they wait for the opinion of the law as between them and you.

"You have led an armed force into the village and murdered a harmless citizen.

"You have despatched other armed men to take property from them by force, and without any justice of legal proceeding.

"Your attitude constrains the people of Charlevain to put themselves in an attitude of defense. They announce to you their determination to resist any further encroachment with all their force."

He left the letter unsigned, since as a matter of fact he had no right to place his signature on the paper. But he said to the gamekeeper: "There is a message here from all the people of the village. Take a separate message from me to your master. Tell him that nothing else matters a great deal to me until I have come to grips with him, not in Charlevain but on ground that is very much nearer and dearer to him."

The gamekeeper answered: "*Monsieur,* my master will know how to answer insolence with a whip!"

The boldness of his own answer turned him pale, but Hampton merely smiled on him.

"There's a right spirit in you," he said. "I grudge you to the marquis. *Adieu.*"

THE VILLAGERS, when they saw the men of the marquis rattling up the road in their great, old-fashioned cart, raised a tumultuous shouting of mockery, which lasted until a bend of the road took them out of sight. Hampton was already on his tour of final inspection, taking with him a score of the best-armed peasants. Those who remained in the open street could be expected to defend themselves well enough because they would have numbers beside them, but it was necessary to post men at the windows in the rear of the houses so that a flank attack might not break in on Charlevain.

At favorable places, Hampton posted these men in pairs, one to start firing as soon as he saw an attack developing, the other to run shouting into the street to bring the alarm. He worked with a tense enthusiasm at these preparations. It did not matter, now, whether he had a claim to Charlevain or whether he were a mere ghost in the town. This was a time for fighting, and his entire nature responded.

He felt, too, that strange sense of obligation to the dead man, and found a pleasure in telling himself that Hugh Massey, if he were a man among men, surely would have done as John Hampton was now doing. Matters had come to such a pass that perhaps even the revelation which Jean-Pierre could make would not be sufficient to shake the attachment of the villagers from him.

But Jean-Pierre, he knew, would never speak.

Hampton was finishing that work when a number of guns discharged at the lower end of the village, and he ran out to find the men of Charlevain shouting, and the women screeching behind the lower barrier. The cause he found the moment he arrived at the barricade, for a furlong down the road fifty or sixty horsemen milled in confusion. The red and blue feathers of d'Alenton glimmered in their hats.

A single figure now emerged from the crowd and rode toward the village. Hampton recognized at once the jaunty figure of de Poncey. The young Frenchman, as he came to the barrier, reined in his horse and called: "Where is the American? Where is Massey?"

"Here, de Poncey," answered Hampton.

"How is it with you in there, Massey?" asked de Poncey. "Do you enjoy stewing around with garlic breath and July sunshine? And how will the others enjoy it when they find that they're cut off from their fields and huddled up in a pen until the law comes and the military behind it to smash the folk of Charlevain like spoiled eggs?"

The harsh, shrill voice of Louis screamed out: "You lie, aristocrat! You lie! You lie! The soldiers fraternize with the people and aristocrats sell cheaper than pork in the market!"

A good big wave of laughter came roaring from the peasants and de Poncey stood up in his stirrups to stare over the barricade. Big Jacques Cartier climbed on the barrier and shouted: "Look at me, *Monsieur* de Poncey. Remember my face. Go back and tell the marquis my name so that he may never stop hating me. I am Jacques Cartier, the blacksmith. I stand or die with *Monsieur* Massey."

THAT GOOD example struck fire from many of the other peasants, who began to clamber on the barricade and name themselves, yelling in a loud confusion until Hampton lifted his hand. The shouting ended at once.

"I apologize for the noise, de Poncey," he said. "But perhaps you can understand the meaning of it?"

"At the first gun," sneered de Poncey, "they will run like rats for their holes."

"You have fifty or sixty guns down the road, de Poncey," said Hampton. "Bring 'em up, man. Try 'em on us."

"I have a letter from the Marquis d'Alenton," said de Poncey. "Take it and answer him, not me. As for Charlevain, I pity it and the people in it. Two cannon shot will open this street."

He tossed the letter over the barricade.

As Hampton opened the letter, Julie, who was sitting on the top of the barricade with her chin in her hand, said quietly to de Poncey: "Is there to be much blood, *monsieur?*"

"Not much, my dear," said de Poncey. "As soon as your men see the red of it, they'll be yelling for mercy."

"Will they?" nodded the girl. "But if I were you, *monsieur,* I would take off all the silver and metal braid that makes you flash so brightly."

"Why would you do that?" asked de Poncey.

"Because it gives you too big a place in the sun," said the girl.

Hampton broke the wax seal of the marquis with the feeling
that he was making history. Then he read:

> Monsieur Massey,
> Out of pity to my poor people in Charlevain, I send them a
> last, formal warning. You are directed to withdraw from Char-
> levain before sunset.
> Before leaving, you will reclaim from the hands of the peas-
> ants all the firearms and the ammunition which you are said to
> be distributing from your stores.
> Immediate obedience to these directions will insure the
> mercy of the law.
> Failure to obey will cause me to proclaim you at once a rebel
> and a traitor to the king and make you a man outside the law
> with whatever price I find it convenient to place upon your head.
> He crumpled the letter in his hand.

"Friends," he said to the villagers, "my lord the marquis orders
you to give up your guns. Otherwise he makes me an outlaw
with a price on my head."

Here Louis screeched in his raucous voice: "A dead de Poncey
would be the clearest answer to send to the marquis!"

The crowd yelled out a sudden agreement; and as suddenly
was silent.

Hampton looked into the pale, narrow face of the cripple,
who was sweating with an unquenchable thirst. He glanced
away again. Then he said to de Poncey: "You see what their spirit
is? Tell the marquis whatever you please and say that it comes
from me. *Adieu*, de Poncey!"

"Poor Massey!" answered the Frenchman. "God pity you more
than I shall be able to when we meet again. *Adieu!*"

He turned his horse away and returned at a brisk gallop
towards his troop. The long tongues of the peasants still were
unrolling their choicest insults when Hampton picked out

from the crowd a plump, cheerful man, one Gaspard, who had a genius in the making of wine.

He said: "Gaspard, how far have you thought through this thing?"

"Monsieur?" asked Gaspard.

"Have you thought as far as soldiers coming to put down a revolt?" asked Hampton.

"Monsieur, the clever fellows in Paris can do my thinking for me," said Gaspard.

THAT ANSWER, it was plain, seemed entirely satisfactory to the village of Charlevain. If there were barricades in the streets of Paris, it was right that there should be barricades in the streets of every village in France. The entire nation seemed to look to the capital city as a body towards its brain.

That finally reassured him that no act of his could have checked the revolt in Charlevain. His leadership merely had hastened the uprising.

He went to sit down under the great tree and put his thoughts in order. No one came near him except Julie, who brought some fruit and white wine and put them on the table beside him.

He said: "Julie, why am I unhappy?"

"A brave man cannot be afraid, before fighting, but he can be happy about it," said the girl.

"You are wrong. I rather like the thought of the fight," said he. "Tell me why I am unhappy?"

"Look at me, *monsieur.* You have a burden on your soul, perhaps. And that is a pity."

"Julie, I think there is going to be fighting, as a matter of fact, and if a bullet should clip me between the eyes, I want you to know that I am not Hugh Massey."

"No, *monsieur,* you will be only his spirit, then; and I shall have a broken heart."

"Julie, I am not Hugh Massey. Hugh Massey feeds the fish in Le Havre. Jean-Pierre knows that I'm not he."

"All our fathers! All their saints! What sort of a game have you been playing here? And yet you play it in earnest, too, as though you owned the stones you were willing to fight for!"

"The fact is that I love Charlevain," said Hampton. "But all that I have in this world, Julie, is my pair of hands, and my sword. Why the devil don't you show a little horror, Julie?"

"How can I show horror when my heart is enchanted?" asked Julie. "To a gentleman with a fortune, of course I'm nothing, but to a gentleman who hasn't a penny in his purse, don't you think that a good cook and housewife has a certain value, *monsieur?*"

"Go away," said Hampton. "I thought the news would strike you blind with astonishment; but it only makes you laugh like a silly girl. Keep the word to yourself."

HE HAD no chance to prepare new measures for the representatives whom Cartier had called in from the other villages on the Alenton estate now arrived in a group. They came from Maraigne, Vailly, Clausonne, Alenton itself, Barbesieux, and Riaux.

No doubt they were representative of the best brains and the greatest prosperity in the other towns; for that very reason their haggard faces and pinched bellies spoke more eloquently to Hampton of the way famine had been sucking the blood of all France. When he offered them food, they ate like wolves and then looked around at the well-fed peasants of Charlevain as though they hated the sleek faces they saw.

They brought something a good deal more important than this news. One of the men, a certain Bertrand Chabrol of Clausonne, gave to Hampton a letter which some of the men of Clausonne that morning had taken from a man of the marquis who had been halted when he was "riding too fast and too far to have any honest purpose," as Bertrand Chabrol put it.

The letter was short and highly to the point. It was addressed to General the Count Menal, commandant of the garrison at Epivent, not far down the river.

It ran:

My dear Joseph,

Can you spare me some two or three hundred men for a day or two? I know that the countryside about you is a little uneasy, but here I am faced with the danger of a vicious peasant uprising.

Consider the strangeness of fate! A rude boor of an American appears in my village of Charlevain and incites the uprising. The peasants flock around him as around a savior. He preaches blood to them in the streets.

Come to my aid if you can. Two or three cannon would settle the whole matter quickly. They would not have to speak three words apiece before the peasants would understand that there is still a law in the land, and masters to wield it.

Adieu. I kiss the hand of the lovely Adelaide.

  With affectionate gratitude,
    Your friend and true believer
      Alenton.

All the hot blood of courage rushed to the heart of Hampton as he read this letter to a close; and his brain remained as cold and clear as an autumn morning. He faced the lordly forehead of the château across the lake as he turned to the delegates from the villages.

Of one of the delegates, a ragged, squat, wide-shouldered man, he asked: "What is your name, friend?"

"Pierre Decretot, *monsieur.*"

"Does the thought of soldiers frighten your village?"

"*Monsieur,* we have known those devils in uniform before. Even to have them quartered on us as friends is worse than a plague."

"Very well," said Hampton. "If we act quickly, the entire trouble may be ended before the soldiers could be sent for a second time and arrive. Will you stand with Charlevain, all of you?"

"*Monsieur,*" said Decretot, "we have starved under the marquis while Charlevain grew fat under you. If you speak, every man in my town of Barbesieux will answer you."

The whole chorus of delegates spoke out after the same fashion.

Hampton said: "In the morning, at prime, I shall ride to the gates of the château and ask for the marquis. If he will speak with me, I shall put before him a petition of rights that will give you the land you have been farming. In the meantime, within two hours after dawn, you will be ready in the woods below the château. The men of Charlevain will be there waiting for you. We are leaving our barricades! It is time to strike before we are struck."

One of the representatives, a man whose eyelids never seemed to cover the glare of his eyes, replied: *"Monsieur,* if you put your head into the mouth of the wolf, what will keep him from biting it off?"

"The fear of the men in the forest will prevent him," said Hampton.

"He will see that by killing you, he shoots us through the brain," said the peasant.

It was Louis the cripple who answered: "Well, no one can make a bargain unless he's ready to risk a little money, or blood."

"When did you ever risk either?" demanded the harsh voice of Julie.

"Ah, Julie," answered the cripple. "You're such a pretty child— why will you spoil your face with foolish talking?" Then, fiercely: "Have I not given a leg already?"

THROUGH THE evening and then on through the night, Hampton remained in the judgment chair, for every few minutes there was a call for him. Deputations came from the villages of Clausonne and Vailly. One man impressed Hampton greatly. He was tall; his cloak was as long as a priest's cassock; his face had the meager, white look of the ascetic. He said: "My name is Claude Laustruc. If you give me a musket, I shall carry it until I am dead or until I have killed one of them."

"You expect to die, do you?" asked Hampton.

"I know that I shall die!" said Claude Laustruc. "Hunger

killed my family. Now it is my turn. But who can tell? I might even see the marquis himself while I am carrying a gun."

The best Hampton could do was to give over his own pistol.

He said at the same time to all of them: "We are going to settle this whole matter peacefully, with a little talk, tomorrow morning."

Laustruc said: "I hope not, *monsieur*, but we are in your hands."

These deputations got no firearms because there were no spare ones to give but they received some extra spikes from Charlevain together with a good quantity of coarse flour, for if they went to the fight with full bellies they were apt to do much more before the château.

SOME TIMES during the night Hampton was able to close his eyes for a few moments but he hardly slept an hour between dark and dawn. About three in the morning, Julie brought out to him toasted bread and some frothed chocolate. He said to her: "Why are you so sullen, Julie? What's happened to you?"

"What do I matter?" she asked.

"To me, you matter more than all the rest," he told her.

"More than all the rest of the village," she answered. "But when you come to the château… when you see that they are your own people?"

"Who have tried to murder me, Julie?"

"Murder? Your heart will find another word for it when you see *Mademoiselle* Marguerite."

He remembered that long, long afterwards.

Shortly after dawn, he marshaled the men of Charlevain in a long column that stretched far down around the bend of the street. None of the men looked at him. They kept their eyes straight before them on their own thoughts. The sun was up and then hid its face in a cloud as they marched out from the village. Children were strictly kept in the rear but twenty or thirty women walked behind the column of men, all carrying weapons. Some had butcher knives, several carried hayforks.

"We won't need you, *mes amis*," said Hampton.

Big Marie Duchamps, striding along like a man, flourished a hatchet as she answered: "If our men kill some venison, we can at least carve the meat for them, *monsieur.*"

Hampton got on a horse and rode up to the head of the column. Here he found Cartier, as a matter of course, but he was amazed to see Louis, the cripple, among the foremost, helped strongly along by several of his friends.

"What are you doing here, Louis?" asked Hampton.

"I thought I might be able to strike a blow with my crutches," said Louis. A grim smile distorted his mouth.

"Also, he could talk for us, if there came a need of words," said one of the men.

They rounded the lake, pouring up through the woods beneath the château. Still in the midst of the forest, they heard the treading of many feet from the south.

"Charlevain! Charlevain!" screeched Louis, the cripple. "Who goes there?"

The entire column took up the shout so that it swept like a storm through the woodland. "Charlevain! Charlevain!"

Other shoutings answered them out of the distance: "Maraigne! Maraigne! Vailly! Maraigne! Clausonné! Clausonné!"

All the villages of the Alenton estate poured out their men in the sparse woods that sloped down from the castle. They made a sound like gathering waters and as Hampton glanced towards the château through the tree trunks, he had, for a time, an illusion that he was staring down, not up.

CHAPTER XXVII

FOR THE GIBBET

BY NINE IN the morning, the villagers had gathered. In number they were well over twelve hundred men. Two or three hundred women and even a scattering of children attended the host. Hampton sent the children back under escort; he ordered the women well to the rear. He was obeyed readily, though the majority of the people never had seen him before. The humming murmur attended him everywhere: "The American! There he is!"

Every man from the other villages looked as though he had not eaten within a month. They clumped along in wooden shoes with patched and repatched clothes hanging on their bodies. They looked out at the world through a screen of clotted fore-locks, and with the bright, quick, desperate eyes of hunting beasts. It was their mood and their need for the day to have a leader like Hampton; but he knew that he was nothing to them. They were grown children who tolerated him at the head of the table. But what if no food appeared? In the meantime, they were looking to their guns, chattering together, burying their own fear in the sense of their numbers.

In the mid-morning, when the assemblage was complete, Hampton told the leaders that he was trying to make his way into the presence of the marquis; that he would leave them at once. He begged them to wait quietly. Only the men with guns should show themselves at the edges of the trees from time to time. When he was about to ride away at last, big Cartier said

to him: *"Monsieur,* let me go, and thirty of our best men; they will think more of you if they see you come with a bodyguard."

Hampton answered: "Thank you, Cartier; but if I go up under the walls with some of our people, their lack of order and their clumsiness will make the soldiers on the battlements think very little of our army. They have cannon up there, and they have sixty or seventy men who know how to shoot straight. We must not let them see us too closely, Cartier. If I go alone, it will show more confidence. You understand that if I succeed in bargaining with the marquis, it will be because he is afraid of the force that is behind me; and if this bargain is made you will be free men on free land forever!"

They heard this in a greedy silence, unlike anything he ever had seen on the faces of men before.

He was barely outside the line of the trees when the voice of a girl shrilled out: "Shall we cheer him? Can't we send even our voices along with him?" He had not set eyes on her, but he knew the voice of Julie; and the whole forest began to roar with shouts and cheers that went booming after Hampton all the way to the gate of the château.

It rose so loftily above him that he felt like some Lilliputian figure made to fit into the hand of a Gulliver. Stone carving lightened the massive walls and the gate-towers were like miniature Italian campaniles. Out of a shot-window a voice called: "Who goes?"

He had not prepared himself for that simple question.

"I am Hugh Massey from Charlevain," he said at last. "I have come to speak with the marquis."

A bawling, insolent voice called to him: "Does the noble marquis expect your call, *Monsieur* the American?"

"If he can't see me alone, tell him I have two thousand armed men in the woods who would like to come in with me if they have to tear down the gates to do so," shouted Hampton.

"It's late in the morning for a cock to crow," yelled the other.

Someone laughed and another voice was barely audible, saying: "We'd rather let him in than out. Open the postern for him."

THEN MORE voices repeating a command, a noise as of a gun butt grounded on stone, the creaking of a key in a lock, and the postern opened in the left gate-tower. A man with a musket at the ready stood in the shadow.

He said: "Say goodbye to your horse and come in, *Monsieur* the American!"

Others, unseen, laughed a little; their laughter went out under a sudden word of command.

Hampton, as he dismounted, looked back towards the edge of the woods where men stirred in the shadow of the trees with little quicksilver slashings of light on their weapons. He took his foot slowly from the left stirrup. A wise fellow, perhaps, would put his horse at full gallop to get back to that company of friends, after hearing the voices which guarded the gate of the château. Fear turned the pit of his stomach cold; and then pride stiffened him, put back his shoulders, stretched his mouth with a smile, and marched him forward through the little arched doorway.

The moment he had passed through it into a short, winding

hall, two more of the defenders fell in behind him and showed him out into the tower room where he saw de Poncey. Three fine lines of amusement formed between his eyes as he laughed at Hampton.

"And sometimes stray fish are caught in the lake," he said. "Where could they come from? Heaven, I suppose!"

Hampton said: "I want the marquis, not one of his bright young men. What amuses you so much? Do you expect the honest marquis to murder me out of hand?"

De Poncey merely laughed again.

"No, *monsieur*," he said. "I think God intends you to be my dish… Bring the fellow after me!"

Hampton was walked out into the court with a musket on either side of him and a pair of drawn swords behind. He could not have been more a prisoner if there had been shackles on wrists and ankles. He knew by the cold of his face that he was pale and for that reason carried his head higher. In the windows around the court faces appeared; the one he saw most clearly was a female servant, laughing and pointing. They passed through a doorway where a pair of men leaned on muskets and stared at Hampton with broad grins.

The sweep of the stairway rose before him like a white road with intricate little carvings along the balustrade. When he looked up, the coffered ceiling seemed to be rising still higher above him. In the hall, an indecent Leda leaned over her swan, and a satyr danced with a bunch of marble grapes. He had a glimpse through the windows at Lake Charlevain which held some of the white clouds and blue of the sky; then they entered a small room where the guards halted with Hampton. They stepped back into the four corners of the chamber with the precision of veteran soldiers accustomed to guard-duty, but their young leader after a glance nodded towards the door.

"You can wait outside for me," he said. "*Monsieur* Massey, I go directly to the marquis; while you wait, I recommend the view, and the name of Georges Francois de Poncey, who hopes to have a closer knowledge of you, before long."

He gave Hampton a bow and a sneer before he went out and left the American alone, his exaggerated courtesy and scornful disdain very apparent.

THE VIEW which de Poncey recommended showed the village of Charlevain straight across the lake. In spite of all the turmoil, all the breath-taking suspense of this day, half a dozen little fishing-boats moved slowly on the water with not enough wind to smooth the wrinkles in the sails. He turned abruptly from this because it was to him like the view a prisoner has from the window of his cell. He preferred to examine the furnishings which enriched even this little apartment.

On the wall, two half figures of nude girls, sexless, vaguely smiling, offered brackets for the candles. The legs of the table rested on gilt lions' paws and swelled at the top into the heads of seraphs in full relief, framed by their upward wings; even the chest of drawers rested on carved supports, bent slightly inwards like the legs of a deer about to spring; and a little Persian prayer-rug glowed dimly on the floor.

A door opened with a sound like a caught breath; the dress of Marguerite de Fréron swirled about her as she shut the door and turned again on Hampton. The fear that whitened her face made it easy to read. Even a period of mourning for a dead father could not reduce a great lady to perfect simplicity of dress. A drift of black Chantilly lace softened the grim effect and diamonds crusted her shoe-buckles. He bowed to her.

"I've sent the guards away," she said. "You must not stay. I can show you how to leave."

"I have come to see the marquis," he answered.

"But don't you understand what he is and what he'll do to you?" she asked. "He's laughing with de Poncey now! I heard them together! Will you come, Hugh?"

"And let murder happen as it happened at Pont-le-Vair?" he asked.

"Murder! Murder! Murder! That's what I'm talking about! It *will* be murder and not a legal hand in France can touch him for it. There's only this instant; will you come—for your life—for God's sake?"

"*Mademoiselle*, you are a saint to concern yourself about me," said Hampton. "The truth is that I don't deserve your consideration. I am not what you think, *mademoiselle*."

"Hugh, are you in God's name going to bargain and haggle? What do I care what you are if I can know that you're safe?"

"Nevertheless," said Hampton, "I can tell you a thing that will remove your concern for me at a single stroke and then it will be as though your hands were washed... Will you give me your oath that what I tell you will go no farther?"

"I'll swear by the saints—"

"I'd rather have you promise by your pride and honor as a lady of France and a Fréron."

"I promise, Hugh. With my hand on my heart."

"*Mademoiselle*," he said, "I am not the heir of a great American estate. I am a penniless adventurer with no more claim on Charlevain than I have on heaven. My name is not Hugh Massey."

It took a moment for the understanding of these words to work on her spirit. Then she whispered: "Do you mean that you're not fighting for your own property and your own people? Hugh—are you only playing hero and friend to the poor, blinded peasants—"

Before he could answer, the second door in the room opened behind him. He turned to see young de Poncey bowing.

"*Mademoiselle*, I beg your pardon if I interrupt," said de Poncey, "but the marquis wishes to see the American at once. I shall tell him that I had to tear *Monsieur* Massey from his talk with you. *Mademoiselle*, again, forgive me. *Monsieur*, follow me if you please."

She slumped against the door with her eyes closed, and Hampton followed slowly on behind his escort.

"Marguerite is a kind girl," said de Poncey. "She has one of those hearts that keep on beating for the under dog, even an American breed of the same."

AS HE finished speaking, he opened a door and they passed into a large bedroom. In the four poster reclined the Marquis d'Alenton among pillows which billowed against him like full sails.

"Ah, *Monsieur* the American," he said, lowering the book which was in his hand. "And what do you think of this rascal? He writes: 'Love is the passion of youth, the recreation of maturity, the despair of old age.'"

"If the mind remains young," said de Poncey, "why should there be the despair?"

"In any case, possession is the least part of passion," suggested the marquis.

"As the kill is the least part of the hunt," said de Poncey.

At this the marquis laughed with an unaffected whole-heartedness.

"You're an amusing fellow, de Poncey," said he. "What keeps you so bright?"

"Continual use, my lord," smiled de Poncey, and the marquis laughed again.

Now he turned his head carelessly towards Hampton.

"And you, *monsieur?*" said he.

Hampton took back his attention from the bed at which he had been staring, the azure background carved and gilded, with four eagles in relief, the vase-shaped knobs, the drapings of blue and golden taffeta, the valances of the bed finished in the same materials, with golden fringes all around. A smaller canopy inside the larger one was draped with gray taffeta finished off with gold silk fringe and lined with Avignon taffeta. The brocaded curtains were now fastened back to the posts. In this setting, like an ugly ivory carving in a fine jewel casket, the marquis seemed perfectly out of place except that his self-satisfaction never permitted him to lose face.

"And you, *monsieur,* what will you have with me?" the marquis was repeating.

"It's written out here," said Hampton.

"I detest handwriting," said the marquis, without stirring hand to touch the paper. "Tell me what it's all about?"

"An agreement for your signature," explained Hampton. "In it you sign away your rights over the entire estate except the family holdings immediately around Charlevain."

"I sign them away?" said the marquis.

"Yes," nodded Hampton.

"Really!" said the marquis. "Say something, de Poncey. I must laugh and I don't wish to seem rude."

"In America, my lord, they have quantities of everything except a sense of humor."

"My dear young friend," said the marquis to Hampton, "tell me what possible reason I could have for surrendering a fortune?"

"To do justice to the thousands of people in your villages," said Hampton.

"Ah, you have decided that it would be justice?"

"Also to save your neck," said Hampton.

"More cogent still," said the marquis. He folded his hands before his head and smiled on the American. "Otherwise what will happen? These desperate fellows will pull the château about my ears, stone by stone? Is that it?"

"Have you heard the story of Pont-le-Vair?" asked Hampton.

The smile of the marquis went out.

"Let us not forget," said de Poncey, "that there were hardly forty men inside the castle at Pont-le-Vair, and no cannon at all."

"*MONSIEUR THE* marquis," said Hampton, "you have a hundred souls inside the château, but how much food is there for them? You have sold a great deal during the recent time of high prices. How long could you stand a siege?"

"A siege? By those scoundrels?" asked de Poncey. "And what would they live on during the siege?"

"On the provisions that remain to me in Charlevain," said Hampton.

"Those could not last long," declared the marquis.

"After that, as lichens live on stone and air, your peasants will live on the hope of tasting your blood," said Hampton.

"This insult..." began de Poncey, loudly.

"Be still, my dear lad," broke in the marquis. "When we bargain for horses, we name all the points. How many fellows have you in the woods?"

"About thirteen hundred, my lord."

"Thirteen hundred? I don't believe it!... I beg your pardon!"

"A perfectly obvious and manifest lie," remarked de Poncey.

"You used to have a mind of your own and a tongue strong enough to speak it, my lord," said Hampton. "Do you need this greyhound to howl in my face and lick your feet?"

The sword of de Poncey came half-way out of its sheath. He bit at the air in a catlike rage, but the marquis said: "There, there, de Poncey! Be at rest... and as a matter of fact you may let me talk for myself from now on."

De Poncey pushed the sword slowly back into its scabbard, as though he were driving it through some hard material.

"To tell the truth," said the marquis, "there are a good many little things that you and I could talk over, Mr. Massey. By the way, did you come to me under a white flag?"

"*Monsieur*, I did not," said Hampton.

"Ah, but wasn't that an oversight?" asked the marquis.

"When I talk to a man who uses women in his murders," said Hampton, "I realize that flags and promises are worth nothing."

"Ah?" said the marquis, sitting up in his bed.

"This is what I expected," broke in de Poncey.

"And what would you do with him?" asked the marquis.

"In the name of his treason and our king, I'd hang him off the southern wall so that his friends could see him hanging there. That would answer to them and their petitions. As for a siege—that is a thing for laughter."

"I think you may be right," said the marquis. "In fact, I'm rather sure. So take him to the southern wall but just delay things like a good fellow until I have time to dress."

"Good!" said de Poncey, and instantly shouted: "Enter!"

Here a curtain pushed aside and three armed men entered the room, stepping with a reverent softness on the Persian carpets.

CHAPTER XXVIII

RABBLE IN ARMS

THEY TOOK FROM Hampton his sword and pistol; they tied his hands behind his back.

"Not too quickly, de Poncey," said the marquis. "I must be there to see if that fine American brown turns a little yellow before the end. How Rousseau would have loved this, de Poncey! To see one of his noble savages in such a tough twist of affairs!"

Afterwards, they got Hampton out of the room and down the hall. When they came into the little chamber beyond it, he saw Marguerite de Fréron standing exactly as he had left her.

"Georges! What does it mean?" she cried out at de Poncey.

"It means that our American friends want to strip the marquis of six villages and all his rights over them," said de Poncey. "We are getting him out of the château as quickly as possible."

"You won't harm him, Georges? There'll be nothing dishonorable?" she pleaded.

"Dishonorable? Nothing but duty, *mademoiselle,*" said de Poncey, and made a bow to her.

She looked to Hampton with a desperate inquiry. A tremor of weakness came up through his body and worked in his throat. He dared not speak. He had to set his face and so go by her with his head high.

They were in the big hall beyond when de Poncey murmured: "So very well done that I see manners are taught even in America. If you die in the same manner, *monsieur,* you will be remembered by gentlemen, which is better than living a long life as a king over dirty peasants, is it not?"

Hampton never could tell how his feet reached it, but they came at last to one of the gate-towers in the southern wall. One narrow window looked out towards the trees; a second gave on the court and the noble peace of the château's facade. They sat down on wooden benches placed there for the guard, and de Poncey's acid tongue went on without pause.

"The marquis will soon be here, *monsieur*. He is very quick-handed when it comes to matters that are near his heart.... I noted that Lady Marguerite was much disturbed about you. How true it is that a woman keeps a tender place in her heart forever for a man she has made a fool of!... That was a good leap you made the other night. Did the horse have the idea, or the brave American? I had you exactly at the end of my pistol. I could have sworn that you carried away a little gift of lead from me but you were not wounded, it appears. But when you think of it, how interesting that all the life in this great body and all the breath in that big, arching chest can be let out in an instant by the prick of a needle or the point of a sword."

"*Monsieur* de Poncey," said Hampton, "you are a clever fellow but I should like to be at peace for a few moments. If it is possible, I'd like to have paper and a pen to write a letter."

"Why think of paper and pen now?" said de Poncey, grinning at Hampton like a cat. "It's too late to add much now to the proud record. And if you wrote a letter, who would send it on its way?"

"By God, you enjoy this more than a cat does cream!" exclaimed Hampton.

"**DO YOU** wonder why I hate you?" asked de Poncey. "I wonder, also. There is no justice or true proportion in my feeling about you, *Monsieur* the American. Here am I with a certain gift of brain and hand, one who dances well, sings well, and fences, I think, with a certain dash of inspiration; with not enough learning to make me heavy in the wits and yet not ignorant enough to be found a fool even when philosophers are talking. And yet in spite of all of this, when I saw you among the ragged peasants behind the barricade, I felt a certain touch of pain—jealousy—yes, jealousy! I must be frank, because you are about to die, and if truth hangs on the lips of dying men, it ought to be in their ears, also. In fact, there is something strange about you, a mere savage American, who comes to Charlevain and is able to make the marquis curse and walk the floor at nights, able to cause our beautiful Marguerite to scream and then to weep on account of the ambush into which the clever girl has led you, and finally and above all, able to touch the soul of this Georges de Poncey with a little sting of jealousy. It is all very strange. I dare say that in your entire life you never have said two clever things, and those by accident, and yet for a moment, as I looked at you over the barricade, I thought I was seeing a king among his people. *Monsieur,* you are about to die, and therefore I may tell you the truth!"

The marquis came in, at this moment, tucking a lace handkerchief into his sleeve.

"Well, here we are, de Poncey," he said. "Have you arranged the rope?"

"There is one ready on the wall," said de Poncey.

"There is nothing to delay us, then," said the marquis. "Let us have the thing over. By the way, I met Marguerite and found her rather excited. Can you tell me why, de Poncey?"

"Yes, *monsieur.* When a man loves a woman, he is one of her possessions and a careful girl throws nothing away."

"Very well reasoned, de Poncey," said the marquis. "And yet—for this—"

He examined Hampton carelessly with his eyes, then turned his back and led the way out onto the wall, where an eighteen pounder carronade peered through the battlements.

"There is the rope, as you see, tied to the gun," said de Poncey. "Should we have a little roll of drums and a fanfare of horns?"

The marquis considered Hampton again and then shook his head.

"Not for a common troublemaker and raiser of revolt," he said. "The law, de Poncey, wishes to apportion the dignity of a man's death to the quality of his life."

He turned to Hampton.

"Can you tell me something of peculiar dignity in your life, *monsieur?*" he asked.

AND HAMPTON, looking inward on his mind, kept his face calm while he groped desperately for some delay. If a chance of whatever nature should make the peasants show their full force on the edge of the woods it might very well change the mind of the marquis. In the meantime, he needed time. All the years of his life would be as nothing compared with the exquisite essence of a few minutes now.

He said: "Why, my lord, I dare say that this day has more of the peculiar dignity about it."

"In what manner?" asked the marquis.

"He is killing time," suggested de Poncey.

"Perhaps," said the marquis, "but I've been at war, de Poncey, and always I've been intrigued to know what passes through the mind of a man when he is about to die. Your soldier of France has some oaths, a prayer or two, and a bit of screaming now and then. How does an American die, then? So I ask you first, *monsieur,* what gives this day its peculiar dignity for you?"

"To lead twelve or thirteen hundred armed men is not a bad thing, you know," said Hampton.

"No? Of rabble?"

"Of your own rabble, my lord. And raised against you by a foreigner."

"A poor, helpless, handless lot of creatures, Massey. But I admit one point with a sting in it. Eh, de Poncey? There are my own, and he has rallied them. Twelve or thirteen hundred? That is nonsense, of course!"

"They are there to be counted," said Hampton. "Twelve or thirteen hundred. Every able-bodied man in your villages."

"I deny it," said the marquis. "Many of them were true men."

"There is not a soul on your estate," said Hampton, "not even a child old enough to speak, who fails to detest you."

"The hatred of animals for a brain and eye that controls them," said the marquis. "Even an American should not pride himself too much on leading a herd."

"A herd, plus some tools which may open your castle before long," said Hampton.

"Open the castle? What tools, Massey?"

"I ask you to suppose two cannon posted on the edge of the woods, just inside the trees, and trained on the castle gates," said Hampton.

"Nonsense!" cried de Poncey. "There is not a cannon of any sort on the whole range of the estate!"

"Certainly not," said Hampton. "But think of the highroads, de Poncey, where troops and artillery are passing every day toward Paris. Have you thought of them? Unescorted guns rolling toward Paris."

"Do you mean that you have seized artillery on the king's highway?" cried de Poncey.

"I won't believe it!" exclaimed the marquis.

"Not cannonades," said Hampton. "Not short-barreled cannon, but long guns that shoot like a rifle to the mark. Guns of the newest make. What would they do in half a dozen rounds to your castle gates, *Monsieur* the Marquis? And once the gates are down, how long before the mob would sweep through?"

"There are no artillerymen in the villages. There is not a man capable of managing a field piece," argued de Poncey.

"Have you heard that the soldiery are fraternizing with the people?" asked Hampton. "Two men could point three guns, could they not? With plenty of hands to work for them?"

"By God, it may be true!" gasped de Poncey.

"We should have had word of it!" said the marquis. "The thing is impossible."

"Who would carry you word?" asked Hampton. "If one of the villagers cared to carry news to your advantage, he would be torn to pieces by his own family and thrown to the dogs."

VOICES SHOUTED from the trees. From their verge a figure darted out into the open and ran for the gates, dodging like a snipe. A small wedge of pursuers pulled out after him from among the shadows and then halted while the fugitive sprinted for his life and screeched for help.

"I think that's one of the assistant game-keepers, isn't it?" asked the marquis.

"It is," agreed de Poncey.

"But if the peasants have come here for war, why should they let one of my people come through to the château?" asked the marquis. "Perhaps *you* can tell me, *Monsieur* Massey?"

"Because it is still peace while I'm in the castle," said Hampton. "They are waiting for me before they begin the attack; but they will not wait much longer."

The marquis nodded.

"He speaks with a certain dignity, de Poncey," he said, "a thing I have noted before this in men who are about to die."

"For an American, *monsieur,* he is almost a gentleman," said de Poncey.

"I consider it," said the marquis. "Stand the American on the edge of the wall and arrange the rope around his neck. His talk about cannon is absurd…. But one of you call up the assistant gamekeeper."

The marquis walked up and down with his hands under the tail of his coat, flipping it out at every stride or two.

"The rights of all the villages—to give them free land, de Poncey. Do you remember?"

"And asked for with confidence! Like a judge speaking of justice!"

Hampton stood in the embrasure with the toes of his shoes jutting out over the edge of the wall, as the rope-end was being knotted to fit his throat. He wanted to do what he had heard of other men: review the whole course of his life in a few glimpses, for it had been a happy, cheerful life. The only picture that came to Hampton was of himself running through the years, his mouth agape with laughter. He could see that he had been a fool and a child; but he could not keep his mind even on John Hampton or on his God. The thought of Julie went through him, a blurred and faceless stroke; he saw Marguerite de Fréron for a flashing instant; and then nothing existed except the present moment as the chafing spines of the rope worked against his throat. The casual manner of the marquis made it easier to die. He dismissed a life as he dismissed his valet and made the world of no moment except for fine clothes, formal manners, large estates.

The voice of de Poncey said, beside him: *"Monsieur* Massey, what last thoughts will you confide to me?"

Then someone was panting heavily close by. And the marquis said: "Ah, here he is! Do I know your name?"

"I am Andre Thierry, my lord," said the other.

"And how did you happen to get through the hands of the wild fellows over there in the forest."

"My lord, I can't tell—I don't know—I thought I was to die—Their eyes pushed into me like knives—And then I was free again."

"Now, don't be a fool, Andre," said the marquis. "Did they say nothing to you when they let you go?"

"Nothing, my lord. Except that I was to say in the château that they were tired of waiting for the American and that they would come after him very soon unless he appeared."

"They would come after him? How many of them are there to come?"

"Thousands, my lord!"

"Andre, you are an idiot! How many with guns?"

"Hundreds and hundreds, my lord. I swear that the flash of the gun-barrels blinded me."

"They intend to come after the American?"

"Yes, *monsieur.*"

"All of that is of slight moment," said the marquis. "But what of cannon, Andre?"

The heart of Hampton sank.

"Cannon, *monsieur?*" echoed Andre.

"Yes—cannon, fool! Cannon! The things that shoot rounds of iron as big as your head and just as full of brains. Did you see any cannon?" asked the impatient marquis.

"Now that I think of it—yes—"

"You lie!" shouted de Poncey. "And you lie like a fool, Andre. How could the peasants have cannon?"

"God give me grace and save me," groaned Andre. "I only tell you what I think. Through the brush I think I saw the gleam of a huge, black—"

"That's enough," said the marquis, shortly.

He gave Hampton a last, lingering glance and turned from him.

"Take *Monsieur* Massey back from the edge of the wall, de Poncey," commanded the marquis. "He may be valuable to us. We must think a little."

THE TWO men at the elbows of Hampton drew him back a pace. In that single step he covered more than a thousand leagues.

"So! So!" said de Poncey, staring eagerly into his face. "Now that you have a little reprieve, you taste death with a finer tongue, eh? It makes a cold drink, *monsieur,* does it not?"

"See the swine, de Poncey," said the marquis. "See them come huddling out into the sunlight… St. Denis for France!… Where did the blackguards find all of those guns? But hush—hush!"

As the throng of peasants rolled out from the forest, all along

the battlements of the château, muffled exclamations of astonishment broke from the retainers of the marquis.

"Do you hear, de Poncey?" asked the marquis. "My men are
troubled."

"I hear them but it's an easy thing to reassure them. They
think a gun makes a man a soldier," said de Poncey.

The marquis caught by the arm, suddenly, one of the pair who
had been guarding Hampton.

"Why are you so damned white, you rascal?" demanded the
marquis. "Why are you shaking? Here you have stone walls to
help you and yonder they are a poor, groveling rabble."

"Ah, my lord," said the trembling voice of the guard, "also they
had stone walls at the Bastille and at Pont-le-Vair...."

"They're still pouring out of the forest," said de Poncey. "This
is like the old Greek myth. The armed men spring up out of the
ground.... There's the end of the firearms but those other fellows
with their scythes and clubs and pitchforks could strike a few
good blows if they came to close quarters."

The marquis put in at this point: "Imagine you with your
small sword and your twenty years of careful schooling against a
two-pronged hay-fork. Imagine that, de Poncey. Does it shorten
your breath a little? Does it pull in your stomach a trifle?"

De Poncey laughed. "The idea goes through and through me,
my lord," he said.

The peasants came on slowly, pausing now and then to
compact their ranks, moving a little ahead, pausing again.

De Poncey said: "They are in point-blank range, of course.
A good round of grape from these guns would do something
to them."

"There in the center," said the marquis. "That crew keeps good
order, and they have twice as many guns as the other companies.
Is that a girl walking beside the leader? A girl carrying a drum?"

"Those are the men of Charlevain, my lord; and that is Julie,
the niece of Marceau, the inn-keeper," explained de Poncey.

"Ah, yes—Marceau! I remember him," murmured d'Alenton.

"And his niece no doubt remembers you," said de Poncey. "Now we can hear her drum—a brave girl, my lord!"

For Julie stepped at the side of big, lumbering Cartier, and now began to roll out a marching rhythm on the drum which was tied at her hip. In a pause of the drumming, the sticks flashed above her head, spinning brightly in the sunshine. She caught them without a wasted step and resumed the drumming on the proper beat. The men of Charlevain began to laugh and cheer.

"Grape! Grape!" said de Poncey. "Now is the time to let them have it, my lord."

"You are brave, clever, and you love battle, de Poncey," said the marquis. "But you are young! This moment that you think is for bullets as a matter of fact is the time for words.... Send out the peasants at once and tell them to come not a step closer to the walls, for the American and I are negotiating here concerning their rights.... *Monsieur* Massey, I have been looking forward to your death as a child looks to Easter but it seems that we must talk a little, after all.... Here, fellow. Set free the hands of my American friend!"

CHAPTER XXIX

A FRIEND LOST

THE MARQUIS TOOK Hampton straight back into the library of the château, sat him down on the far side of an espagnolette (one of those tables decorated with female figures at the four corners), and drew up a chair in the most business-like manner, but even at this moment he did not allow haste to appear. He first waved to the old ivory of the vellum bindings that lined the walls and said: "Are you for this sort of thing, *monsieur?*"

"I've never done much with books," said Hampton.

"But that Shakespeare; you know him like a father, I suppose?"

"He has at least two ways of saying everything," answered Hampton, "and that sort of thing tires me a little. I prefer Mr. Pope."

"Mr. Pope is beautifully exact," answered the marquis. "He writes almost like a Frenchman—pray forgive this vanity! But now let me see this contract which you have drawn up for me."

When Hampton produced it, the marquis turned immediately to the end to sign.

"You should read it first," suggested Hampton.

"But why?" asked the marquis. "Your French may not be perfect, but I'm sure that your intentions are thorough. I understand that by this act I release the peasant from every feudal due? Well, the thing is done!"

He signed his name with a broad flourish and sanded the ink, then he looked up to Hampton with that stone-cut smile.

"And so, *monsieur,* you are contented?" he asked.

"I have to ask for another thing," said Hampton.

"But this concludes the bargain, does it not?" asked the marquis. "For this you came to the château? Or am I wrong?"

"When I was standing on the edge of your wall," said Hampton, "I had some new thoughts. Among them, I remembered your son. May I see him now?"

"Totally impossible," said the marquis. "Your country is new, *monsieur,* but in this France of ours we reserve certain judicial rights to the head of a family. My poor Jean-Pierre, who needs the teaching of adversity, is not even in the château."

"Will you tell me where he is?" asked Hampton.

"Oh, in a safe place. You recall our little adventure on the road? The day before that, I sent him away, quietly, by night."

Hampton lifted his eyes for a moment to remember.

"It was his ghost, then, that was heard singing in the château?" he asked.

"That I do not understand," said the marquis.

"Neither do I," said Hampton. "If you'll call him into this room, perhaps he can explain matters to us."

Even the smile of the marquis was not proof against this moment. It died from his face, leaving a rigid immobility of features. Here a door jerked open with such violence that it shuddered against the hand of the servant who appeared on the threshold.

"They have come on—they are almost under the wall—our men are afraid to shoot—" cried the man.

The marquis looked silently from the door towards Hampton. The American said: "Send word that I am coming to them within a few moments and that I expect them to remain quiet."

"That is all," nodded the marquis. The door shut with an impolitic slam and the fellow was gone.

"You see that I have only a moment or so for Jean-Pierre,"

said Hampton. "I must go out among the people to prevent mischief."

The marquis was smiling again. "To produce my son from a distance and in an instant, that would be a feat of real legerdemain, *monsieur.* But I shall attempt it."

He went to a bell pull, and when the call was answered he said to the servant: "Bring the viscount to me at once."

"The viscount?" repeated the gaping man.

"Go to Hebert," said the marquis. "He will understand everything."

AFTERWARDS HE said to Hampton: "What difference the seasons make! If there were snow on the ground, those fellows of yours would not be standing under the wall. The cold wind would blow sense into them. Winter would say to them what Socrates said to the sophist: 'I see your pride through the holes in your cloak.' But are you familiar with Socrates?"

"I am not a scholar," said Hampton. "I know that Socrates had a pug nose and a good heart. That's about all."

"Perhaps that's enough to know," said the marquis. "When the times grow hard and full of action, it may be best for the mind to go in light marching order. And here, I think, is your friend."

For the door opened, rather slowly, and the slender figure of Jean-Pierre, Viscount of Charlevain, came into the room. He was pale. His wide eyes seemed to see nothing. A thin lock of his disordered hair curved like a wound across his forehead. Slippers covered his feet; his lean calves were unstockinged, his shirt open at the throat.

"Hebert!" exclaimed the marquis.

The hard-faced man who walked behind the viscount jerked himself to attention.

"Are you bringing me a peasant out of the fields or the son of my house?" demanded the marquis in that terrible voice which the American never had heard before.

"I brought him only in respect of speed, my lord!" said the trembling Hebert. "I omitted ceremony, my lord, to bring him instantly."

"Get out of my sight!" said the marquis. As Hebert vanished he added: "Your American wanted to gladden his eyes with you, Jean. I only hoped that it would be a better picture."

Hampton already was gripping the hands of the viscount, running his eyes over the lean face and the forehead so finger-marked with intelligence.

"Are you well, Jean?" he asked.

"Wait till I learn to use my eyes on you again," answered the viscount. "They've been dieted on four gray walls and a patch of sky with bars across it. But now I begin to see all of you once more. I tried to come back that day, but my lord the marquis decided otherwise. Has he reached his claws at you again in the meantime?"

He spoke as though his father were not in the room. Never once did his eyes regard the marquis.

"He's reached for me a time or two and barely missed," said Hampton. "Tell me, Jean-Pierre—will you stay with him or go with me?"

"Stay with him? Ask one of the burning souls if they'll stay in hell! But will he let me go?"

"I have ways to persuade him," said Hampton.

"It means your inheritance, Jean," said his father, without emotion.

"Whatever I inherit from you will be the lash of the whip and never the handle," said Jean-Pierre. "But what does it mean, that you are here, Hugh, and at peace? Have you learned how to scratch the tiger so that he'll purr?"

"Tell him, *Monsieur* Massey," urged the marquis.

"In brief, Jean-Pierre, the peasants have risen and I'm march-ing at their head—"

"They have been *raised!*" said the marquis. "And this is the man who roused them. Two thousand of them are standing under the south wall and your American has forced from me a resignation of every feudal right—my right, *your* rights, Jean-Pierre!"

"Rights? Damn the rights!" said Jean-Pierre. "And as for the peasants rising, they're been beaten into it by the hand of my revered father. But you, Hugh—you're not with them—you're not there in the dirt with them, are you?"

"I am," said Hampton. "I saw Marceau stoned to death in the stocks with my lord the marquis throwing money to the soldiers who were murdering him."

"Is that true?" said Jean-Pierre. He hunted the face of Hampton with painful care. "I know there's nothing *but* truth in you. But even murder is not cause enough for a gentleman to join the *canaille*. My God, Hugh, if you stain yourself with such fellows, the dirt will never be out of your soul."

"I've put myself on their side," said Hampton. "I've put myself with them with all my heart, too. If the common people cannot be trusted, there's nothing left to trust. I can't draw back. But it doesn't mean that you go to them when you leave the château with me. It simply means that you step out of the trap. Will you come?"

"Are they under the wall now?" asked Jean-Pierre.

"They are," said Hampton.

"And in arms?"

"Yes. Whatever I could furnish them."

"The insolent dogs!" cried the viscount.

The marquis began to laugh, softly.

"Do you hear me, Massey?" cried the viscount. "Every good word and hour that ever passed between us is canceled out, by this. If I meet you again, my hand is against you. If you were my brother, I'd tear you out of my flesh! By God, the walls of my cell are four fine faces, compared with yours."

He turned his back on Hampton without a farewell and flung open the door into the hall. Hebert and another were waiting in the corridor.

"Take him, Hebert," said the marquis.

And the door closed behind the viscount.

HAMPTON LOOKED blankly at the future and saw nothing but the face of Jean-Pierre. For it seemed to him that all the faults and the virtues of the French aristocracy were gathered and distilled in the person of the viscount.

Even the pride which had made him scorn the American, just now, would also prevent him from breaking his promise never to reveal the true identity of Hampton, and that adventurer knew that the oath of Jean-Pierre was stronger than any other human rock on which he could build. But it staggered him when he realized how completely a revelation of his identity would solve this situation for the marquis. It would scatter the peasants like leaves before a wind and leave d'Alenton invincibly the master of the situation again.

"Ah, well, my friend," said the marquis, "there is nothing much for you to hang the head about. Blood exercises a high control in France."

Hampton straightened his shoulders and drew a long breath.

"I'll go out to the villagers and show them their grant of rights," he said. "Do you go with me, *Monsieur* the Marquis?"

"With all my heart," said d'Alenton, and commenced to laugh again as he accompanied Hampton from the room.

CHAPTER XXX

THE STORMING
OF THE CHÂTEAU

WHEN THEY CROSSED the court to the gate-tower, Hampton heard the voices of the peasants beyond the wall, a rain of meaningless sound, with sudden outbreaks of anger in it. De Poncey appeared, exclaiming: "It's time, my lord! In another three minutes, I think they would have had their ladders against the wall. But as for the cannon, that was a lie!"

"Well, you could have pushed them off again, I dare say," answered the marquis. "And the words about the cannon were a fiction? If you will see our American friend out…. *Adieu, Monsieur* Massey. To have known you has enriched me. Forgive me if I hope that our acquaintance may become a thing of the past."

"*Monsieur* the Marquis," said Hampton, "I understand you well enough to know that as long as you live, your hand will be reaching for me somewhere in the dark."

"Nothing is more pleasant than a perfect understanding," said the marquis.

They exchanged bows and de Poncey led him through the winding passage of the gate-tower to the postern.

"*Monsieur,* I look upon you as one who has risen from the dead," said de Poncey. "But do not rise so far that you may fall again. *Au revoir.*"

From the postern, Hampton stepped out almost into the arms of a dozen peasants, all with their heads back as they stared up the height of the wall. When they saw him, they raised a huge shouting that beat back in sharp echoes from the gate and the towers. In that confusion of sound he raised his hand until a silence began to spread around him.

Then big Cartier came striding, dragging along another huge fellow. Together they swung Hampton up onto their shoulders so that he viewed the faces of the mob as they shifted and crowded, like the waves on a lake. They were agape with expectation, all of them.

"Here it is in my hand!" cried Hampton. "All the lands attached to the villages, he gives back to you."

He expected a flood of applause but he heard only a low murmuring. A vague emotion worked in the faces he looked down upon.

He shouted: "When you walk in the field, you'll be stepping on your own soil. When it turns over in the furrow, it is your own earth. You will not give half the grain or half the grapes to the marquis. It will be yours. It will all be yours!"

An elderly woman on the far outskirts of the crowd raised the first cry, a long, thin, wavering note of joy drowned long before the end by the roaring of every voice in the throng. Understanding came to them in fresh waves, re-uttered in new boomings. Hampton looking up, saw the white smile of the marquis in a narrow window of the gate-tower. He slipped from the shoulders that supported him, and called to the people nearest: "We've got what we came for. Home, now! We'll all go home!"

In this manner he started a small movement, a gradual drifting of men away from the wall, but the general confusion and noise was so great now that the major portion of the villagers milled idly around and around, laughing, striking at one another with foolish, happy hands.

THROUGH THAT confusion Hampton heard the thin, penetrating cry of Louis, the cripple:

"He's given back the land, but when will he give me back my leg that he took from me? When will he give us back Marceau from the grave? Etienne, where is your father that disappeared into the cells of the château three years ago? Paul, where are your children that died in the famine?"

The joyful yelling died away in patches; the voice of Louis spread farther and farther through the crowd like the raucous note of a crow through the merry chattering of song-birds in the spring.

"He gives us something for tomorrow," yelled Louis. "But what about all our yesterdays? What about the long winter nights with no fire in the house and the days with not even beans for the pot? You, there—where has the flesh gone from your face? *Mademoiselle,* who put the white streaks in your hair?"

"Louis, Louis—be silent!" shouted Hampton, but the deep growling of the crowd half covered his voice. The drift he started away from the château ended and the peasants now were staring up at the walls, especially at the round, black mouths of the carronades. Yet through this tumult the voice of the marquis cut clearly down to him, saying: *"Monsieur* the American, I have given you meat for your pack; now take them home to their kennels before we have to whip them away!"

"Do you hear?" screeched Louis. "He calls us to our faces 'dogs'! The noble marquis is right. We are only dogs. We have been beaten so much that we know our corners; and so we'll crawl back into them again. He gives us back the land, but famine is killing France and we'll be dead before the next winter. We'll chew the bark of trees. The children will die. We'll creep to the château and give back our rights to the marquis for the sake of a little bread, while he laughs at us—"

"Stop the mouth of Louis!" called Hampton, pressing through the crowd towards the cripple. "We have what we came for. Now home with us all. Louis, do you hear me?"

He was close enough to see the cripple clearly, now, as two men raised Louis high in the air. In both hands he held up one of his crutches like a flag. His words convulsed his face to a flashing of teeth.

"Go! Go!" screamed Louis. "Go home and wait for the whip

of the marquis, but I'll stay here behind you. We never dared to climb the hill before. Now that I'm at the top of it, here I'll stay!"

"We'll stay, too!" called others. The cry grew: "We'll stay here for our rights, for our rights!"

What additional rights they could ask none of them knew, as Hampton was aware, but when he tried to shout his way into their attention, a fresh outburst stifled his words.

This time it was fear that set them yelling and pointing towards the top of the wall. The pale marquis watched everything from the same window but he was not the figure that terrified the crowd. At his command the three cannon which commanded the approach to the gate had been depressed until the muzzles pointed straight down towards the crowd. Through the embrasures, Hampton had a glimpse of the cannoneers at work; he saw the thin fuming of a lighted match and then noted that the marquis had lifted his right hand. When that hand fell the three guns, loaded with grape shot, would sweep three horrible channels through the peasants. He knew it as perfectly as though the marquis had spoken the words at his ear.

Only a part of them saw the danger that threatened overhead. Some tried to take to their heels but were caught in the thick of the crowd like fish in a net. Others stood helplessly fixed. Still more were unaware of the danger; they listened to the piercing voice of Louis as Hampton looked desperately around him.

If the crowd started to flee, the fine shot that loaded the cannon would sweep them with greater effect. The safest place by far, for the moment, was close under the foot of the wall. A big peasant beside him had spotted the aimed guns above his head and stood rooted in a strange gesture of defiance, holding half-raised a huge axe, double-bitted and heavy as a sledgehammer.

HAMPTON SNATCHED the axe away from him, shouting: "Follow me, brothers." His voice was no more than the sound of one wave in the tumult of a storm. His example might have a clearer effect. As he ran in, he saw de Poncey on the wall above, laughing, clapping his hands together. Julie was close by. He caught her up easily inside one big arm and as he ran in close to the postern door of the gate-tower, the three cannon roared above them. It seemed to him that the heavy wall shuddered to its roots; the air trembled and dazzled; and near and far he heard the small shot flog the ground. Then the sound of screaming went up through his brain like fire through a dead tree. He struck the postern gate with all his might. One bit of the axe crunched like glass against the scroll of heavy iron that protected the oak-wood.

He ventured a glance over his shoulder. It seemed to him that half the crowd was on the ground in three fan-shaped scatterings which told where the guns had been aimed. Of all the pictures, one remained with him: a woman holding her body with both hands as she sank to the ground with a scream stretching her mouth to one side. And all the rest of the villagers scampered here and there, brainlessly milling. How soon before the gunners reloaded and fired again from above?

He swung the axe again with the good edge turned to the mark. It cut into the hard old oak above the lock. He wrenched it clear. He commenced to sling long, powerful strokes, swaying at the knees.

A gun barrel thrust out at him through a narrow slot. He drove the gun in with a blow from the flat face of the axe and felt the musket stock ram into flesh. Afterwards, the yell of pain from the arrow-slot pierced his mind with a special music. A drum began to toll right at his ear. He had a glimpse of Julie at work with the sticks and, beyond her, of the villagers flooding in towards her summons and the safety of the wall. The drum called them at a run. His axe at the next stroke clove through the wood above the lock. He began to hew powerfully at the plank beneath.

Left and right, he saw the ladders set up against the wall. In glances he saw them as his body turned half around with every blow he struck. A three-legged cat scrambled up one ladder. That was Louis the cripple with no weapon in his hands, but gripping a knife between his teeth. Other men swarmed up after him.

Something plucked at the shoulder of Hampton. It was Julie, pointing straight overhead, and he saw as he glanced up the muskets that had been thrust through the machicolations of the battlements. He saw that. He heard faintly the cry with which she warned him, and without pause he struck the axe once more into the wood of the postern. For he felt as though bullets could not harm him. They might as well shoot into the ocean as into the immense sea of his anger.

Something snatched the hat from his head. An invisible wasp stung his shoulder, biting flesh away. The drum commenced to roll again, close to his ear.

To each side, the defenders pushed out the scaling ladders with long poles. Some of them slid sidewise down the face of the wall. That which had Louis near the top rocked straight back, wavered at a balance, then pitched towards the ground. They crashed, other men in a frightful heap, Louis unharmed on top of all!

But Hampton did not turn his head to make sure. The second bit of the axe crumpled against iron. He had in his hands now only a blunt-headed club, yet with the next stroke, he beat in the whole section of the plank and the lock it supported.

A dozen hands instantly tore the door open. Out of the inner shadow a pistol pointed its long finger at him. He smashed down the face behind it. Both barrels of a fowling piece spat fire. The hot smoke scorched his face.

BUT THE first man was down. His foot stepped on loose flesh. He felt the snapping of a bone under his stride. The second face in the narrow passage was gone; now, he saw the back of the poor devil who screamed and tried to flee but was stopped by the others before him. With the flat of the axe he struck down that figure. Hands gripped at his legs as he strode on. The rolling of the drum filled the narrow winding of the passage....Julie was there behind him, somewhere... then he ran out into the light of the court yard.

He paused one instant to wipe the blinding tears from his

eyes, for the powder-smoke had scorched them; and the rolling of the drum flooded out through the court, with rattling echoes showering back from the surrounding walls. That was Julie, still beside him, while past her the villagers ran out into the open one by one, like bees issuing singly from the narrow mouth of the hive. Beyond them he saw a half dozen of the men of the château re-pointing a pair of small cannon that stood in front of the inner gate. Hampton started for them on the run. The rolling of the drum followed him, staggering but never-ended. Before him raced barefooted peasants. They reached the guns. They whirled in a dreadful tangle. He saw a villager leap into the air to give greater force to a club stroke. Then through the arch of the open doors, the peasants ran on leaving crushed bodies on the pavement near the guns. From the great hall inside, echoing voices poured back to him; and the endless drum-beat maddened the air in the court.

He paused again, to look back. Half a hundred peasants were in through the postern by this time. In the tumult he could not distinguish individual voices but he saw the screaming joy on every face as they rushed on through the open door of the château. Along the outer walls and from the gate towers, the defenders fled back towards the main building. He saw them throwing away weapons as they ran. From half a dozen scaling ladders the peasants poured over the battlements. Their yelling filled the sky. He saw a half-naked brute pause in the charge to break into a frenzied dance of triumph. The gates were being beaten open. Out of the upper windows around the court a few muskets fired—as though at a tidal wave of the advancing sea. Still through the open postern where he had made the breach, the single thread of peasants ran in upon the château. The flow checked for an instant, then he saw Louis the cripple swinging along on his crutches, helped on by two other men of Charlevain. His face was half white, half crimson from a head wound.

Even in this moment the tumult, diminishing in the court, boomed and rushed through the inner reaches of the château like a mighty water through a cave.

And the rolling of the drum would not cease beside him. He put his hand on the arm of the girl.

"Be quiet, Julie!" he commanded.

The drumming ended. Hundreds upon hundreds of the peasantry, bursting open the main gates, now flooded through the court shouting: "Victory! Down with the marquis! Victory! Down! Down!" Women were not the last. They even had climbed the scaling ladders among the first. Now they ran and leaped and screeched in the wide stream that invaded the château. He saw wounds reddening on many of them.

But the contorted faces meant more than blood.

As that tide of maddened peasantry streamed through the court, hundreds of them remained eddying for an instant around big John Hampton to screech out a thanksgiving to him before they rushed on their way. But he, penetrated by a new and strange pain, could not move from his place but remained there, leaning on the great axe with its shattered edges.

CHAPTER XXXI

THE CRIPPLE KING

IT SEEMED TO Hampton that the peasants had overtopped more than walls of stone. It was as though his axe had opened a way through a barrier of centuries and let the new time flood roaring in. All the names of lords and ladies whirled out of the past like a dust in his face as he turned into Charlevain at last... Julie had disappeared.

He ran on through a great hall of windows and mirrors overworked with gilded arabesques. At the farther end half a dozen bodies strewed the lower steps of the staircase; three of the men lived. Hampton turned to the stream of peasants who blew on wings through the hall. He caught by the arm a woman who carried a gun barrel that had been broken or shot away from its stock.

"Here are sick people. Will you take care of them?" demanded Hampton.

She fought against his hand.

"Devil, devil, let me go!" she screamed. "There is gold on the mirrors! I can fill my hands with diamonds!"

"We pile all the loot in one heap and then we share it," said Hampton. "Will you take care of these poor fellows?"

He gripped her by one shoulder and shook her violently, as she struggled.

"Will you do my bidding?" he thundered.

"Monsieur, forgive me! I did not recognize *monsieur!"* she gasped, turning limp.

He left her with the wounded and ran up on the stairs. Yells and gunshots sounded far before him through the château. At the head of the long steps he glanced back. The peasant woman already had deserted the wounded. The thick stream of feet pounded over them. Perhaps their cries of agony mixed with the universal yelling. Joy, pain, victory sounded all on one note. He ran on towards the noise of gunfire.

Not a tithe of the peasants went on to the fighting. The loot on the way over-tempted them. He had glimpses of strange pictures—the feathered hat of a woman on the head of a man—two peasant girls struggling for a brocaded bed covering that ripped apart in their hands—a villager with a gilded chair on his shoulders—a woman of the château household dragged by the hair of the head with a knife raised over her. He jumped into the doorway to stop that murder but the knife already had fallen.

When he ran forward again, the noise of the guns was ending, and so he came to the long gallery which links together the mainland and the island portions of the château at Charlevain. A barricade of heaped furniture, shoulder high, stopped him at this point, and the peasants were gathering more material to strengthen the barrier. Farther down the long hall a similar barricade rose. In between, half a dozen bodies lay in pools and streaks of red blood. Only one of them wore the livery of the marquis, for in this narrow way discipline and swordsmanship had counted. The marquis had saved one half of his house from the first onslaught. If only Marguerite and Jean-Pierre were safe in his hands, now!

Gunfire outside the building drew his attention. From a window he saw a score of the little skiffs and fishing boats cruising under the walls of the château on the island. Muskets kept up a fire from those boats on the windows of the old building; answering guns puffed from the walls above them; gradually the small craft fell away from this unequal battle.

He turned from the window and heard through the rooms all about him the stamping of feet, furniture dragged stuttering over polished floors, and always those yelling voices which were pitched on a single note whether for agony or for joy.

He stopped a peasant.

"*Vive Monsieur* Massey!" screamed the fellow. "*Vive l'americain!*"

"The Lady Marguerite!" demanded Hampton. "Where is she? Has she been seen?"

"Ah ha, *monsieur.* You do not know the new France. We all shall have as many women as we want! If you want ladies, you shall have ladies, too! *Hola! Hola!* A lady for our brave American!"

Hampton left the madman and went on. He had led the attack that captured Charlevain. He had broached the way for the others to enter. But now he was only one among a great swarm of ants. A brainless horror began to overmaster him.

HE STARTED to run once more, though he hardly knew in what direction to go. Continually he had in mind that picture of the poor domestic dragged by the hair of the head and the knife poised over her. Marguerite might have died like that. He tried to tell himself that the gold of her hair was a wealth that would stop any hand from murder; and then he remembered the trampling feet that crushed down the wounded at the bottom of the stairs. The first step to this liberty, this new freedom, was murder.

A sound of horns, often repeated, led him into the great hall of the castle. Hundreds had preceded him, every man, every woman with plunder of some sort. The huge dimensions of the room dimmed the bright fountain of voices, made the people small, and yet his glance found at once Marguerite de Fréron in all the crowd. She wore a dress of black but it was not this that enabled him to pick her out. It was the sheen of her hair, first, and then her face framed in a ruching of thin white stuff. She carried her head with such pride that it seemed to Hampton she was looking up at him as he stood at the head of the stairs. He started down them at once, still with his eyes fixed on her and the huddle of peasants around her.

He had come to the bend of the stairs before the rolling of a drum began, ceased, and then the voice of Julie cried out: "It is our *monsieur!* See where he comes!"

A wild, unending uproar answered her. Every new-stolen hat and cloak and every bit of rich drapery waved above the heads of the crowd. It seemed to Hampton that every gesture was loading on his shoulders the blame for the murders at Charlevain.

From his raised place on the steps Hampton charted the different parts of the mob. What mattered to him most was the small cluster of prisoners who had been taken during the rush upon the château; for Marguerite stood among them, to the right of the dais. There was a serving girl in the group; the rest were men wearing the château livery. And off to the left, farther down the hall, their irons being taken from them one by one, were all those rescued from the château dungeon, a score of men and women, with Hebert, the jailer, among them. With hands still red from butchery, the peasants lavished every kindness on these victims of the marquis. While others worked at the irons, some were giving food, others held wine at their lips. Only one in the group received not the slightest attention. That was a tall, slender fellow standing close to Hebert, and in another moment Hampton made out the features of the viscount nearby.

Hampton was about to push into the crowd when he was stopped by the sight of Jorry Cartier at the farther end of the hall, standing on the dais which supported a canopied chair like a throne. The duties of a throne it once had served, in fact; for Henry of Navarre had been seated in it after he was king of France. Big Cartier commanded attention by swinging above his head a cutlass which still dripped blood onto his hairy arm, bare to the elbow.

AS HE shouted, the tumult in the great hall died away in patches and let his voice come through.

"We've come for our rights, and we've put our teeth in some of'em!" yelled Cartier. "Who opened the way for him?"

"The American… *Vive l'americain!*" roared the crowd.

"Ay, cheer for him," bellowed Cartier. "But he's served his turn for a while. We want a judge, now. We've been judged all our days by aristocrats. Now we'll have aristocrats judged by the people. Who'll be our judge, eh?"

Someone yelled from the side of the room: "Louis, the cripple! He kept us from going home with nothing but words on a piece of paper! Louis! Louis!"

He appeared, thrust up high by several peasants. Hampton saw him laughing with pleasure but making gestures with both hands to push away the proffered honors.

Some of the crowd laughed, others cheered, and a small group of men forced their way through with Louis carried on their shoulders until they had placed him on the throne.

Louis himself was laughing, and waving his crutch. That voice of his cut through wider, larger noises with a knife-like ease.

"I ought to be judge; I ought to be king," laughed Louis the cripple. "Because an aristocrat gave me this sceptre!"

He waved the crutch still higher.

"Ay, and he's brave, too," said voices near Hampton. "No fear in his body; none in his soul. He'll make a judge for us!"

Hampton stepped down into the rearmost ranks of the throng.

Louis was calling out for silence, which in part he gradually obtained.

CHAPTER XXXII

DEATH BY A ROPE

"CITIZENS!" HE CALLED. "Now we can hear the prisoners of the marquis. They are only a few pages torn out of a great book but they may tell us something worth knowing."

That suggestion pleased the people at once. There were a number of men and women who had been imprisoned within recent years. These, the moment their irons had been taken off, were welcomed back enthusiastically by groups of friends but the center of interest remained in the older figures who had been taken from the cells. Most of them were not recognizable. The first that Louis selected was a white-haired man with a shag of beard that flowed almost to his waist. Even when he stood erect, his back retained the curve that came from sitting year after year cross-legged on the floor. This gave him the bent, long-legged figure of a crane.

"Who are you, brother?" asked Louis.

"I am Robert Drouet," said the other.

"Louder! Speak up more loudly, brother," called many voices.

"You see, citizens," interpreted Louis, "how the irons have eaten into his wrists and ankles? So the silences of the prison has gnawed away his voice. What is the use of speaking with a human tongue when there are only rats for company?... He says that his name is Robert Drouet.... Why were you imprisoned, Robert, my brother?"

"The marquis was hunting and one of his hounds took a little dog that belonged to me by the throat. I beat the hound over the head with a club and the hound died. I have spent the rest of my time here."

"Because he beat a dog to save one of his own!" cried Louis, and then canted his head to listen to the deep growling that ran through the hall, as a musician listens with a far-away look to the sounds that come from his own violin.

He took the others one by one, sometimes repeating their husky stories to the crowd, sometimes casting in little comments.

One said:

"I am Leonard Flammont. Instead of sending all of my crop of grapes to the winepress of my lord, I kept one cartload to press at my house for the use of my family."

"How long ago was that, Leonard?"

"I don't know. I was twenty-eight years old, then."

"Look, citizens! He is covered with time like a house with icicles; and he has been in the prison since he was twenty-eight—for the sake of a cartload of his own grapes!"

And another:

"I am Marie Girard.... What does it matter why I am here? But, ah, my God, where are all the young men that I used to know? Have I grown as old as this? Have I lost my good years? *Monsieur* the cripple... help! All you that have loved me, tell me your names; help me to tear away this covering—there must be a beautiful, tender body beneath it—"

And another:

"I am Quintin Cortey.... Quintin Cortey.... Quintin Cortey...."

Someone shouted: "Take his horrible face away! His brains are gone!"

"Yes—true—his brains are gone," said the cripple. "They weren't dashed out with a club, but the four walls of a prison cell crushed him, and leaned on his mind until it was gone. That was how he died, above the eyes.... Hebert, tell us why this man was thrown into the prison."

Hebert, the jailer, who knew that he stood on dangerous ground, looked cautiously around him, studying faces. But Louis screamed at him: "Don't feel your way with lies, you dog! Speak out quickly."

"Why, the truth is that I can't remember why Quintin Cortey was put in the prison," said Hebert.

"You lie!" shouted Louis.

"You lie! You lie!" yelled a hundred voices. Many hands suddenly placed old, tottering Cortey in front of the jailer.

"Do you remember him? Look at his face. Did he ever do you any harm, Quintin?" pleaded many voices.

Poor Cortey, after staring at Hebert for a moment, threw his hands up over his eyes and fell on his knees, moaning.

"That's not because I ever beat or harmed him!" shouted Hebert. "Citizens—kind friends—why do you look at me like this? I swear to the kind God that I never have harmed old—"

A FROWSY, square-faced woman had been watching and listening without the slightest indication of understanding what went forward around her. Now a glint of comprehension entered her eyes. She lifted the two-pronged pitchfork on which she was leaning and plunged it into the middle of Hebert's back. He fell forward on his face, but writhed about on his side at once, gasping: "There is still life in me, friends. There is the breath and the mercy of Christ still in me. Save me, save me, friends…."

"If you knock in his head, his bleeding will stop," said Louis.

A peasant dropped the butt of his musket on the head of Hebert, and he fell flat on the floor. With a studious face the peasant raised the gun again and brought down the butt, hard. Afterwards he looked up, smiling like a child.

"Like cracking nuts, eh?" he said.

The murder started the crowd babbling. Those who could not see the last strokes could hear them; and the outcry was all of joy except for the shout of protest from Hampton.

Then, realizing that his voice was wasted, he put back a hand against a baluster of the stairs and hung his head, for his brain was still spinning with a horrible darkness.

Louis was remarking: "By the dry look of him, who would have guessed at so much juice? Like some of those October pears, eh? But the killing of one beast like Hebert—what does that mean? Shall we inquire into the minds of the great aristocrats who are in the hall here with us? Or do you think that they would condescend to answer our questions?"

The peasant woman who had speared Hebert now banged the butt of her fork on the floor.

"If they won't talk, we'll have out their tongues by the roots!" she shouted.

"Sister, you are great-hearted!" said Louis. "Attention, citizens!"

"Attention to Louis!" she screamed.

"Attention…" called the diminishing voices.

Hampton thrust himself suddenly forward through the press. He came to the place where Jean-Pierre was standing, closely guarded.

"Jean-Pierre," he panted, "trust me. I shall manage to save you."

"*Monsieur,*" said the viscount in a loud, clear voice, "if you save me from them, how will you save yourself afterwards from me? Murderer!"

"Save him? Who talks of saving him?" growled one of the guards near the viscount.

He fronted Hampton with a bloodstained face, scowling.

"*Monsieur* the American, this is French business, for Frenchmen only!" he declared.

"True, true!" said his neighbors, looking with equal darkness on Hampton.

He knew that his power over the villagers was utterly gone, for the moment, at least.

"Bring the viscount of Charlevain," said Louis. "Perhaps

he will talk even to simple people like us." They thrust Jean-Pierre quickly before his judge. *"Monsieur* the Viscount, I would kiss your hand except that the crutches make me so clumsy.... *Monsieur,* my lord, we beg you to tell us for what cause the noble marquis put you into his prison?"

THE VISCOUNT, lifting his head, seemed about to answer. Instead, his glance roved on past the cripple and over the faces of the crowd. Sudden malice overwhelmed the cripple. He drew in his breath through his teeth. The hall in the meantime had begun to dim, for rain clouds drifted over the sky, piling on the southern horizon until a dark wall of rain began to fall from under the chin of the clouds as they accumulated towards the north.

"If the fool won't talk, what shall we do to him?" asked the woman with the pitchfork.

"String him up by the thumbs," said someone. "That'll make his tongue wag along fast enough."

"Hush! Hush!" said Louis. "My dear friends, speak more softly. Suppose that a word of this should come to *Monsieur* Massey...."

"Well, what of it?" demanded the woman with the fork.

Murder had given her the authority to stand forth.

"But *Monsieur* Massey considers the viscount his friend," said the cripple. "And we must not anger our American, must we?"

"The American can go and hang himself," said the woman. "He may have comforted your ribs in Charlevain, but I got devil a bit of good out of him until he knocked open the door for us, today. Are a thousand men going to crawl forever because a man opened a door for them?"

"Who accuses the viscount?" called out Louis.

"I accuse him of never spending a day in the village," said one of the peasants of Charlevain. "Even when we were starving."

"I've never seen largess from him when we were dying of a winter famine or a summer plague," said another.

"Ay, and that's the truth," agreed Louis, licking his thin lips. "We never had so much as a sou out of him."

"If you had had the money then, and the blood now, a fat, filthy bargain you'd have of it, wouldn't you?" demanded young Jean-Pierre.

"Do you hear the beast? There's no shame or modesty in him!" shouted the woman of the hayfork.

"Hush, friends. He is only the son of the marquis!" exclaimed Louis. "He cannot help it if his heart is as hard as a stone. It is in his blood. When the frost was in the stump of my leg and I crouched by the roadside with the tears of pain on my face, I have seen the viscount go riding by, laughing, pointing me out to the others. Nature does as nature is, and when the old fox—"

This speech had excited the peasants to such a point that two of them gripped Jean-Pierre suddenly from either side. One kept easing and re-gripping a butcher's cleaver which he held high in his right hand.

"Now?" gasped the man, rising a little on his toes to give power to the stroke. "Now? Shall I split that damned aristocratic skull of his now?" He surged forward impatiently.

"Hush and don't be a fool," protested the lady of the pitchfork before Hampton could shout. "If we have the viscount, we should have him as a show for every one to see. Why kill him in a huddle of a corner in the dark of the day? Wait for the morning. His belly will be empty of pride, then, and he may come to hand very prettily. Tell them to take the viscount away, Louis. Hang him by daylight, with the sun on his fine face. That will be something for us to remember. The dungeon will keep him cool and fresh for us overnight."

"No man that ever took part in such a thing," said Louis, "would ever be forgiven…. Citizens, citizens, do you hear? Shall we keep the viscount until the morning and hang him off the wall as a sign of sworn brotherhood among us? Or shall we smoke old foxes out of their dens and let the young ones breed freely in the same places?"

"Root them out! Throttle them by families!" roared hundreds of voices.

A NUMBER of kegs of wine had been rolled out from the cellars into the great hall of the château and these barrels drew continuing streams of men and women. Those who lacked red blood stains on their clothes as a proof of their valor soon had wine stains at least. Strings of big dry sausages, whittled up into great chunks, filled up the bellies of the people with strength and a confident courage. This eating and drinking went on upon a busy note that never grew very loud. The peasants conducted themselves quite decently on their free fare. From time to time hunger left them and they gave all of their attention to the procedure at the end of the hall where Louis now had the place of honor. The trial of the viscount pleased them very much. They began to shout: "To the prison with the viscount. Leave the fruit on the tree till the morning. To the prison with the viscount."

A dozen men hustled him instantly from the hall.

"Who else is there that we should treat with special care?" demanded Louis, fixing his eyes steadily on Marguerite de Fréron.

The girl shivered, tried to look away; and found, terribly, that she could not. His awful gaze drew hers like a magnet, potent and evil.

Andre Coumier, the charcoal-burner, bellowed: "Bring the Fréron woman here to the feet of Louis, the cripple. Let him be a judge for her!"

Some of the men protested a little, but they were drowned out by the joyous howling of the peasant women. A number of these dragged Marguerite de Fréron before the raised chair. Louis writhed in his chair and, resting his elbows far forward on the arms of it, looked hungrily down on the girl.

"How could poor Louis be the judge of such a great lady?" Louis asked.

"Judge her! Judge her!" cried the peasants.

"But what's known against her?" asked Louis. "I have nothing to say. I was simply beaten and maimed because I did not hold her horse still. But that's to be expected from the great people. Who has anything to say against her? You can see for yourselves that her *skin* is clean enough. You, there, Victoire—you are her maid. You can tell us how kind she is!"

Some of the village women dragged Victoire forward. Her eyes rolled in her head with terror and she kept whining: "Our Father, help me! I've always said my prayers! Our Father, save me."

"Save yourself, you minx!" shouted a peasant woman. "You've wallowed in the fat of the land long enough. Save yourself with your own tongue, if you've got one. Did this precious lady ever lay hand on you?"

"She's been like a kind mother to me!" cried Victoire.

"You fool, you're old enough to be *her* mother," said the peasant. "You mean that she never laid hand on you and never scorched you with her tongue? Was she always pleased with you?"

Victoire stared helplessly at her questioners; licked her lips with a quick nervous tongue.

"Only when I was very stupid," said Victoire. "I *could* not do the hair right, always! But she always was kind to me. She even let me go every day to see my father."

"Every day? Where was your father?" asked Louis.

"He was in the prison of the château," said Victoire. "My God, what a shame to an honest family."

"Come, now, what had he done to be in prison?" demanded Louis.

"Must I say it before all these people?" groaned Victoire.

"Unless you want this in your ribs!" commented the woman with the hayfork.

"He stole a sheep!" lamented Victoire.

A groan of mingled derision and rage from many voices answered her.

"How long ago?" asked Louis.

"Eleven years, *monsieur.*"

"And for that—how long was he in the prison?"

"Until he died—God rest him—"

"When was that?"

"Last year, *monsieur.*"

"Ten years of the grave before dying; ten years for the stealing of a sheep!" said Louis, looking fixedly at Marguerite de Fréron.

A FULL-THROATED howl of anger washed through the hall and left the echoes dripping from the walls. Louis licked the thin of his lips and grinned on Marguerite like a cat. Then he held up his hand and produced a silence, in which he said: "But aristocrats are aristocrats, citizens. How can they be expected to know that peasant dirt like you and I have feeling in our flesh? When they see us living like dogs, how can they be expected to guess that we love our fathers? They don't think we're human— that we can love as fiercely and hate as proudly and as long as any of them!"

Through the uproar of anger he added: "What have you to say, *mademoiselle?*"

The calm, clear voice of Marguerite de Fréron answered: "What have I to do with this? I did not send the father of Victoire to prison."

The woman of the hayfork yelled, "I'm tired of her pretty, damned face. Let's put an end to her."

The men, on the whole, were silent, but the toothless, wrinkled women screamed their agreement.

"She's a good dancer!" cried Louis the cripple. "By God, we'll see her walk on air at the side of the viscount in the morning. They must die! For the sake of their rotten souls they must die. Take her to the cells. Keep the hands of the women away from her. Beat them away. Keep her whole and pure for her dance tomorrow. Do we want our picture spoiled before it is hanged in the sky?"

He began to laugh. The perfect delight of the moment twisted his body into odd shapes.

Hampton got himself out of the hall into the big courtyard. A small rain was falling but the day was still warm. On the pavement streaks of blood washed into small pools and these started running into one another.

He listened to the laughing tumult inside the hall of the château, the long, braying, uncontrolled sounds of joy.

People came stumbling towards him through the wet and the dim light.

"There's our American," said the drunken voice of old Phillipe Lenoir who had sat as one of the four judges under the great tree of Charlevain. "There's our American! Go back home, American. We don't need you any more. We have Louis. He is enough. Go away. We are not French dogs any more. We are French *men!*"

The whole party went on its way, staggering, laughing foolishly.

CHAPTER XXXIII

FAREWELL!

THE RAIN ENDED. No stars appeared. The humid close breath of the wind promised another downpour at any moment. And at last Hampton went back into the château.

The great hall smelled like a kennel, and was filled with sleeping figures, for the peasants were accustomed to closing their eyes as soon as the full night descended, and after this great day they were exhausted by danger, fighting, and joy. Littered across the floor of the hall and spread over two long tables they slept in every position. Hampton picked his way through the confusion.

Every man and every woman slept with a weapon close at hand. He saw an old gray-headed hag whose naked arms were as muscular as those of a man; her body was wrapped in the torn half of a velvet curtain. Near her, a man slept with his arm around a gilt vase whose top was broken off but which remained a treasure to the thief; here a man with a cut across his shoulder, the blood encrusted around the deep lips of the wound, kept moving his other hand toward his hurt and groaning in his sleep; a fat man laughed, softly, continually, through his teeth and strangled the air with his hands; yonder a wine cask leaked at the broaching spigot and unregarded spread a big red pool on the floor. A child of eleven lay in the center of that pool, its fair hair soaked in the wine; others, on the margin of the wet, were half surrounded by the dark liquid. But they slept on, and a deep groan of snoring never ceased sounding through the hall.

Hampton reached the stairway at the farther end of the hall.

When he looked back, he saw that a dozen resolute men could drive that mob before them.

He climbed the stairs and came to the barricaded entrance to the long gallery that reached between the two halves of the château. Half a dozen guards had been posted there by the forethought of Cartier or of Louis the cripple. Both of them had become far greater men, to the peasants, than John Hampton.

Every one of the six sentinels slept very soundly!

He climbed the barrier. Something slipped under his foot when he was at the top of it, making a distinct noise. Looking down, he could see one of the guards sit up. The man scratched in his beard, grunted, slumped over on the floor again.

Hampton climbed down on the farther side and passed along the corridor. Some of the windows were open. Through them he heard voices echoing flat and dim over the water. When he paused at a casement, he made out the faint shadows of boats that rowed ceaselessly around the château to make sure that the marquis and his men did not escape during the dark night.

A ragged mass loomed before him—the barrier at the other end of the long hall. Then the voice of de Poncey asked, sharply:

"Who goes?"

"It is I, Massey," he said.

"Alone?" asked de Poncey.

"Alone. I want to speak with the marquis."

"Climb the barrier. At this end."

He climbed the barrier. Three figures closed around him. "Watch him closely," De Poncey ordered. "You've seen what he can do."

"No fear, *monsieur*. We'll watch him."

That was the voice of the gamekeeper.

"You have come, Massey," de Poncey said, with exultation in his voice. "But when will you go again?"

"Get me to the marquis!" commanded Hampton. "Let him decide whether I'm to come back or not."

A DOOR opened before them. They passed into a faintly lighted hall. A stack of pikes against the wall. Some cutlasses lay on a chair. A bloodstained bandage, curved to fit an arm or a leg, hardened with old blood, had been flung into a corner. His guards walked with him, limping. One had a cloth tied about his head. De Poncey, walking ahead, kept his head high and his step light, but his clothes were in tatters. By the bandages, Hampton marked the three wounds which he bore.

They passed down a flight of stairs and de Poncey knocked on a door. He waited, standing back, eyeing Hampton. Some of his smile remained to him, and the three faint wrinkles between his eyes always gave him the look of a cat.

Silence grew through the château. Out of the silence small sounds passed gradually into the consciousness of Hampton. Through a window he heard again the voices over the water of the lake; then a faint groaning that was so dim that it must have issued from a room on the lower floor. More than one voice entered that chorus.

De Poncey knocked on the door again.

"Enter!" called the marquis, inside.

They passed into a bedroom where the marquis lay stretched on a bed with his wig off. He was almost entirely bald and had the look, suddenly, of a very old man. In the warmth he had thrown off all his upper garments, and as he sat up from the bed, Hampton saw a plaster down one cheek, covering a wound of some sort.

The sight of Hampton brought him lightly to his feet.

"De Poncey!" he cried. "Have you snared the scoundrel for me? Glorious work, my boy! That's foraging with a vengeance!"

De Poncey said, reluctantly: "He came of his own accord, my lord."

"Of his own accord?" echoed the marquis. "Did you come to us of your own accord, *monsieur*? Now why in the name of the devil should you do such a foolish thing as that?"

He stood with his hands on his hips, perfectly unconscious of

his strange appearance, and stared at the American. And Hampton watching him, said nothing. For he was amazed to find that the old hatred no longer contracted his heart.

"He has some words to speak that are a little too big for his mouth," said the marquis. "What will they be, de Poncey?"

"Have you a dozen sound men?" asked Hampton.

"A dozen? Ten dozen, my dear Massey," said the marquis.

He walked to Hampton, folded his dry, hard arms across his bony chest, and looked up at the big man with his accustomed smile. He seemed to the American at that moment more the aristocrat than ever before.

"You may have ten dozen in other places. How many men have you with you now that are capable of doing a man's work in a pinch?" asked Hampton.

"An odd question," said the marquis.

"My name is not Massey," said the American. "I am John Hampton. I never had a real right over Charlevain and you were wasting your time when you were so busy trying to kill me off. *Monsieur le marquis,* I am an obscure adventurer whose name has no more value than yours is apt to have before the morning."

De Poncey sent his breath hissing out through his teeth. The marquis bowed.

"Then why have you stayed on in Charlevain? Will you tell me that?" he asked.

Hampton bowed in his turn. "I have been kept here by my admiration of a certain lady of the château," he said.

The marquis looked upon him silently, with a fixed stare.

Hampton said, "Jean-Pierre is still alive—"

He saw the words strike the older man like a fist. That change from smiling insouciance to desperate and unexpected hope astonished Hampton.

"Alive?" asked the marquis at last. "But dying, *monsieur*. Mangled and dying, eh?"

"Alive and well," said Hampton.

The marquis looked up, in silence, and crossed himself. After that, he put on his usual expression like a mask.

"They postpone the murder till the morning," said Hampton. "Marguerite de Fréron is alive and well, also. She will die at the same time unless we can manage something."

"De Poncey, do you hear?" asked the marquis. "Our lovely Marguerite, also? When I said farewell to the thought of her it cost me—well, you have left your herd of wild swine, Hampton?"

"I think a dozen fit and sound men, acting together," he said "might get through to the prison and set them free."

The marquis looked at de Poncey. "Tell him, Georges.... I cannot," he said suddenly.

De Poncey exclaimed: "Tell him the truth?"

"Aye, the truth," said the marquis over his shoulder as he turned away.

De Poncey began to breathe heavily. He pointed to the two men who had escorted Hampton into the room.

"Everyone is here," he said.

"God forbid!" cried Hampton. "What? All the rest?"

"There are three poor devils groaning in the room below us. Otherwise, this is the garrison of the château," answered de Poncey.

The marquis was pulling on a shirt. He said in his ordinary, casual voice: "A fine thing on your part to come over to us, Hampton. But useless, it seems. Or could the handful of us manage a trick or two?"

"Or die trying!" exclaimed de Poncey.

"Come, Georges! Come, come! No heroics!" said the marquis. "As for dying, it's the sort of thing our American would love. He would adore it. To fill both his big hands with action and then to die in the breach—carrying the flag—or the friend in his arms—but you see, de Poncey, that he's not suggesting the adventure for three or four. A dozen or nothing, eh, Hampton?"

THE SINGULAR mixture of railery and admiration in this speech did not offend Hampton. He looked at the marquis thoughtfully as the latter pulled on a pair of silk breeches and began to tuck in the tails of his shirt.

"They have killed my poor devil of a valet," said the marquis, "and I think I might as well die now in the château as live on and have to break in a new body servant—six months of cursing, at least. I can still see that hulk of a peasant running the scythe through the back of my poor man. I hate a scythe, Hampton. The sign of the beast is on it, eh?"

"I'll go back to them—if I can," said Hampton. "If they suspect that I've come to you—God knows what will happen to me. But I hope to get safely back. Then I may be able to devise something. *Adieu.*"

"*Adieu!*" said the marquis, waving cheerfully. "De Poncey, see him out."

Hampton had reached the door when the marquis called: "One moment, *monsieur.*" He stopped and turned again. Alenton came to him with a vaguely troubled face.

"It may be that you may reach one, but not both," he said. "In that case, think of the lady first, *monsieur.* But your heart would tell you that?"

Hampton said nothing.

"If you reach Jean-Pierre," said the marquis, "and have only time for six words, but never mind that—"

He drew himself up and drove some weakness from his mind.

Hampton said: "If I reach Jean-Pierre and have time for only half a dozen words—I say that you forgive him, that you beg him to forgive you, that you send him your love?"

"I despise a maudlin speech," said the marquis. "I despise these revelations at the last moment. As though death could unmask a man! Bah! It's our living that matters, and as for our dying, I thank God that most gentlemen know how to do it quietly. No, take no message from me to Jean-Pierre."

Hampton shook his head.

"Shall we go, *monsieur?*" asked de Poncey.

"He will change his mind," said Hampton. *"Monsieur le marquis,* I am waiting."

"Ah, damn it—then say whatever you please. Embrace my dear boy for me. Tell him that I wish to God this dry, worthless body could die for him.... There, do you see? Sentimentality *will* creep in. In another moment there would be tears in my eyes. Hampton, go; *adieu.* The God of brave men and good men go with you. Farewell!"

CHAPTER XXXIV

A BARGAIN

AT THE BARRIER of heaped furniture, young de Poncey murmured: *"Monsieur,* I have wronged you many times. Will you attempt to forgive me, and to honor me with your hand before we say farewell?"

Hampton took his hand silently.

"These distances between nations," said de Poncey, "and between the people inside their nationalities—all at once they begin to seem rather silly, eh? *Adieu, monsieur!* A safe journey to you. Mind this cursed furniture or it will slide and make a racket. Farewell!"

The last was a whisper, and Hampton stole up the length of the corridor. He got over the other barrier without disturbing the sleeping guard and so through the great rooms and down, again, to the big hall where the few lamps that burned gave the same uneasy moonlight, as it were, to the throng of sleepers. Somewhere a man was whimpering with the pain of his wounds—and sleeping on!

He gained the courtyard. The rain, which had held off for a time, now began to fall again in big, single drops. He crossed the yard, his foot slipping in the slick of something at one point. He passed through the hacked and battered gates. Outside, there was the smell of the green, wet grass, and he walked up and down, up and down, trying to drag from his mind some device.

A whispering footfall came up behind him. *"Monsieur,* are you sad?" asked Julie.

"Well, Julie," he said, "strangers are always sad when they are made to feel their strangeness. Your people have locked me out. Where is that damned Louis, the cripple?"

"He's general and king together. He sits in a room with the men from the villages—the ones who came to see you. They've made themselves into a parliament for this new King Louis. He sends out orders. He keeps the keys of the château. Everyone thinks of nothing except of obeying him."

"Well, it will be a good party in the morning, Julie, won't it?"

"What party, *monsieur?*"

"The murder of Jean-Pierre and Marguerite de Fréron."

"An execution, *monsieur;* not a murder."

"What's their crime?"

"*Monsieur,* your heart is so very big that you have room in it even for bad things."

"Like Jean-Pierre?"

"Yes, and the lady."

"Is she bad, also?"

"To me she is very bad," said the girl. "But she makes you still love her, does she not?"

"How can a man love a girl who despises him, Julie?"

"A woman with her children, a man with his woman; there is no such thing as reason about it. Love is love."

"How much do you know of a certain night when I rode out of Charlevain?"

"*Monsieur,* I saw you returning—on foot."

"But you know nothing of what happened on the road."

"I was not there when the guns fired on *monsieur,* but I know."

"How could I care for a woman who would trap me in such a way?"

"*Monsieur,* if it is not for her, why is your heart breaking now?"

"True," said Hampton.

"Ah, I knew!" whispered Julie.

"Because," said Hampton, "when a thing we once have loved must die, something in us dies and is buried also."

"That is true," she said. "Is it painful to you to talk about her?" she added.

"No."

"What are the good things you have seen in her?"

"Courage, Julie. And a good brain."

"Old Mother Guinnet—did you see her during the attack today? She is as brave as any man, and almost as wise. But you would not love Mother Guinnet. What else, *monsieur?*"

"I don't know. What do you hold against her?"

"Pride, *monsieur.*"

"It is born in her blood. Also, there's a virtue in pride."

"Cruelty, *monsieur.*"

"She has paid for that, today. She could be tender enough, perhaps, if she had a little teaching."

"Perhaps. But without perhaps, she is beautiful. Ah, what a strange thing it is that the face of a girl should do such things to a man! Even if she has bad elbows and knees that stick out like broken sticks and ugly hands, it doesn't matter. The pretty face is what they read, chapter after chapter, verse after verse.... And so you love her because she is beautiful—and there's an end of it!"

"**YOU KNOW**, Julie, I don't think she's a whit lovelier than you."

"I? I am nothing, but she is like the day, all golden and blue and bright!"

"Twilight is better than the day, Julie. It is darker, but one thinks farther into it."

She began to laugh softly, but the laughter stopped at once.

"I've heard other women laugh like that when men say things that they wish to hear—they cannot be true, but we wish to hear them so much."

"But it's the truth, Julie."

"I think you're smiling a little at the things you've been saying to me."

"Smiling? No. I'm wondering if we could finish my work and then go off together away from Charlevain."

He thought of Marguerite de Fréron and took Julie in his arms.

"Ah, if this is a lie… I shall love you even for the lie! But ah, my God, how big you are! The pounding of your heart makes me tremble. But what is the work we must do?"

"So far as the villagers are concerned, my hands are tied and my tongue is tied, also. They will not listen to me now."

"Not for a little while. That is true."

"And my friend Jean-Pierre must not die."

"Monsieur le vicomte—the poor young man! And the lady, *monsieur?"*

"Can we save her, also?"

"When I think of her, what a jealousy sets my teeth on edge!"

"Tell me, Julie. When she and Jean-Pierre are free and done with, shall we be happy together?"

"Happy? I laugh when I think of it. All the poor creatures who think they've been happy before us!… When we are together the angels will wake up and rub their eyes. 'Hush!' they will say. 'There is a star burning on the breast of the earth! Let us go down and look!' *Monsieur*, we shall hear their wings whistling.… But I, alas… I have only poor, dark hair. I am not a Lady Marguerite!"

"I don't think of her," lied Hampton. "Except to keep her throat from the hangman's rope."

"Dieu!" murmured the girl. "My bones and my body, my soul and my breath, what a joy is entering them!… And yet are you not lying to me, *monsieur?"*

"Do you think so, Julie?"

"I shall not let myself think. If it can endure only from now until the morning, I shall throw the rest of my life over my left shoulder and let it fall where it may. But what can we do to save them?"

"We must have the keys, Julie, if we wish to work quickly and without much sound."

"Louis keeps them."

"Do you know where to find them?"

"They are tied around his waist."

"Let us go to him, then. Where is he, Julie?"

"I'll take you at once."

"Danger may come to you from this, Julie. I thought I might have some power over them by myself, but you see that I must lean on you."

"They love you, *monsieur*, but it seems to them the will of God that the blood of the aristocrats should be poured out here at Charlevain."

"And that seemed right to you, also?"

"It doesn't matter what I thought before," said the girl. "The other Julie is dead. This is a new hand in yours, a new body inside your arm, a new light in this soul. Do you see it, *cher monsieur?*"

CHAPTER XXXV

A TRICK

ALL THE HAPPINESS scattered through the life of Louis the cripple, if it had been drifted out from the common ore of his misery as gold is salvaged by the fingers of quicksilver, could not have equaled a tenth part of the joy that had been heaped and gathered into this single day.

The good God was not a very bright reality to Louis but he felt that some power from above must have been with him from the moment his voice stopped the retreat from before the southern wall of the château to the moment when he fell with the scaling ladder, and landed unharmed.

But perhaps all the triumph was made clearer to him when he sat at the end of the day in conference with the head men of the villages and planned with them what they could accomplish that night or the next day in an attack on the island portion of the château. He had been accepted, mutely and generally, as the brain which would control everything, perhaps because it was hard for others to be jealous of a poor cripple, and because everyone could see that one mind must guide everything.

As for the big American, he was a happy legend with which they could dispense.

"After all," said Louis, "he is one of them. He is one of the aristocrats. When I first saw him, he gave me money; but how did he give it? Like brother to brother? No, but as a man throws a bone to a dog! And we have been like dogs to him, ever since."

"No, Louis, he is a kind man," said Claude Lanstone, of Veilly.

"And kind men are good to dogs" said Louis. "Are they not? I say he threw me the money, as you would throw a bone to a dog! I picked up the silver. Who is Louis to ask how a gift is given? You know, citizens, that I have a humble heart!... But you will see tonight or tomorrow that everything will go well in the attack, even without him."

A good, solid volley of rain roared at the windows of the room and set the long, stiff curtains trembling faintly.

"We will have," said Louis, "the marquis, de Poncey, and all their men to hang along that southern wall in a row with Lady Marguerite and Jean-Pierre. *Ah hai!* Now your eyes shine! Well, you shall see it done!"

Here there was a knock at the door. One went to answer it.

"But Monsieur Massey," said one of those at the table, "is a useful man in a fight. I saw the bullet strike blood from his shoulder, but still he swung the axe! As though he were made of metal, and shot would glance from him! It made my heart laugh in me. I thought that God had sent us the man!"

"It is Julie!" said the man at the door. "Come in, Julie. She has a right to be where she will. Eh, Louis?"

"Well..." said Louis, joining his brows in one dark line.

She came laughing to him. "Listen to me, Louis—and send them all away. I am going to bring him in to you; and you will be amazed!"

"Who will amaze me?" he asked, his frown never relaxing.

"Monsieur Massey."

"What do we want with him?" demanded Louis.

"Ah, but you never would guess what he has in mind! However, he will never talk, except to you. He says you're the cleverest brain of them all."

"But he's in a fury, Julie. He's tried to see the prisoners and been refused."

"*Con*fused, not refused. He is not a very quick mind, Louis. He is not suspicious but simply worried a great deal."

"Is he standing now outside the door?"

"Would I be such a fool as to bring him to the door until I knew that you would see him? I've left him at a distance but I'll bring him instantly as soon as you've sent the others away."

"Why should I send them away?"

"If more than three people knew what he has in mind, Louis—but wait! You shall hear!"

"About what?" growled Louis.

"Well, about the marquis and de Poncey."

"He hates *them*, at least," agreed Louis.

"What he thinks of doing to them, you cannot guess."

"It means what?"

"Louis, no one can tell you except himself. I've promised to be silent about it."

"What is a promise to a stranger?" asked Louis.

"I have sworn," said the girl, lifting her right hand.

"My leg-stump feels like bad weather," said Louis, "but...."

"And there *is* rain, isn't there?" asked the girl, laughing. "How long do you keep him waiting?"

That tall, white-faced man in the long cloak rose from the table. "It concerns us all, Julie, does it not?" he asked.

"It does! It does!" cried the girl.

"Then let the rest of us go; receive him here, Louis, and you can tell us afterwards. When a man like the American thinks at all, his thoughts are sure to be big. Come, brothers!"

THEY BEGAN to drift from the room, and Julie among them. From the door she looked back upon the cripple and found him in such deep thought that he was carving marks on the inlaid face of the table, and blowing the chips of his carving out of his knife's way.

When she came again, John Hampton entered behind her.

He said, in a hearty voice: "I get somewhere at last, Louis. The confounded people have addled brains. Is it the taking of the château or the wine they've been drinking? They knew nothing. They could not even tell me where to find Louis—until I found Julie just now."

The girl was locking the door behind him.

"*Monsieur*, there is a confusion that goes with all great happenings, is there not?" asked the cripple twisting a smile on his face. He got up from his chair and stood, resting the stump of his leg on the seat.

"You were a brave fellow today," said Hampton, coming to his side, "and I hope that people won't forget it."

"*Monsieur*, we do what we can," said Louis.

"Do we choke, sometimes?" said Hampton, catching the scrawny neck of Louis at the nape. "Do we strangle sometimes, when we do *more* than we should?… Be quiet, Louis. One screech out of you and I'll break your back and put an end to the murder that's in you!… Take the keys, Julie."

The eye of Louis reluctantly left the face of the American and traveled to Julie. She met the glance with an undaunted smile.

"The devil devour me and spit out my brains!" whispered Louis. "Have I forgotten what my grandmother told me? That men are fools and cannot read the faces of women! Julie, you have done this!"

"She betrays you only a little, Louis," said Hampton. "How much have you betrayed me? She makes only a small fool of you; but what a great one you were making of me!"

The girl took the keys from the hip of Louis and sorted them rapidly. She sang under her breath, detaching three or four great keys from the rest. A fever burned in the face and the eyes of Louis. His whole body quivered like the tremor of a flame.

"Slut!" he said, as he watched her.

Hampton pinched the nape of the cripple's neck. He shrank, with an arm lifting to guard his face, but his breath kept on whispering vileness as he stared at the girl. Hampton watched her, also.

"Are you unhappy, *monsieur?*" she asked suddenly.

"If they so much as suspect you, Julie—"

"They will never suspect. The keys are my warrant. And I can keep laughing—like this, do you see? So that it will seem that I have a great secret:"

"Julie, you are a most exquisite thing. I shall be praying for you!"

"And something a little different from prayer, *monsieur?*"

"That also, my dear."

"Adieu, poor Louis," she said, and left the room suddenly.

HAMPTON, FOLLOWING, turned the lock behind her and went back to the cripple. His head lay in his arms, his stiff fingers were buried in his hair.

"Patience, Louis," said Hampton. "It may be that we'll not have to throw you to the dogs, after all. You know, you were a brave little cat today, hopping up the ladder on your three legs...."

Louis looked up from between his hands. "You could have kissed her, just now," he said. Hampton frowned.

"Her head was back, waiting," said Louis, his voice a soft groaning. "And I... after today I would have been something. Their eyes have been trailing after me. They all have looked up to me. I thought that even Julie—And now it is lost forever! And I never have touched a woman's mouth!"

CHAPTER XXXVI

ESCAPE FROM MURDER

WHEN JULIE CAME down to the lower corridor, the guards started up from a lunch of cold veal and good bread and white wine. Their full mouths were still munching as they glared at her. She rattled the big keys in their faces.

"They want the viscount and Lady Marguerite," said the girl.

Henri Patay, the large-handed miller, had charge of the guard and he did the talking. He was a man incapable of haste, and first he washed his mouth clean with half a pint of wine, then dried his lips with the back of his hand. For fear any of the delicious wine should be wasted, he rubbed it gently into his skin.

"Who is it that wants the pair of them?" he asked.

"Louis and the rest," said the girl.

"And who are the rest?"

"All the heads of the villages. Hurry, Henri Patay."

"He who hurries today will lie abed tomorrow," said Henri Patay. After he had quoted the saying, he looked with satisfaction on his comrades.

"Well, let me go to their cells. I have the keys," said the girl.

"*You* have the keys? And where did you get them?"

"From Louis, of course."

"Did he give them to you?"

"Do you think I could take them by force?"

"Well, women have their ways of taking things. Some have

good ways and some have bad ways; but they take things. Eh, *citoyens?*"

The men grunted; they still were feeding, since one of their number was willing to do all the talking for them.

"A good woman is like a clear fire on the hearth," maundered on Henri Patay. "But if you want the flame to rise, you must keep on feeding it."

"Then let me have some of that wine," said Julie. A cup was filled for her.

"What makes your mouth dry?" asked Patay.

"Impatience," said Julie and raised the cup to her lips.

"Impatience sweeps the floor and leaves the dirt behind," said Henri Patay.

"I drink to all good citizens!" called the girl. "And death to aristocrats!"

"… death… aristocrats…" said the peasants, accepting the toast.

She only had half drained the cup, so she passed it to Henri Patay.

"There is a kiss left in the cup for you, Monsieur Patay."

"No, no!" laughed the miller, swashing the wine around and around. "This is worth more than kisses. When I taste the richness of this wine, now, I think of all the good manure ploughed into the ground and how the rain and the sun works on it."

"Citizen Patay, I am waiting here. Shall I go back to Louis and say that you will not give up the two prisoners?"

"Yes. Go back and ask him why he sent a *girl* to fetch them."

"Because he would not send men to fetch away Lady Marguerite, of course."

"A woman to get a woman?" echoed Henri Patay. "Does that make sense?"

"Ay, and a thief to catch a thief!" laughed Julie.

Henri Patay laughed also.

"Well, well, I suppose the keys are the warrant," he said. "What does the poor American do?"

"He walks through the château, still. Or else he tramps up and down, up and down before the gate. Nobody will tell him what he wants to know," explained Julie.

"Well, he has a strong hand and a strong heart," said Patay. "But there are no good brains outside of France. Is the poor fool still wandering? Well, I hope they give him a bottle of wine to keep him company."

HE TURNED down the corridor. It was rough-hewn from the rock. The noise of dripping water walked up and down the length of it by day and by night. On each side were the doors of the cells with the small, barred windows through which the prisoners drank what little air there was. A foul odor, incredibly stale and old, crept into the lungs. Henri Patay beat on a door.

"Citizen Jean-Pierre!" he called.

"Well?" asked the quick, sharp voice of the viscount.

"You are to take a little walk, *monsieur*. We are going to give your nobility a little air. Pride needs a big house because it takes such long steps. Eh, Julie?"

"Henri Patay, do you remember every wise saying in the world?" she asked.

"Oh, I have picked up just a few little things and saved them. Wisdom is lightly carried, but it strikes harder than a stone eh?"

"Good!" said Julie.

The key groaned in the lock. The door swung wide. The tall viscount stood in the arch, blinking at the torch.

"He can stand straight enough now," said Julie, "but I think he'll learn how to bend his knee and bend his tongue, too, before they're through with him. Do you sneer at me?"

She struck the viscount across the face with the full swing of her arm. The peasants laughed. She had hit with such a hearty force that a trickle of blood started from the mouth of Jean-Pierre. He licked his lips and said nothing.

"I was lower than the latch of his shoe yesterday," said Julie. "But now I'm as tall as his master, eh?"

"He's ridden a tall horse; he must have a hard fall," chuckled Henri Patay. "Here… take him by the arms. We don't need the work of putting iron on them when we have hands like these to hold him."

"If he tries to stir from me," said one of the guards, laying hold on the arm of the viscount, "I'll break his bones like reeds—so—so—so!"

"Careful, man, or you'll be breaking them in fact," said Henri Patay laughing.

"Well, and what of it?" demanded Julie. "How many bones of poor devils have been snapped and smashed by the men of the marquis?… Well let's have the female aristocrat."

"She's here," said Patay, opening a door on the opposite side of the corridor.

When it swung open, Marguerite de Fréron fell on her face before them.

"Ah-ha, and ho, ho, ho!" laughed Henri Patay. "Her cell was not fit for her to sit in eh? She had to stand on her cloak behind the door, did she? Ay, till her silly knees trembled, and the brain rocked in her head. Well, there she is on the floor. Even a fool can keep his feet but only a wise man knows how to rise again when he's fallen."

Julie kicked the fallen body. "Get up, golden hair!" she cried. "Get up, lace and satin! Get up, beauty! Get up, disdain!"

She kicked the body with each phrase until the miller brushed her aside with his long, heavy arm.

"No, don't bruise her till she has her wits about her," he said. "There's no use giving pain to a creature that won't wake up. Now, then!"

As Lady Marguerite began to moan, he took her by the hair of the head and turned his wrist slowly. By sheer force he lifted her to her knees. The pain got her suddenly to her feet. When she fell, a jag of the pavement stone had cut her forehead. A thin line of red now ran down her face.

"Now when you look at the white of her," said Henri Patay, "you don't see very much. It's like seeing a city through a fog, all dim. It's like what old age does to them. I never see a woman keep her looks past five married years. Three or four children and the good is used up out of her. Here now. A pair more of you take hold on her. Don't be trying your strength of hand or you *will* break her, for sure. And yet she has pretty good bone, eh? If you felt bone like this in a mare you'd call it pretty good bone, wouldn't you? Hard and flat. And the joiner that made this knee was a master workman! Well, the day'll come when we test things like this in our own beds."

THEY TURNED back down the corridor and, with Julie in front, climbed the winding steps that led into the upper chambers. They had reached the story above the great hall when the tall man with the long cloak and the death-white face turned a corner of the hall and stopped them.

"What have you got there?" he demanded. "Who's told you to have the pair of them out of the prison? The morning's the time for that!"

"Yes, but this is another thing," said Julie.

"By whose orders?" asked the tall peasant.

"By the orders of Louis, the cripple," said the girl.

"He is going a long, far way, if he gives such orders all out of his own single will!"

"The thing is to make them talk a little," said Julie. She took Marguerite by the chin and with the palm and back of her other hand slapped the face rapidly, back and forth.

"And *will* you talk, *mademoiselle?*" she demanded.

Marguerite de Fréron murmured: "Our Father, give me death when You will!"

"Do you see?" asked Julie of the tall inquisitor. "She has enough flesh and bone to her but no heart at all. A soft sick thing that's no use, except to whine and pray. How long will it take them to make her tell everything that's in her heart?"

"You may be right," said the village leader. "But she looks near fainting to me. The strength in some of these proud fools is as small as a sword, but it's as sharp, also. It will kill them if it cannot save them. Get on with her, then."

So they went to the door of the appointed room, and Julie rapped mysteriously upon it, holding her ear close to listen for the answer. Then she whispered over her shoulder: "The door will open only a foot. Thrust the woman through. Then the viscount after her. And be quick!"

"But who's inside that's not to be seen?" demanded one of the villagers.

"Hush! Will you be a fool?" gasped Julie.

The door at this moment pulled open not more than a foot or so and through the gap Lady Marguerite was thrust first; they flung the viscount more roughly after her, and Julie slipped in behind, whispering over her shoulder: "Wait here in the hall; you may be needed!"

Then, closing the door behind her, she slipped the bolt home.

John Hampton already was lowering Marguerite de Fréron into a chair. The viscount stood over her.

"Have the beasts killed you, Marguerite?" asked the viscount, on his knees beside her.

"The filthy darkness, Jean-Pierre; the taste and the stench of the air—"

"*Mademoiselle,* look up if you please," said Hampton. "You are half a minute from freedom and no more, I think. Julie, will you speak to them at the door? No, Louis will do it for us."

Julie, standing near the table, kept her eyes upon two objects only: Hampton and Lady Marguerite, until the latter swayed from the chair to her feet with Jean-Pierre close beside her. It was the viscount who began to understand, first of all.

"Do you see, Marguerite?" he said, quietly. "It has all been schemed for us—even the blows in the face—and now Hugh Massey...."

Hampton, picking up the cripple in his arms, strode to the door and banged on it with his fist. In his left arm, then, he cradled the slender body of Louis lightly while his right hand lingered at the peasant's throat. He whispered.

"Citizens!" called the broken voice of Louis.

"Louder—with a clear voice!" commanded Hampton.

"Citizens! Do you hear me?" called Louis.

"I hear you Louis..." came from without.

"Quickly call everyone to the great hall—everyone from the entire château—a great thing is about to happen."

"By whose order, Louis?"

Hampton pulled the bolt of the door and opened it a trifle.

All the others in the room could hear the gasping murmur of Louis: "By order of all the village leaders—but be swift—call everyone—"

"Except from the gallery, Louis?"

"From the gallery over the lake, also. And quickly!... If you are slow, the whole plan may be ruined!..."

A RATTLE of footfalls answered him, and the American closed the door again. Louis, weeping, beating his face with his hands, was whispering: "May the marrow rot in your bones and burning oil be placed in them! May the crows pick out your eyes before you are dead! May swine eat your flesh!"

"Hush, Louis," said Hampton, replacing the cripple in a chair. "When a fellow has as much power as you, he should expect to use it for others now and then. See how strong your word is! Listen to the working of your command!"

He held up his hand. From far and near a rumor of footfalls had commenced through the château and was running steadily towards the lower part of the building.

"Go into the hall, Julie, and tell us when the way is clear," said Hampton.

She paused for only one more glance at Marguerite de Fréron; then she went slowly from the room with her head bent as though in deep thought.

"It *is* true!" breathed Lady Marguerite. "He is giving us our lives."

"There is blood on her face, Jean-Pierre," said Hampton. "Have you a handkerchief to take care of her?"

"Hugh, you are pulling a ruin on your own head in trying to save us!" cried Jean-Pierre. "Marguerite, I have despised him, but he has forgiven me. Hugh, my heart is crucified with pain…" He strode towards Hampton, throwing out his hands.

"Americans are a thrifty lot," said Hampton. "We don't throw away friendships, you know; we fight to keep 'em. How could you expect to wash me out of your life with words, eh?"

"If you make me weep," said the Frenchman, "I must begin to curse you all over again. Come with me…. Marguerite, do you see him?… No, you never can see him till you open your heart to look at him."

"Yes," said the girl.

He said: "The most noble—the most glorious—"

"Hush!" said the girl. "He has just said that words don't matter."

Jean-Pierre took the hand of the girl and the hand of Hampton. He looked from one to the other.

"Now what does this mean?" he asked. "If you lift your head any higher, you'll break your neck with pride, Hugh; and yet your hand is trembling. So is yours, Marguerite. At the same instant—together you blush. Do I understand? Or am I child unable to read?"

Hampton knew that Jean-Pierre spoke the truth; his love for Marguerite de Fréron could no longer remain hidden. And he, too, had noticed Marguerite's blush.

The voice of Julie said from the doorway, coldly, steadily: "The way is clear; the wasps have gathered into their hive. We can go on, now, and take our golden honey-bee to safety."

They heard the weeping murmur of Louis the cripple: "Let me die! God, God, let me die!"

"Carry his crutches, Jean-Pierre," said Hampton. "We'll make better time if I carry him."

"Do we take the snake with us?" asked Julie, looking with an earnest wonder at the American.

"If we leave him here, they'll tear him into shreds and eat them," said Hampton.

The cripple, in the great arms of Hampton, moaned softly for every step of the way: "The devil seize you the way a chicken seizes a worm!… May there be winter in your veins!… May your brain rot and an idiot sit in your eyes!"

CHAPTER XXXVII

ADIEU, LIBERTÉ

AS THEY PASSED into the hall, footsteps still were thronging down from the upper reaches of the house and the great murmur increased towards the hall, but the corridors were empty that led them to the gallery across the lake. They climbed with considerable noise over the barricade; the roar of the rain covered the sound. Through the windows, Hampton saw no boats on the lake.

As they walked down the length of the hall, vaguely behind them they heard the murmurs from the landward part of the château. They reached the second barricade and an unhooded light flashed.

"Jean-Pierre!" cried the voice of de Poncey. "And Marguerite! *Monsieur l'Américain,* what have you done for us?"

"He is our miracle-worker," said the viscount, "Where is my father?... Quickly!"

They passed inside the barricade, through the dim hall, down faintly lighted stairs, to the corridor below. Hampton put the cripple on foot again and gave him his crutches.

"Watch him, Julie," said Hampton, "for God knows what he'll attempt if he sees a chance to make trouble."

"Ah, kind *monsieur,*" said Louis, "if there was a madness in my brain, forgive it in the name of God!"

"Be quiet Louis," interjected Julie. "He'll take your skin safely out of this but every look at you, every word from you is poison to him."

The marquis appeared in a long plum-colored coat with a wig as white as winter snow when the wind has fluffed and blown it into translucent waves. A smaller plaster now covered the wound on his face. He paused at the door to glance over them, saying calmly:

"Welcome! Welcome! Marguerite, they have spoiled your clothes a little and that is a pity." He bent over her hand and kissed it. "And Monsieur Hampton, our man of honor. The pretty Julie, also; and one poor, crawling reptile?"

He turned his head at last to Jean-Pierre and for a moment maintained his smile, his poise of exquisite indifference; but suddenly some spring in the heart forced his arms to open. They embraced, silently. A shaken voice passed the lips of the marquis, saying:

"There *is* a God… and I thank Him!"

"You have given them to one another again," whispered Marguerite. "And that is almost worth the ruin and the blood."

She touched his arm as she spoke and looked up to him in a way that placed him again on the white road with the moon darkening the forest and the nightingale's song afloat in the valley; but something kept his own face grave and when he lifted his head he was aware of the searching eyes of Julie.

"We must go," said Hampton to the marquis.

"It is an honor to obey you in everything," said the marquis. "De Poncey, use your wits and your feet. We start at once."

"Do we leave everything?" cried Jean-Pierre, throwing out his hands. "Sacred God, do we give it all up to be fouled and taken by those animals!

"The jewels are half the fortune, my dear boy, and I have them," said the marquis, "and now that Monsieur Hampton has cleared my eyes, I see that the other half is you, Jean and Marguerite. Quickly! Quickly, Jean! Gather the servants. Send everyone to the dock, while I show our friends down to the boats!"

AGAINST BAD weather and winter, one long boat was kept

housed on a small canal, cut back from the lake and protected by
the wall of the château. In this they laid the three wounded men
of the marquis, then opened the doors and pushed the boat out
into the lake. The rain was ending in a small drizzle and already
the stars commenced to show in the north, toward which they
aimed. Ten miles down the river would bring them to Epinfort
where the small garrison of regular soldiers remained under the
command of General Menal, the friend of the marquis.

The boat slid out into the black of the lake and Hampton
looked back with an expectant dread to the casements of the
château above them. At any moment the peasant leaders would
discover that Louis and the prisoners were gone.

They hoisted their sail. It filled. The boat leaned gradually and
as the oars were shipped the water commenced to make a rapid,
rushing song, lipping the gunwales as it slid past. The marquis
himself held the tiller. It was he who said in a clear, strong voice:
"Adieu, Charlevain!"

Then the wind freshened and the boat had to run a little
more full before the wind to keep the waves from lapping over
the weather side.

They dropped far down below the village before a confused
rumor blew down to them upon the wind. Now, as Hampton
looked back, he saw lights flickering across the windows of the
island portion of the château; a moment later an arm of darkness obscured that scene as the boat round the first bend below
the lake into the river that flowed northward.

Charlevain village was out of sight. Perhaps everything was
lost to him for it seemed to Hampton that he had passed all his
years in a pleasant twilight until he had come in sight of the
château and the village. Now another life would have to begin.

As he sat at his oar, pulling heavily, he tried to put his thoughts
in order, but the music of a name sounded continually in his
mind until all thinking ended.

"John! Can't you hear me?" called the voice of Jean-Pierre
just behind.

"I hear you, Jean."

"Is it true that you stood at the postern and smashed a hole in it while they shot at you from above? Marguerite, did you hear of it, also? And how my lord hosed down the peasants with grapeshot? And how they stood up to it, and how John showed them a way? Well done, old fellow! If you had battered the castle down around our ears—still, well done! Father, if there's not enough room in the world for a fellow like Hampton, he shrugs his shoulders and makes a place. Will we deny him the right?"

The wind hummed in the sail; the water went hushing down the side of the boat; and in that whispering moment the voice of the marquis sounded clearly from the tiller: "Why deny the door to a man who is strong enough to knock down the wall, Jean?"

The people laughed. Amazement pressed like two hands against the temples of Hampton. Who under the sky could laugh at such a moment except the French? The marquis, who loved money more than blood, had suffered on this day incalculable loss; but yet he made *mots* and the others had heart enough to laugh at them.

FORWARD IN that boat, deliberate choice had placed Marguerite de Fréron at the side of Julie but they had been silent until this moment. Then, as the wind failed them at a bend and the monody of the straining oars began again, Marguerite said: "Where were you then, Julie? Did you see him at the postern?"

"Yes. I was beside him," said the girl.

"But beside him there in front under the guns?"

"He is an easy man to see and follow," said Julie. "That is not hard to understand, is it?"

"I understand," said Marguerite, humbly.

"If he wished, he could have stayed and been lord over everything—the *monsieur*. For the revolution has come to France and will not leave it. What would the new brains in Paris say of such a man as *monsieur*? They would make him a great leader, would they not? But he gave up the chance for glory in order to save you. *Mademoiselle*, do you love him?"

Marguerite was silent.

"Why not be open with one another?" asked Julie. "You know, that *I* am not ugly, either, and a pretty girl feels that even though she may not be born a princess she may marry a king?"

"Yes, Julie."

"But if you will have him, have him you must. I cannot help seeing you with the eye of *monsieur,* like a jewel with a light flowing out from inside. *Tiens, tiens!* Ah, God, what a pain that is to me! But do you love him?"

"I do," said Marguerite.

"Ah hai, what teeth are cracking my heart like a nut."

"Julie, you love him with a great, full heart!"

"I am not a fool, *mademoiselle.* When I see such a man, I have the sense to love him instantly…. Once, for your sake, he took me in his arms… what arms and what hands to hold a woman's body so that even her soul cannot escape! Has he held you so in his arms?"

"Yes," said Marguerite.

"Then you love him, *mademoiselle.*"

"I love him," said Marguerite.

"Ah—ah—" sighed Julie. "Then it is the end. Oh Julie, Julie, I wish to God that his big feet never had walked down the street of Charlevain with your heart in the dust under them!"

"Julie…."

"Be still! Do not pity me with one word…. There are the lights of Epinfort…. You will drink the wine together, tonight…. Ah, what a small, choking, black, dirty world is left for me to crawl in! There is not enough sweet air in it to fill my lungs once!"

WHEN THE boat slipped in alongside the river pier at Epinfort, Julie appeared at the elbow of Hampton, saying: "I am not going ashore. Louis and I will stay in the boat and drift down the stream…."

"Julie, do you forget? We are not parting."

"Why should we keep on playing a game of suppose?"

"It is not a game, Julie."

"Monsieur, does she love you?"

"She? No, no, Julie!"

"Then she lied when she told me so just now?"

"Julie, wait for me here. I am coming again," said Hampton. He climbed up out of the darkness to the brightness of many lights along the pier. A squad of soldiers moved along the pier with a single footfall, like the beat of a heavy drum. Others with slung muskets went here and there quickly to obey the orders of the commandant of the garrison, for he himself had come down to welcome that good and old friend, the marquis. They stood side by side now, smiling on one another.

"And this is the man," said the marquis "General Menal, Monsieur Hampton."

"Monsieur Hampton, I have some excellent Tokay, and I expect you to amaze me tonight while we are drinking it…. Alenton, if I took the best of my men and forced a march across country, and took the murdering scoundrels by surprise…."

"Dear Menal, the dogs are still too hungry to sleep very well. They have muskets now for every man of them. The beast would loll out a red tongue and lick you down with all your brave little swarm of fighting wasps."

De Poncey touched the arm of Hampton "Are you wounded?" he asked. "Your face is white."

"Just a scratch on the shoulder. That's all," said Hampton.

He turned away to Marguerite, who hurried towards him and whispered: "She is leaving us, John. Do you wish her to go?"

It was hard to penetrate the darkness at the side of the wharf but he managed to peer down through it to the small landing-stage.

He heard Marguerite de Fréron saying: "Except for Julie…."

Then he made out that the girl had cast off the boat. He sprang down the steps. His weight set the landing-stage swaying. The water sloshed and lapped at the edges of it as he stood on the verge with the cool, wet breath of the river in his face The boat already wavered beyond leaping distance with the cripple holding a pair of oars and Julie standing up in the stern sheets.

He called to her: "Julie, what under heaven's the matter? Come back!"

"Down the river I have an old cousin, a good woman. She will take me in," said Julie. She spoke so quietly that her voice barely lifted above the river noises and was nearly stamped out by the footfalls on the hollow wood of the pier. "Louis will be safe there, also."

"You both stay with me!" commanded Hampton. "Do you understand? With the peasants you won't be safe."

"Would we be safe with *your* people, *monsieur?*" asked Julie. "We were only the sheep and you were the shepherd for a while, but now you go back to your own kind. *Monsieur, adieu!*"

The boat had drifted away another pace. He held out his hand to draw her back. "Julie, do you hear me? Return!"

"*Monsieur,* it is more than kindness that I would want. I will not be a stray dog in a strange house. Listen!"

For here the voice of Jean-Pierre began to shout out of the distance: "Hampton! Where's Monsieur Hampton? John, where are you? John! John!"

He turned his head toward that outcry and when he looked again Louis the cripple was giving way with the oars; added veils of darkness were covering the slender figure of the girl rapidly. He heard her voice cry out a word which he could not decipher; then the little craft disappeared around the head of the pier.

In after years Hampton would often think back to this moment, wondering what the word was which Julie had cried out to him in heartbreaking farewell.

Hampton turned and leaped up the stairs again; but even as he ran he knew that there was nothing to do. If he pursued the girl with another boat, he would need more than force to bring her back with him. So, when he stood on the pier again, he remained fixed in place, staring before him at Marguerite de

Fréron, while the image of Julie drifted down the swift, black river of his thought.

"She is gone!" he said to Marguerite.

Jean-Pierre came striding to him. "I missed you, John," he cried out. "It was like missing my right hand, for a moment. Come along, old fellow. Come on, Marguerite. What's the matter with you two, staring at one another? And what the devil do I see in your eyes, my dear? Tears?"

"Hush, Jean. Be still!" said the girl. "Take your chatter away."

She took the arm of Hampton and they moved together with slow steps leaving Jean-Pierre, amazed, behind them. Once or twice she looked up at Hampton as though she were about to speak, but no words came. He felt that he was moving step by step into a new life.

THE MOMENT the boat passed the end of the pier, the deeper current caught hold of it and swept it rapidly down stream. Julie held the tiller; now and then with a stroke of the oars Louis straightened the nose of the craft.

"Shall we put up the sail, Louis?" she asked.

"No. Let's go down the stream quietly," said the cripple. "I have lost something out of my hands, tonight. A thousand men. That is all. A little thing in the life of a beggar and cripple. I was a general at noon. At night I am a mangy dog. If the peasants catch me, they will tear me to bits. If the noble gentry take hold of me, they will use me for dog-meat."

"Well, Louis," said the girl, "it's better to have been rich once than never to have been rich at all. When you're an old man, you'll still have this day to remember; and if you die young, it will keep you from a lot of three-legged misery."

"How full of mercy and pity you are! What a sweet Christian!" said Louis.

"Compared with my loss, what have you suffered?" asked Julie.

"*Monsieur l'Américain?* Bah, he would have used you and turned you out of doors in a week!"

"That is a filthy lie!"

"There is enough truth in it to make *you* screech," said Louis. "Do you know something? It would take you a year to make your hands like the hands of a lady."

"Louis, you are a beast!"

"He is holding the hands of Lady Marguerite, now. He says, 'The silly little fool of a peasant girl is out of the way, at last.' She answers, 'But remember how useful she was, Hugh. Give her her due!' He says, 'Sweet Marguerite, how charitable, how like a saint....'"

"Be still!" cried the girl. She began to sob.

The cripple presently groaned: "Julie I lied. It is not true. His heart is breaking for you at this minute! How could it help but break? My God, he is human, I hope; he has eyes to see you and ears to hear you. So don't weep for him. When I hear you sobbing because of another man, it tears my heart to pieces; it burns the flesh from my bones. Julie, if I had had two good legs under me, and if I were a little taller, do you think that any woman ever could have loved me?"

"Poor Louis, you will find a good girl who will love you, one day."

"Damn the good girls! I want someone beautiful, with a terrible sharp tongue like yours, Julie!... My God, my God, what pain to hear you weep for him... and what a joy to row you down the river away from him forever!"

"Ah, Louis... forever?" she sighed.

"No, no! Not forever!" cried Louis. "He is a man, is he not? He has the heart of a lion. Do you forget him thundering with the axe at the château? Such a hero never will let you sink out of his life forever. He will find you. He will give you such a dowry that you will marry a duke, at least."

"Hush!" said the girl.

"This cousin of your is rich?" asked the cripple.

"She has three cows and some sheep... yes, she is quite rich. She has three rooms in her cottage.... That stubblefield there on the left, what a sweetness blows from it over the dark river. Perhaps we are meant for unhappiness except when God sends to us some happy memory."

ABOUT THE AUTHOR

MAX BRAND IS a Californian who saw the West first in the central valley of the State, where the Coast Range ran low on one side and the Sierra Nevadas on clear days were green and brown over the foothills, and blue or glass-white above. He learned something of cattle and cattlemen among the great grasslands of the foothills, but he never was so deep in that Old West winch is a golden legend today, as when he spent a few weeks with two old trappers near the Diablo Mountains, close to El Paso, in Texas.

Nick and Alec had fought Indians, ridden range, prospected for gold, made fortunes for others, and had never been able to spend all the wealth that had poured in upon their minds. Some of the glory of mountains and desert remained with them as a perpetual heritage. Nick, at seventy-eight, had a body bent and twisted by age; Alec at eighty was straight as a stick, with no visible sign of the passage of time about him. But Alec was apt to blame his inability to read upon a defect of his eyes.

They quarreled constantly. To Max Brand, Nick reported that Alec was just a touchy old idiot—who could not even read! And what is a man capable of when he cannot read print? Alec, with equal fervor, reported that poor Nick was not to be blamed for weakness of temper and mind, for, said Alec, when a man's body is bent his brain is sure to sag also! But in spite of their wrangling, the two loved one another with a perfect devotion. And the long tales which they told in the evenings, making sixty years of Western history breathe and repainting mountains and deserts, have never been out of the mind of Max Brand. Nothing is more vivid to him than the memory of the little shanty near the "tank," the small stretchers on which the skins of coyotes and bobcats were drying, and the wrangling voices of old Nick and Alec.

Max Brand has been a traveler for a great many years, from the Pacific Islands to the deserts of northern Africa, but when he searches for stories, he

Max Brand

most often goes back to that shanty in Texas, and the voices of the two old men pour up in his mind. That is why Western themes generally have come off his typewriter during the last sixteen years. In fact, he has written more Western stories than any other author. He is forty years old, was born on the Coast, spent twenty-three years in California, and since that time has lived east and west in diverse parts of the world.

THE ARGOSY LIBRARY ™

SERIES 5 INCLUDES:

* WORTS * SHEEHAN * SERVISS *

* BRAND * PERRY * ROSCOE *

* BEECHAM *

* WIRT * FORSYTH *

* ROUSSEAU *

THE BEST FICTION
FROM THE FRANK
A. MUNSEY LINE